POLLUTO

Polluto is published twice a year by Dog Horn Publishing.
Visit polluto.com or doghorn.com to subscribe or for submission details.

Contents © the contributors.
Selection © the editors.
All rights reserved, 2012.

Editor-in-Chief: Adam Lowe
General Editor: Victoria Hooper
Designer: John Eckert
Acquisitions Editor: Chris Kelso
Creative Director: Michael Dark

Polluto 9 $^{3/4}$
Witchfinders vs. The Evil Red
ISBN 978-1-907133-09-1

Dog Horn Publishing
45 Monk Ings
Birstall
Batley
WF17 9HU
United Kingdom

A copyright record for this title exists with Nielsen BookData/Bowker and the British Library.

If you enjoyed this title, please share it with your friends.

POLLUTO
WITCHFINDERS
vs.
THE EVIL RED
ISSUE 9 3/4

CONTENTS

Editor's Letter		4
Embers & Emeralds	Cris O'Connor	5
Elseworlds	Gareth Durasow	7
Hempish Love	Gio Clairval & Erin E. Stocks	8
The Colours	Max T. Hawker	15
Subway Mandala	Robert Lamb	22
The Causeway	Aliya Whiteley	26
Red Riding Hood at Fifty	David R. Morgan	30
Before This Happened	David R. Morgan	31
The Desire of Things	David R. Morgan	32
I Forget Who Was on Whose Side	J. J. Steinfeld	34
The Espionage Agent	J. J. Steinfeld	36
The Meaning	Nicole Cushing	38
The Green Eyed Breath-Vampire…	Mike Aronovitz	40
Somnambulist – Southside	Chris Kelso	54
Give 'Em The Finger	Steve Conoboy	56
Hecate	Claire T. Feild	62
Host	Claire T. Feild	63
The Edge of Darkness	Claire T. Feild	63
Wild Rose	Claire T. Feild	64
Wraiths	Claire T. Feild	65
Professor Dingleberry and the Peripatetic Coxcomb Abode	Marshall Payne	66
Dissemblance	Douglas Thompson	73
Nothing Will Be Good Enough For You	Kiik Araki-Kawaguchi	76
Today, Paradise	Kiik Araki-Kawaguchi	77
What We Call The Night	Kiik Araki-Kawaguchi	78
The Ballad of the Bullet Holes	Erik T. Johnson	79
Daggi Comes Ashore	J. Michael Shell	89
Salt and Pepper	Jacob Edwards	94
Favors & Grudges: A Tale of Sister Merciless	Garrett Cook	103
Think Tank	Dan Nichol	118
Crescents and Pentagrams	S. R. Dantzler	127
Food for Thought	Medusa Graves	138
The Secret Stealer	Sam Wood	144
Fireflies	Richard Thomas	150

EDITOR'S LETTER

Wow. I don't think we've ever had quite such a thought provoking issue, or at least one so steeped in blood. On the surface, many of these stories and poems are rather violent; naturally, 'Evil Red' gives rise to thoughts of blood, pain and war. This is the sadistic, brutally honest side of the Evil Red. Looking deeper, however, it perhaps seems to be the quieter tales that leave the more disturbing aftertaste… stories and poems that tell us something about our own ability to rationalise extreme suffering, to hide it away and lie about it, to pretend that it's necessary. This is the manipulative, two-faced, and ultimately more dangerous side of the Evil Red. In these stories, Red encapsulates all that is frightening and different, that must be controlled or destroyed. It is no accident that sexuality, particularly sexually dominant and powerful women, feature strongly in this issue. We can hear the accusatory cry of 'Wiiiiitch!' echoing down the ages. And bad news readers… it seems they're still amongst us.

Time to call in the Witch-finders!

Turn to page 8 for our Editor's Choice story for this issue. 'Hempish Love' is a wicked, feverish tale with one of the most unusual narrators we've come across. This is a very clever story that deliberately plays with and then twists the reader's expectations, and it is not afraid to break a few rules. Filled with dark humour and sexuality, this story is simply delicious. Prepare for rope-burn as our narrator spins his depraved, vivid, and Hempish tale.

So, slip your arms into that long, black trench-coat, tug down the rim of your hat, and load up on the rock salt; it's time to hunt some Witch. But careful, stalwart hero, as the danger of the Evil Red lies ever close, and infests even the purest looking heart. Keep your eyes peeled for signs of communism in our midst; hold the line against all urges and sexual desires; ward yourself against all that is feminine and female, for their wily ways will bewitch you! Stay vigilant, Witch-slayer, for the Red is everywhere: blood, violence, sadism, magic, Mars, women, socialism, communism, even consumerism.

And while you're at it, set fire to those damn ruby slippers!

–Vicky

EMBERS & EMERALDS

CRIS O'CONNOR

"My skin! Oh my God. I'm melting!"

Edward stares blankly back at the woman – worn celluloid streaming behind his eyes.

"My baby, please take him."

The woman's hands shake as she holds out the rotten husk of a son; their skin fused together. Edward takes the corpse by the head and pulls it from the woman, tearing the merged flesh like a father releasing his child from the womb.

"Protect him." She collapses to the floor, her skin bubbling, the blood staining her once pale body. Edward lifts his hand above his head, the corpse dangling above him.

"I can't have you disappearing again Toto."

Edward strokes the rotten head of the child, ash staining his hand, and pulls a purple lead from the front compartment of his suit. He ties the lead around the dead child's neck, puts the boy on the floor and continues walking west.

"Pick your feet up, Toto. I'll happily drag you all the way there and you won't like that will you?"

Walking through the charred city, Edward ignores his surroundings, his eyes focused on the furthest westward point from himself. He doesn't see the nothingness around him and doesn't notice the silence. He only stops at a decaying post office when he feels a tug from Toto.

"I know it's hard, but we have to keep moving."

Toto's lead is caught on loose paving slab fragments. Edward walks to Toto and begins the awkward process of untangling him.

"It won't be long and we'll be there. I'll kill her and we can go home. Just me and you."

As he yanks on the lead the boy's hand snaps off at the wrist and for a split second Edward sees it; sees a world ravaged by war, sees the corpse of a young boy caught in a purple lead, his charred hand on the dusty ground beside him. Edward sees it all for a split second.

"Toto, I've had enough. Come on!"

Edward pulls hard on the lead, freeing Toto from the paving slabs. They continue towards the edge of the city. Toto's hand, their breadcrumb, waiting behind.

The sound of his tin suit no longer gnaws the corner of Edward's mind. The sound of Toto scraping across the ground behind him doesn't bother Edward either, but one thing that he can't ignore is the weeping of a small girl.

"What's wrong Dorothy?"

"My name is Lucy…"

"What are you doing without your red slippers?"

"'I don't know what you mean…"

"That's okay, I'll get them for you."

"You're scaring me Mister…"

Edward leaves Toto with the girl and runs towards the nearest building. Without hesitation, he thrusts his fist through a window and collects the glass shards.

"I've got them!"

Edward charges towards the girl, glass shards scratching against his tin covered fingers. He gets one piece and forces it into the sole of the girl's foot. Her screams, like the nuclear fallout, can't penetrate the tin suit. Edward forces her to the floor and continues to force glass into her foot. Putting his full weight on her chest, she has little room to fight.

"Look how they're turning red."

The pressure restricting her breathing.

"Please…Stop…I…Just…"

The floor around them is no longer a war torn grey, but now a muted crimson. Piece by piece he forces the glass into her feet until there's none left.

"There. You should be fine now."

The silence echoes around his tin helmet.

"Dorothy?"

The girl lies motionless, her face a pastel blue.

"Careful, Toto, the witch is near!"

Edward's movements are erratic; his eyes trying to view everything around him at once, his hands trapped in spasms, forcing his fingers to form a fist.

"I'm leaking again."

Small droplets of orange liquid break through the rust of his crotch panel, pirouetting down his leg and forming a small pool at his left foot.

The sound of a music box brushes his ear and Edward tilts his head to catch it.

A table forms in front of him, a used cream colour with only two items on its surface: an almost empty, emerald green perfume bottle and a small box. The music is coming from within. Edward watches as the box opens. Inside, a small girl holding red roses spins. The mechanism is aged and the spin isn't as fluid or as graceful as it once was. The girl looks close to falling at regular intervals. Edward sees himself, at the tender age of seven, moving a chair towards the table and climbing on it; arms stretched towards the box. Just out of reach. Edward rests his knee on the table and his fingers can just feel the polish of the wood. A noise startles the young Edward, he slips and as he falls he instinctively grabs the table. The young Edward looks up from the floor. He can smell the perfume; smell his mother diffusing into the carpet, the broken glass trying to hold what remains. The girl continues to spin, but the music is muffled like tears into a pillow.

"You heartless child! Get Out!"

Water builds in the corner of Edward's eye, hidden behind the slightly corroded eyepieces fitted to his helmet.

"We have to keep going Toto."

Edward presses forward towards the Witch of the West.

ELSEWORLDS
GARETH DURASOW

Summer of '47. Roswell, New Mexico
Ranch hand Mac Brazel stumbleupon'd a crash site
It broke his heart what the Reds could intern and shoot into space
Sucking its thumb with the might of a scaffolder's grip
Tantrum of a colossus in the astral crib
Flashforward to '62.
Kennedy to mobilise the blue boy scout
Full-throttle cobalt at a thousand dpi
Emblem embroidered in Pepsi Cola script
A fatherly noogie and the good to go
I can keep the brinkmanship up all night
And as for Charlie, he lights 'em like matches
according to Kilgore's account of heat vision in practice; it burns
Faster than a paper tiger
Has its own smell
Like no victory of this earth.

HEMPISH LOVE
GIO CLAIRVAL & ERIN E. STOCKS

Our 'Editor's Choice' Story

I never wanted to be an executioner. My maker twisted me with habile hands, and as though it weren't enough, he twisted me some more until I became the perfect tool for the cruellest tasks. Maybe, if a fair woman had caressed me, singing words of love, I would have grown into something peaceful, I would have held flowers or led white foals to the water. Instead, here I am, hanging from a hook in this windowless chamber, ready to imprison wrists and shake limbs until my victims confess imaginary deeds. After thirty years spent performing the *strappado*, I wish my body unravelled, but when I appear to be tired my master strokes me with beeswax to soothe me, and I am like new: the perfect rope to extort false confessions.

Oh, yes, I wanted to die, my dear Polletto, until I saw the female of my dreams. I spied her first this morning as I hung from my ring fixed to the ceiling: a Dominican friar called Guido burst into the forensic vicar's adjacent office, towing Gostanza behind him.

He said, "Vicar, this woman slaughtered a new-born babe!"

The magistrate looked up from his codex. "Do you have proof of this, Fra' Guido?"

The good Dominican bowed. "Early this morning, I was walking across the *Piazzetta Del Casseto* when Gostanza came out of a house, her hands overflowing with rue and vervain, baskets dangling from her forearms. The incense of moscata walnut and pumpkin clung to her hair unbound and flowing like a young girl's mane despite grey streaks. I offered aid, and she allowed me to relieve her of two baskets.

"'Was that Mona Astrea's abode?' I asked. As I balanced the baskets, bottles clinked together with ill-fated chimes. 'How went the birth?'

"'It went well.' But a frown creased Gostanza's features. At the moment, I did not understand why, but a suspicion gnawed at my heart. I yanked a bottle out and unstoppered it. I was right, vicar! Concoctions smelling like oil of bartram, crushed cloves, madreselva and betonica herbs ... all ingredients used for unholy spells!

"Then the devilish woman flipped open the lid of the third basket. 'Accept this offer to quench your hunger,' she said in a sly tone. 'Duck baked with prunes in tuber oil.'

"The aroma of roast bird tickled my nostrils. No sooner had she placed a palatable morsel between my lips than my senses fled. When I regained consciousness, I was alone in a mossy alley, slumped against a wall. I stumbled back to Mona Astrea's house, following a worrisome inspiration.

"Astrea lounged upstairs, her belly slack with recent birth. The maga Gostanza, lips and hands stained red, leaned over a cradle. Inside it, a babe, pale and still. She had killed it!

"I suffered kicks and scratches," the

friar concluded, "as I dragged Gostanza out of Astrea's abode and up the hill to this Palazzo."

The accused's eyes shone like little suns. Dried blood marred the corners of her mouth.

Upon hearing the friar's words, the soldiers who stood in the audience hall grimaced, whereas I died to taste such a woman–one of the evilest suspects ever. You see, Polletto, I've always wanted to torment an accused that had actually done something bad.

Guido bowed again, and from my vantage I noticed sweat beading on the friar's forehead. Now, the sweating could have been caused by the unseasonable heat, couldn't it?

The forensic vicar then sent for the inquisitor of Florence, Dionigi da Costacciaro. When the brown-robed Franciscan arrived, my master the executioner brought the accused before him, in this same chamber, my home. I was yanked from my perch, and laced twice around the witch's delicate wrist bones. My braided cords shivered in ecstasy. I wondered whether Guido's accusations were grounded indeed, for her skin had the texture of guilt.

Gostanza lifted her chin–the portrait of good faith offended.

"I'm innocent! My trade is about bringing babes into the world. The women tend to die without my help–you know that. This is what happened. I was coming out of Mona Astrea's home. I was damned tired 'cause our noblewoman had taken ages to lay her precious egg. The friar approached. He stared with eyes like toads, ser. And he stank. He stank so much my nostrils got all stoppered up all by 'emselves.

"'Stay away, you unwashed crack,' I said.

"He smiled more. The idiot thought I'd whispered words of love, so thick he's got that head of him. You must know how he plays with them children in his parish, ser."

Fra' Guido cut in despite the magistrate's gestures to make him step back and let the accused finish. "You of all accuse me?" Guido cried. "I know what you do to innocent babes. You suck their blood. And you defile holy wafers!"

He yanked the accused around to make her face him.

Gostanza yelled, "Let go, applejohn!" To the vicar, she said: "He wanted to lie with me, the lewdster, and buy my silence 'bout the children. And look at the boarpig. I bet he wishes to drink me like his mamma. But I'm twice his age. Will be sixty-two this autumn come, tho' I dunno when I was born 'xactly."

That granny is remarkably well preserved, I must say, with a narrow waist and round hip.

But let's not get distracted, O propitious demon. She went on, recounting how the "mammering miscreant" had shoved her against a moist wall. Rough stones bruised her shoulder blades. I pictured a rising sun and thin clouds brushing rosy smears of feathers. Such an image she saw, I suppose, like a fresco painted by her distraught guardian angel. I also imagined her mouth crushed under wet lips. In my hempish mind, I saw her wiggle, jerk her knee up, hitting Guido's jewel cases. He leaned back to administer a blow. Her head hit the wall. Pain in her cheek darkened her sight, yet she managed to bite the friar's hand.

Crying something like "You'll regret this, Jezebel!" he released Gostanza and disappeared into Astrea's abode.

Once the poor woman (I was beginning to find Guido unsympathetic) had rearranged her bodice, sensible thoughts returned to her: she would retrieve her medicinal herbs after the ruttish friar had blessed the babe; those she did not worry about. But her tablets–recipes she kept of potions and concoctions, including formulae to cure the plague–

she did not trust the "moldwarp" to leave those alone.

Then a woman's scream from upstairs stabbed her delicately shaped ear. (Like two small seashells, those ears are, but I digress.) She heard: "My babe! Dead! Dead!"

The friar's heavy steps resounded in Astrea's chambers. Gostanza hurried upstairs to see the babe in his arms, lifeless.

At this point, the accused made a big show of pulling her hair out, to impress the judge. "He did it, inquisitor, to discriminate me!"

She surely meant, "incriminate" me.

" I 'cuse Fra' Guido of murdering an innocent soul!" She screamed on and on, like a harpy, and my master the executioner had to gag her.

This is what the woman said. As for me, I trembled with hemp-lust. I knew she was guilty, of something at least.

The Franciscan commanded everyone be gone and the woman to be submitted to the *strappado* torture every accused expects during the trial. My rough coils squeezed her narrow wrists as the executioner hoisted her upward, arms tied behind her back. She dangled with me from the hook set in the ceiling until excruciating pain oozed from her skin—sweeter than the beeswax used to make my fibres slick. When the executioner released the clamp around my lengths, Gostanza dropped for several feet before my ends snapped taut. She screamed as all the accused do when their shoulders are dislocated from their joints.

The wise specialist of torments repeated his ministrations twice.

I absorbed her pain with quivers of joy.

"Enough!" she cried. "I'll tell you the truth. I'm guilty of killing babes, I am. The plague, the dead, all of it—'twas me."

It is the usual outcome. It is the way humans fabricate confessions, but this time, against everything I hold true, I wished she were guilty, to be able to sense her pain without feeling guilty myself.

"Untie her," the inquisitor ordered. The executioner allowed us to collapse in a heap on the terracotta tiles.

"Woman, your story."

Gostanza, sprawled on the floor like a broken puppet, began her narration. For truth's sake, I will recount what she said, making it less raspy to your ears, O Polletto.

Last month, her neighbour, a gossiping woman, invited her to a reception. Gostanza clothed herself as best as she could.

The neighbour gripped her wrist with surprising strength. "One condition, though," the woman said. "You must promise to utter no devout words or holy names on this journey."

Curiosity silenced Gostanza's questions. She wanted to discover why her friend had proffered such strange terms. So Gostanza climbed astride a donkey and followed the neighbour's mount through the *Piazzetta del Casseto*. But where the *Flusso di Vita* babbles its cool waters, Gostanza saw only a cloud of fog heavy with dew. She feared the mounts would trudge blindly into the stream.

Her companion reached over and drew Gostanza's donkey to a halt. "There we are."

The fog lifted. She thought they were standing atop the sun, for the ground glittered with the resplendence of dawn. Shards of light pierced the fragile flesh of her eyelids. She cried out and covered her face, only to have insistent fingers clamp around her wrists and draw her arms down.

She heard: "Gostanza."

The voice transformed the fear in her mouth into a buttery cake flaking apart on her tongue. Her heart sang a madrigal that pulsed through her most hidden places as she turned to behold a strange creature.

Un angelo? Un demonio? His well-formed features, framed by ebony locks, appeared to be carved of copper. Rich velvet cloaked human limbs, but curled around his ankles gleamed a silvery tail. "Who are you?" Gostanza whispered, although she knew.

"Call me Polletto. Welcome to my country." She was talking about you, my marvellous friend!

She stood in a golden city unlike any she'd ever imagined, aye, even more gilded than Florence. Graceful towers rose from palatial mansions and punched through the clouds. Beneath the crystal ground rushed a citrine river. Strangely, a wind carrying odours redolent of sickness blew over them.

The creature's tail slipped under her skirts, scales sliding up her bare legs until she shuddered.

"Mona Gostanza, you conjured the plague and sucked the blood of innocent babes. A great banquet will be held in your honour."

Your arms lifted the woman. Your feet left the crystal ground. The two of you (the neighbour disappears from Gostanza's story from this moment on) flew above the tallest towers while wisps of cloud plucked at Gostanza's garments. You alighted upon a golden balcony and gestured at open glass doors. "My palace."

Tables draped with silks and jewels bowed from the weight of platters of steaming sweetmeats, bowls of fruits, and decanters of bubbling wine. A gay set of pipes recanted the tale of a shepherdess and her lover lost to Hell. Merry light danced about, yet, frozen in the jaundiced gold of the walls, mouths gaped–puckered faces of children locked in silent screams. The stench of death bloomed from the blossoms of foliage wreathed above her head.

Polletto, your robes vanished. She beheld your body in awe and terror, the power of your tail, the command of your gaze which entranced her in a fearful stupor. You threw her across the hard gold of his throne and rammed holy wafers into her throbbing nature.

Shall I disrupt my report by noting that the two men present in the torture chamber were now sweating abundantly?

Gostanza said, shuddering, "When the puttock had finished taking me, I laid–"

"Lay, she means 'lay'," I cried from my perch, but of course nobody could hear me.

But lo! Interrupting her narration, the witch glanced at me in terror. Did she hear my voice?

Tears streamed down her cheeks, and I understood. Nothing of what she'd said was true. She intended to escape the pain caused by my loving coils and run straight to the burning stake. Disappointment flooded me. But you, Polletto, will give her to me for more interrogations, won't you?

"That's what I did, inquisitor," she continued. "I pissed on God and all the Saints. Hear my confession, and my soul will be saved." She struggled to her feet, pain crumpling her face.

A cloud of mist settled around a shadowy figure. Yours, Polletto!

Your very voice resounded. "Who called my name?"

Gostanza took a step back. The inquisitor pinched his nose and addressed the executioner. "What's this stench? Open the window."

The executioner complied, as blind to your supernatural presence as the inquisitor.

You set your eyes on me, the speechless but observant rope, and gave me the ability to relay everything I'd heard in this room, which I just did, staunchly, almost word for word. Now, most noble Polletto, surely my tale rang true enough for you to grant–

Your raised hand silences me. Why do you seize Gostanza's chin between your golden-tipped thumb and forefinger? Polletto, don't touch her, I beg you, for she's been mine from the moment I caressed her wrists, still raw from my affectionate ministrations.

"You told the truth about her beauty," you say. "She's desirable." With a flourish, your fingers stroke her arm. "She's coming with me."

Gostanza pulls away. "I'm so *not* coming, you bare-arsed chicken!"

You fix your gaze on my woman. "Gostanza, let me bring you to my golden city. Well, it didn't exist till I heard your story, but it exists now. Ask, and I'll give you everything you demand."

"I demand to go home. Go rot in Hell yerself." Behind her, the executioner moves forward, but the inquisitor holds up a hand. The two men watch her shake her head frantically.

You brush a fly-sized devil off your scarlet sleeve. "You won't be in Hell, sweet child. What use would you be to me as a bodiless soul? I need you here to bring the plague to every door."

"I'm a healer, not a killer."

"Be my queen for a day. Dance in my golden palace in the sky." You extend a hand, palm up, and crook a forefinger, to call her forth.

"Stick that finger up yer back door, devil!"

Your eyes glaze over. "Foul mouthed as I love them." You leap onto the roughstone wall. "Be healed, Gostanza."

Her shoulders relax. She lifts her arms to the frescoed ceiling.

The inquisitor, I expect, will acknowledge this sign of witchery, for ordinary people do not retain the use of their limbs after suffering the *strappado* torture. Nevertheless, the Franciscan only looks unseeingly at the tip of his own nose, as does the executioner.

My coils unravel in despair. She deserves me. Bind her!

You, handsome devil, disappear from the wall where you've been prancing and reappear next to the inquisitor to whisper in his ear. I try to sway close, but your words elude me.

The Franciscan shudders as though dispelling a bad reverie. "You have told us a wreath of lies, woman. As Tommaso d'Aquino teaches us, demons are incorporeal and cannot mate with human beings."

Gostanza glances at me, surely fearing the inquisitor will order more torture to punish her lying tongue. (Yes, yes! I'm ready.)

"I told the truth! Polletto made love to me, and I got more satisfaction with him than with my late husband."

Polletto, now you puff up your chest like a journeyman bragging in front of his whole guild about the perfection of his tools.

My witch snorts. "Although his cum was ice-cold."

You take on a saddened countenance for the briefest moment then stomp your foot. A cloud of flaming sprites shivers around you, like tiny lapilli out of a volcano mouth.

The Franciscan rolls his eyes to the ceiling frescoes of naked infant angels and martyrs draped in togas. With a solemn nod, he signals he has made his decision. The executioner steps up to the door and pushes the heavy panels open. *San Miniato's* forensic vicar, two soldiers, Fra' Guido and a clerk file in. Guido flashes victorious glances at Gostanza, and my core twists with hopeful aching. She will be given to me again. I prepare for the verdict.

"This woman claims to have lain with an incorporeal demon." The inquisitor steeples his hands. "How could anyone believe such nonsense? Furthermore, her witchery as cause of deaths in *San Miniato* is an inane supposition, for it is the same sickness which struck most of Italy three years ago. The dead babe was discovered to bear signs of the plague, not of sorcery. You, Gostanza, invented a fancy story to escape torture and die quickly. This, alas, happens often, even though the Holy Inquisition tries to avoid such errors. I thereby discharge you from the accusation of ensorcelment against the child and Fra' Guido, and any other sorceries."

A smile smoothes lines from Gostanza's visage.

Polletto, stop this madness. I need to caress my witch. Now. Please.

Your grin tells me you will do nothing. I writhe on the floor but no one heeds my pain—as if a rope moving of its own accord were no prodigy. All gazes are riveted to the inquisitor.

"Although you're innocent of the charge of witchery," the Franciscan continues, "I shan't condone your midwifery. You, a woman, cannot be a physician. From this day on, restrain from practicing your impious trade. Never again shall you administer potions and spread ointments, and neither will other women. Go free, God's creature, and do not sin again."

"But…ser, I've brought to life hundreds of babes." She runs trembling hands through her greying hair. "And I'm a healer. My tablets…you must see what I can do. I've found a way to fight this plague!"

"There are physicians in San Miniato, and everywhere in Tuscany, who heal people and bring babes to the light much better than an uneducated woman could ever imagine."

"By bleeding women with leeches? To weaken 'em till they die–"

A soldier backhands Gostanza, who falls to the floor. Her svelte figure lies there, throbbing with sobs. Perchance the vicar will punish her impertinence with my loving coils. If I were a man, I'd hold my breath in hope.

But no.

The inquisitor raises his hand to stay the soldier. I pray to God that one day Guido's fellow friars will lead the Holy Inquisition. Strict Dominicans would do a better job of punishing heretics than these soft-hearted Franciscans.

Guido grabs my witch by the arm. "Come! You have wasted enough of your betters' time."

He pushes her out of the torture chamber. The soldiers fall in after them as the executioner threads me through the hook in the ceiling, my perch and home. In sadness, I gaze out of the open window. Gostanza is still deserving of me, for what is midwifery but sorcery in disguise?

A crowd has gathered to learn about the witch's fate, but the human wall gives way before Guido, who drags Gostanza towards his mule. Polletto, ill-omened devil, you weave around my woman, you… hellcat of my doom.

While Guido mounts his animal, the light changes. Over the hill on which the *Palazzo dei Vicari* roosts, farther than the dales quilted with the variegated green of crops and trees, across terracotta-striped fields, beyond a stretch of landscape that turns violet where it meets the sky, clouds of red meld into gold.

The clouds surge and pile up as the sun sinks.

"Don't worry about that over-zealous Dominican," you whisper to my woman. Even from a distance, your voice teases me, Polletto, for I am tied to you by your spell.

"Come with me, Gostanza."

A flurry of sparks explodes above the piazza. The air crackles. A jolt of lightning splits open the sky and the sparks draw apart curtains of air to reveal a city floating in a cloudy sea: tapered towers and crenelated parapets, cupolas fruiting with spires and belfries. Rays from the setting sun pierce honey-tinged walls and refract on minarets and domes, rippling to the ground like liquid topaz.

Several women in the crowd fall to the ground. The men point at the city in the sky, and cross their chests.

"I ain't coming, devil," Gostanza

says, "but look at this handsome man, who worships you."

The Dominican's eyes show too much white. "What is this place?" Guido gasps.

Gostanza clutches his black sleeve. "Travel to Polletto's golden city. For the best of pleasures."

Fra' Guido licks his lips. A thin dribble seeps from one corner of his mouth. "Pleasure?"

"Lots. Look at the Prince here. He'll give you all you want."

A smile tugs at your lips, devious devil. "Yes. The friar craves me. Very much so."

You snap your fingers and your person glows from crown to foot.

Guido sees you for the first time. "Who *are* you?"

"Your beloved Prince."

The city in the sky sparkles ten times more.

People gasp, cry, and run away in terror. Fra' Guido spurs his mule, which leaps ahead of all but two, a small child in rags and a nun. The nun–alerted by galloping hooves–veers towards the child to protect her. But Guido steers his mount over at the same time.

"Out of my way!" he shouts.

Hooves tap the nun's heels. The woman falls over the child. The mule tramples them both, but Guido doesn't stop, his distorted face riveted to the city.

Cries gush from the crowd. "The friar! He's possessed!"

Gostanza's voice resounds high and clear. "I saw him bleed a new-born babe! Sorcery!"

The sun withdraws its fingers of light. Ivory towers and domes melt into wisps of cloud as the city vanishes.

From my high-perched home, I see the vicar and the inquisitor hurry out into the courtyard. On the vicar's order, the soldiers tear after Fra' Guido and drag him off his mount. They pull the Dominican back toward the Palazzo. A tablet falls out of his robes. Guido lunges for it, but another man picks it up and hands it to the inquisitor.

"Sorcery!" the inquisitor says.

I am jerked off my hook. A manservant brings me outside, panting, as if I were an effort to carry, and a soldier lashes me around the Dominican's sweaty wrists.

I don't like the friar. O envious devil, I demand you return my woman. Now. Now. I crave her smooth skin.

But you do not answer, for Gostanza's beauty no longer stops your tongue. You stroke the friar's cheek. In your execrable fickleness, you have chosen another lover. And you will watch his torments with delight, surely to liberate him later and win him over? He is already yours, can you not see? Ah, the Devil woks in tortuous ways.

While the soldiers lead Fra' Guido back to the *Palazzo dei Vicari*, with me coiled around his wrists, I strain for any glimpse of *my* beloved. People mill about, demanding answers, justice, the return of the golden city.

Then I spy a lone figure hurrying on the beaten path around the Palazzo's western tower. Her long hair blows freely behind her. I remember the frailty of her skin, the feel of her wrapped within my bonds. O Polletto, venomed idle-headed giglet, my strands will fray in bereavement.

Now I wait for Gostanza, the woman I love with all my hemp. I know she will be back, for she shall use her herbs again to save someone. She is guilty. Women like her will always be.

# THE COLOURS
MAX T. HAWKER

I.

'So, Astor human, are you satisfied with this offer?' asks the Zeta grey, sucking smoke from its cigarette. 'You won't find sweeter deal. No, no, no.'

Interrogation-room light fizzes. Astor rubs his forehead, cursing his boss for choosing him for the negotiations.

'An' I keep tellin' yer, I can't go fer sucher trade. It's 1953 fer Chrissake! An' yer gone thinkin' ye-r can wily yerself that much uranium?' The Zeta grey's almond eyes wriggle like East Coast mudsnakes—Astor can read nothing.

'Your suggestion then? You do need this *Patriot*?' The Zeta taps ash away from the end of its cigarette.

'Okay. How 'bout this: twenty percent less uranium and we'll give yer a further, say, five abductions. And yer don't have ter return the abductees neither. Sell 'em, pickle 'em, do whatever the fuck yer creeps do, an' no questions assed.'

The Zeta grey takes another drag from its cigarette. It nods, apparently enthused. It then claps and turns to its associate–another Zeta grey. 'Human know how to tickle us!'

'Yes, yes, yes. Ability commendable. Yes. Stubborn creature. Isn't it, Sue?'

'Definitely.' Sue stubs its cigarette out in an ashtray and turns back to Astor. 'But I'm afraid Clive and I can't accept such terms. No, no, no.'

Astor slams the table he's sat at with a single palm.

'However,' the Zeta continues in its ludicrous, chirpy voice, 'I will accept the deduction of twenty percent of your uranium should you offer us… a substitute item.'

'Whadayahave in mind?'

'Well, Clive and I have been in the narcotics trade for a long time. Yes, yes. But we have never encountered a creation…' the Zeta grey lifts the cigarette butt from the ashtray, 'as delicious as *this*. How about you keep your twenty percent of uranium and give us, say, ten thousand cigarettes instead.'

'Yerferreal? Whadathehell yer want that many cigarettes fer?' Astor coughs. 'Geez, I'd be happy ter agree on those terms!'

'This pleases us. Good, it's settled then!'

Sue and Clive stand, Sue lifting its briefcase from the floor.

What's in there? Astor wonders, standing as well. He opens the interrogation room door and leads the aliens out and down a corridor. Several military policemen pass them by.

After several moments, Sue speaks: '…I can't help but notice that this is your biggest request for *Patriot* since the period of time you call "1945". Has the need for the drug increased so greatly?'

Astor scratches his greying temples… *Damn headache.* He lights a cigarette for himself. 'Times are hard fer this cunt tree. People gotten spooked by the damn Commies. And then there's *yer* lot making 'em think God-knows-what's coming ter get 'em–with yer damned "saucers" an' "cigars" in the clouds. People neeter know they gotta cunt tree ter be proud o'–a home wurf fightin' fer. Use ter be tha' people didn't have no trouble rememberin' tha'.' The image of his boss injecting himself with *Patriot* comes to mind. *Damn addict.* 'But these are times 'o change. Times 'o uncertainty. People don't find it so easy ter remember what the red, white an' blue means anymore. But luckily, we got yer *Patriot* ter give 'em poor fools some meanin'.'

'Indeed, indeed. Yes, yes. This *Patriot* our purest yet. Spread fast if introduced through water. Very thick consistency. Effects: big paranoia; high inferiority complex. Perfect, perfect.'

'Perfect s'long as it does its job.'

'We are not, as you'd put it, "used-car salesmen",' Clive replies with a sound vaguely resembling laughter.

'No, no, no. In fact we wonder if you'd be interested in *another* drug we have recently developed,' Sue follows on from its associate, in a lower tone.

Astor takes several clumsy sucks of his cigarette. 'What kinder drug? Why didincha mention it before?'

'We didn't mention it because it has not been trialled, as yet. But we have complete confidence in its ability.'

Astor glances about him and pulls the two aliens into an empty filing room. '…I'm listenin'.'

'Good, good. Okay. You humans have strong obsession with colour–be it on your skin, your food or your flags. You, for example, do not like political thinking that is "red", so we understand from your planet's communications. You seem to prefer political thinking that is black and white–it simpler for you to swallow the world, no? Well, that's why this new drug we have is perfect for you!'

'Why? Whadoesido?'

'If successful–'

'–and it will be–' interjects Sue.

'–it will make affected life-form colour-blind,' Clive nods.

'More than that! More than that! It polarizes vision almost entirely. Nearly everything in vision become either sharp black or sharp white–grey almost all go away!'

'Ha!' Astor snorts. 'Then yer two would be gone!'

'Wonderful Earth humour!' Sue and Clive clap. 'We would still be visible, but made up of denser black or piercing white. Think though, think–your nasty little "reds"… *poof*…they all gone! No colour, no problem!'

'And no red and blue in your flag to worry about either. No, no, no. Just nice black and white flag for you–easy to understand; *Patriot* work more efficiently with easier job to do.'

'But your decision must be quick. *Other* buyers I think might like this drug, this *Muteye*, as we call it.'

Astor wrenches a final plume from his cigarette before stamping it out. The new drug intrigues him. He could pull a good deal here. Astor's boss has told him not to step beyond the trade restrictions prescribed. But initiative is what wins promotion, so Astor argues to himself, and his career is in its autumn, after all. Besides, any drug with the potential to fix the Commie problem could be game changing in the arena of global politics. The world is tired of conflict; Astor is tired of conflict. Here is his chance.

'So whadayawant fer a drug like this? An' how much of it have yer got?'

'We have already looked at your geo-political map and so recognise which areas are afflicted by "red"–we can have enough of this drug to solve your problem within the next three of your Earth "years",' Clive informs.

'As for cost,' begins Sue, '…there *is* something we desire that we could work out a trade for.'

'Godammit, I tolljer we can't offer no more uranium. Don't be about ter ask fer that.'

'We weren't, we weren't,' Clive shakes its head, raising its hands as though to placate Astor. 'Instead, we wish to utilise the strengths of your species for very special ends. What you think are strongest points of Earthlets? What has help you get this far?'

Astor fidgets with his temples again. 'Hmm, wellemmesee. Our ingenuity—we've developed tools ter help us along. Err. Or our teamwork—couldanuh got far without—'

'You're thinking all wrong,' Clive interrupts.

'Yes, yes, yes. Your species' greatest strength is its blind violence and ability to destroy what it doesn't understand.'

'And we could benefit from such a trait!' Clive chirrups.

'Oh, right… Well then, howjer wanna use *that*?'

'You understand principles of "marketplace"? Well, it not just you Earthlets that have this.'

'No, no, no,' continues Sue. 'Across our galaxy is vast "marketplace" also. And we represent great trade capacity within this "marketplace".'

'What is worse thing in "marketplace"?' Clive asks.

'Err, that'd hahterbe a lacker demand fer whatcher sellin'.'

'Clever human thinking! But no. One thing worse than no demand—*rival competitor*! Yes, yes, yes. This very bad!'

'And we have very bad rival in "marketplace",' closes Clive.

'Okay… go on.' Astor fingers his chin, conscious of where the greys are steering the conversation.

'This rival is other species called Lillitians. They look for business arrangement also on Earth. This is no good. We want them gone.'

'*Gone*?' Astor parrots.

'Exactly,' continues Sue. 'We want your group of Earthlets to take their craft down on sight.'

'Fire on 'em? The hell we s'pposed ter tay down craft like that?'

'We can't offer you any weaponry–the Lillitians would recognise the signature once fired upon. But if you look here…,' Sue hands Astor several sheets of paper from its briefcase. 'You will find details of structural weakness. Exploit.'

Astor takes the sheets and scans the information. He looks back up at the aliens. 'An' if we bring down their crafts?'

'Do what you will with them. Same goes for any survivors,' Clive nods.

'Agree to this and shipments of *Muteye* will begin within one of your Earth "months". You can even test it out on a closed population before dispersing it tactically. That way you see you get good, working product. Then decide if just red go or blue too.'

Astor puts a finger to his bottom lip. The correct action would be to report this new development in the negotiations to his boss. However, his boss is a busy man and does not appreciate being disturbed. He'd probably be too dosed on his private cache of *Patriot* to care. Astor's boss trusts him to this task, right? Surely he'd want to see Astor using his initiative. Perhaps this negotiation is a test of his ability… Initiative then, yes. After all, Astor will have to shine if he is to beat Williams and Parker to a promotion.

'Awright boys, I gotta say, this sounds good. But what if the drug don't work like you say it should?'

'Smart human! If it fail then we reimburse you with other product–you will take pick.'

'But it will work, and when it does—no more red for nasty thoughts to crowd around!'

'Things all simple again.'

Astor smiles. This is his moment. 'Okay, boys. Yoo done got yerselves a deal. Where do I sign?'

'Very good, very good, human!' Sue and Clive applaud.

'Swallow this pill,' Sue pulls out the pill in question from the briefcase. 'It will dissolve inside you and send a bio-signal back to our organisation headquarters, where our administration department will acknowledge your agreement to the deal.'

Astor takes the pill and swallows it. What an odd way of getting a signature. It wasn't necessary for the *Patriot*... The aliens seem enthused. 'How does this thing work?'

'The pill's signal acts like the signature you Earthlets apply to written contracts. It acknowledges that you have read and agreed to be bound by the terms and conditions of the trade agreement,' Clive continues.

'What terms and conditions? Yer never showed me any.'

'Did I not, Clive?' Sue asks its associate, apparently aghast at such carelessness. 'How forgetful of me! Here they are, Astor human. All printed on dead tree as your custom dictates.' Sue reveals an enormous bound document from its briefcase and lumps it to Astor.

'Do not look worry!' Clive chirrups. 'All perfect normal and no bad surprises.'

'We real must going now,' Sue adds quickly. 'As hear, our translator battery life die. Such unfortunate time!'

'Well done negotiate,' Clive smiles, taking and shaking Astor's hand. 'We'll just transport out from here.'

Astor clears his throat and smiles bemusedly as the Zeta greys dissolve in a scuffle of light.

'And that's how it finished. Their translator battery was dyin' an'—flash! They was gone!' Astor finishes explaining to his boss exactly how the negotiations proceeded. Everything told. Everything except the second deal. Astor wants to find his own moment for impressing the boss with *this* news.

'Damn fine job it soun's lie yer done; dunno whatchoo mean by translator battery though, they don't use batteries...,' replies the boss, a highly rectangular man in military gear the colour of Mississippi swamp juice. 'Anyways, looks like I was righ' ter have faith in yoo. Here, have a whisky.' The boss pours a whisky out into a glass and passes it across his desk to Astor.

Astor swirls the booze in its glass with a flick of his wrist. He chinks the boss's own whisky glass and throws the fire down his throat. He can smell *Patriot*... boss must be dosed.

'Boss, why're them two greys called Sue an' Clive?' Astor makes conversation for the sake of it.

'Aww, they go by them names ter make 'emselves seem like everyday folk.'

Astor finds such a feat difficult to achieve.

'Know why I put yer in there with them two creepy sonsuhbitches?'

'I did wonder,' Astor replies.

'Boys higher up won'id 'a test ya. See how ya'd cope with the greys—mos' can' deal with the headaches. They look at a man like ya, look at ya record, look at ya service in the Pacific. They gone lookin' fer a true patriot an' I tell them yer the man. Keeps his hea' down. Follers orders. Quiet an' conten' with servin' his cunt tree. Gives no shi' abou' any 'a tha' promotion chasin'. Hell yer jus' abou' the only guy I know who ain't lookin' fer some way 'a oust me from this here desk.

Williams gits awl starry-eyed when 'e sees my office. Parker jus' lurves bossin' those below 'im round an givin' me the sloppy "Yessirs". Goddamn nice ter have som'un aroun' like yoo who jus' happy ter do his part. Som'un who don't put M an' E above U, S an' A.' The boss swigs his whisky and pours another for himself and Astor. Astor glances down at the volume of terms and conditions by his feet. 'Anyways, I gone gotten off track. Boys higher up as' me if I know any'un trustworthy enough ter help in a matter 'a national security.' The boss stands, holding his whisky. 'An' I thoughta yoo.'

The boss nods and turns around to look out of his window. He separates several segments of a blind before opening it fully.

As the boss's back is turned, Astor quietly lifts the terms and conditions onto his lap. 'Gee, boss. I dunno wha' ter say.'

He opens the cover and looks at the wording inside.

```
Congratulations on purchasing new
bio-altering agent Muteye. Do not
store in temperatures exceeding
30° celsius. Keep out of reach of
babies, cubs, hatchlings or any
      other form of offspring.
```

'So… what is it these people got planned fer me?'

'Wouldn't give specifics, as yer'd imagine. Did a lil bit 'a diggin' ter see what I could find though.'

'And didja find anythin'?'

```
Please carefully read the terms
and conditions to which you must
adhere, should you agree to trial
Muteye. If you are an individual
acting on behalf of an organisa-
tion, but do not have authority
to sign on behalf of said organ-
isation, please refer to a higher
authority than your own.
```

'Couple 'a things. None 'a the meat, as yer'd expect, no doubt. Boys up top wantcher fer an' exchange scheme o' sorts. Somethin' ter do with a new pact signed with another alien species–a kinda peace treaty, so I' heard…'

Astor is only half-listening as he flicks nervously through the rest of the terms and conditions.

```
       STIPULATION 4
The killing of a Lillitian who
has survived craft destruction
can best be achieved in one of
    the following three ways:

1.   Severance of head: as with
many species, the Lillitians re-
quire their heads to be attached
to the trunk of their bodies in
        order to survive.

2.   Pulping of head: the Lil-
litian head is large and soft and
will not long tolerate the pres-
sure of repeated kicks, punches
or impacts from blunt instru-
              ments.

3.   Exposure to high-fre-
quency sound waves: the Lilli-
tians are a telepathic species
and their brains will vibrate and
burst when exposed to the fre-
quency range: 180-200,000 Hz.
```

'…full details are limi'did. I did manage ter fine out which species we gone awl dove-swappin' wiv–the Lillitians. Never seen one o' 'em 'cept in photos. They only one feet tawl an' they got big ol' heeds fer snoopin' inter ours wiv.'

Astor's heart plummets. 'Ya sure, boss? …'Bout it bein' the Lillitians, that is.'

'Yip. Pritty sure. Tha' batch o' Patriot yer jus' done dealin' fer, tha's our las' trade wiv the greys. Shame... Boys up top can't afford what they charge fer their drugs no more. *Patriot... Blaxbane... RightThort...* they's all goin' now. I tell yer–mus' be one helluvah deal them boys made wiv the Lillitians, ter give up wha' we got wi' the greys. Nutin' stoppin' the greys dealin' wiv the Commies now an' the boys above know tha'. Those sonsuhbitches are expensive, but ya get what ya pay fer...'

'Peace treaty, ya said?'

'Tha' it be, from wha' I hear.'

Astor glances down again at the terms and conditions and conspicuously tears through to the last section.

```
       STIPULATION 9
Should the terms of the agreement
be broken by the purchaser, said
purchaser shall be liable to the
        following penalties:
1.     Fine of 500 lbs of ura-
nium-238 and 750 lbs of gold to
be paid within three Earth months
to the broker of Muteye. Fail-
ure to do so will result in the
impounding of the Earth's sole
satellite, commonly referred to
as 'the Moon'. An additional fine
of 250 lbs of uranium-238 will
then be payable upon collection
of 'the Moon'. If 'the Moon' is
not collected from the satellite
depot on Zeta B-316 within one
Earth month, it shall be crushed.
2.     A breaking off of future
negotiations with the purchaser
and negative feedback provided
for purchaser's 'Purchaser ID',
as currently available for view-
ing in the galactic marketplace
             archives.
3.     Full disclosure to all
```

citizens under the authority of the purchaser, of the existence of extra-terrestrial species.

'Hey. Wha's tha' yer got there?' the boss leans over the table, still holding his whisky glass.

'Boss, I, err... there's somethin' else, somethin' I need ter tell yer. Somethin' abou' the greys.'

The boss's face and voice seem to sharpen. 'Well, ou' wi' it then. C'mon, whatcha got fer me?'

'There... there was a second deal between us, well, *me* and the greys. One I made on the spur o' the moment.'

The boss's face flinches. His eyes widen. 'Ya done wha'!? Withou' my permission? Wha' the heel kinda deal ya gone an' done?'

'They offered me a new drug, one called *Muteye*.'

'*Muteye*? The hell's tha'?'

Astor tries to explain the drug's effects.

'Whadaya mean no more red, white an' blue!? Yoo insane!?'

'Think how much simpler things'd be. Bring everyone round ter our way o' thinkin'–simple black an' white. No more red, an' yeah, no more blue neither maybe, but we wouldn' need it anyways. We'd all be the same!'

'Jeeziz Kries! All the same? All levelled inter the same *thing*? Now yer speakin' like one o' '*em*! Hell's the matter witchoo? Thought yoo was better than that! Jeeziz Kries! ...Wait a secon'. I know them crafty, grey sonsuhbitches...whadid they as' fer in return?'

'They wan'ed us ter maker pointer shootin' down the craft o' their main business rivals... Their main business rivals are the Lillitians.'

'An' yoo agreed ter awl this shi'!? Jeeziz!' the boss slams his whisky glass on the desk, cracking it and allowing the fire to seep. 'Whyja do it?'

'I…I wan'ed ter give myself a shot at promotion. I wan'ed ter do somethin' ter help my cunt tree. I ain't one o' 'em who needs *Patriot*; I know where *my* loyalties lie.'

The boss visibly flinches. 'Ferget loyalties yoo crazy sonuvabitch! We gonna have ter set up a meetin' with the greys again, only wi'out the boys up top knowin' 'bout it. We gonna have ter renege on this deal.'

'That ain't gonna be so easy…'

The boss looks narrowly at Astor. '…Hell, yer signed sumin', didincha? Hell, yer didn' swaller one o' 'em damn pills they got, didja? …Oh, shi', yer did.'

'Why's the pill so bad?'

''Cos Sue an' Clive's damn organisation have records o' the deal now. Them pills are funny lil things—they send some weird lil bio-signamajig. In shor', we can't go back on the deal now. Shi'. Shi'. Shi'.' Astor notices the boss glancing occasionally towards a drawer… His stash of recreational *Patriot*? 'An' what's that on yer lap, what I seen jus' now?'

'The terms an' conditions, boss. Bucher don't wanna–'

The boss has marched around and yanked the document from Astor's lap. The page is still open on 'Stipulation 9'. 21.7 seconds pass, then: 'Oh my swee' Jeeziz…' the boss staggers back and collapses against a filing cabinet. 'Thassit… I'mer dead man…' he whispers, before bursting into tears.

Astor looks from his boss to the desk to the window, through which he sees a large, unmarked aeroplane taking off from a runway some short distance into the desert.

Astor sighs, and rubs at the headache slumped over his receding hairline. 'Jeez, boss. I'm sorry. I think them greys gone an' tricked me. They muster known our boys up top was plannin' somethin' with the Lillitians. An' they thought they'd try an' destroy all tha'. Tha's how the market goes, I guess…'

The boss sighs and heaves himself up, rubbing the tears from his cheeks.

'I'm sure I did whadiethor' was own'y righ' though…'

The boss chugs behind his desk and collapses into his chair, staring down.

'It's jus', I been in the Pacific. I seen death. I seen what we can do ter each other when we're ordered ter…'

The boss pulls open a drawer and pulls out a syringe and corked phial with a cloudy fluid in it. He pulls the cork out and sucks fluid into the syringe, and injects it into one of several prominent veins in his wrist. He closes his eyes and slips back into his chair.

'I'm scared abou' where we headin' now. There're always colours owddergeduss. Yeller in the East. Yeller and blue in Europe. An' now red too—red everywhere! Red runnin' the white an' blue outer our flags…'

The boss opens his eyes after several moments and reaches back into his drawer.

'Guess I though' the worl' migh' be a better place if we all jus' saw wi'out the colours.'

The boss pulls out a revolver, cocks it and shoots Astor twice in the chest. He turns the gun around, slips it into his mouth, and fires.

Red marches from three bullet holes.

SUBWAY MANDALA
ROBERT LAMB

The slightest of subworld breezes wafts through the station, carrying with it the ozone stench of trains in their burrowing, the oil of lubricated tracks and a million dark miles of spooring mold. Vortices of litter rise wearily and die. Rodents scurry through the littered waste. And all the while the subway stalactites drip, drip, drip their grey waters and its anyone's guess what oceans they drain to.

Rondo, scruff-faced and bag-eyed, is in full lean against a tiled cylindrical column, tiles that steer one's mind toward questions of color. When does green end and grey begin? It's the faded pigment of hospice wards and communist bath houses. It infects the whole station, even the two strangers waiting by the platform.

Fuck, maybe it's contagious?

Rondo shakes away the thought and jabs the nozzle of his aspirator up his left nostril. He pulls the trigger. Inhales.

Feels.

His.

Mind.

Go.

Tight.

He realizes he looks quite suspicious in his current garb. After all, his grubby trench coat is enormous, swollen with the bulk of his many personal effects. He takes inventory.

• One duffle bag stuffed with sour-smelling garments.
• One toiletry bag, mostly full of supplements and enhancers.
• The ragged remnants of an extremely plaid bed roll.
• Two synesthesopes: one working, one busted.
• A digital recorder
• The sketch pad
• Cache of pencils
• Fuck gun

Luckily he's never had to use the fuck gun. He's always fled when the Red Cops bustle into a station and he can all but turn himself invisible when they move from car to car.

Still, it gives him a certain confidence: Foot-long barrel, flat black, one aluminum charge canister locked into the butt. He tested on himself after he bought it just to make sure it would do in a pinch. Ever black out from an orgasm? Aim for the brain, not the junk.

The synesthesope is the cornerstone of his research, though. He has the busted one sheathed on his thigh, nothing more than spare parts at this point. He keeps the functional model strapped to his belt. Its processer hums and vibrates ever so slightly. He feels its warmth through three sour layers of clothing. Sometimes it slides around to the front of the belt, inevitably stirring an erection. A tube runs up from the processer, down his right coat sleeve and the synesthesope's sensor module itself coils around his wrist.

All he has to do is lift his arm. Aim it at some stranger or object. See what's really there.

Of course, he has to reach into his coat with the other hand to adjust the settings – which creates the ever-problematic illusion of public transit masturbation. An earpiece whispers him the analysis data. Sometimes he has to clutch it, tilt his head to hear it above the train noises.

But the machine works like a charm, slicing away layer after layer of cross-sensory metaphor. It turns sound back into sight, smell back into vision and taste into language. And as long as he stays dosed on the right stimulants, the audio it pumps into his ear gives him flashes of The World As It Is.

The revelations fade fast, so he sketches any pertinent findings straight into his little notepad with all the other sketches – mostly torturous phalluses and vaginas like unfolding orchids. The occasional goblinoid or cydunk enhancement.

Rondo checks his wristwatch and sees it's nearly time for his meet up with Bomb Tet. Tet chronicles the transit system's various food carts. Which ones sell actual food? Which ones deal in reliquaries and black market organs?

Tet has seen what the hot dog vats actually contain. He has unfolded a jelly bomber and uncovered the vile secrets of its filling. He's now a devoted vegan.

Rondo glances at the watch again. It's still a little early, but he has to wee. To the rest room.

Abandoning his pillar, he shambles off toward the nearby alcove. Engraved in the stone above the archway is the unmistakable – and rather graphic – toilet glyph. He passes beneath it and gives a quick glance to the left and right hand doors, to the bluntly anatomical symbols painted to represent the two primary human genders.

But he's interested in neither.

Rondo stares instead at the blank wall immediately facing him and switches on the synesthesope. He raises his right arm.

He winces as the piercing whine fills his ear, but then the sound bleeds out into raw sense data. The stench of the station dims. The lighting dissipates and colors moan like banshees. For one glimmering moment, he glimpses a door where there wasn't one – and this one's emblem features a humanoid groin with an X over it.

He grasps the knob before it can vanish and cracks the door just enough to slink through into the restroom beyond.

The synesthesope flash wears off rather swiftly. The door shuts and the restroom is once more washed in illusion. It looks just like any other, except it boasts 108 toilet stalls.

No one else is here of course. Only his fellow chroniclers know about the secret restrooms. The most important rule, obviously, is never ever attempt to use any of those 108 toilets. Piss in the sink if you have to. Shit in the corner. But each stall only appears to contain a normal toilet. Give it a blast with the synesthesope and you'll glimpse monstrosities of porcelain and steel, plumbing conceived by a madman to drink from thoroughly inhuman orifices. One of them, Bomb Tet assures him, may actually serve as a telecommunication system for a species whose language consists entirely of defecation.

It's Rondo's area of study. Not directly. But a great deal of his work involves synesthesoping strangers on the train for alien reproductive organs. So far he's chronicled 33 non-human genital arrangements, all sketched in black pencil. But are those truly 33 separate species? How many are different genders of the same thing? How many alien? Mutant? Surgical or cybernetic enhancements? Countless others remain uncatalogued.

He occasionally doodles human wangs just to remind himself how much the anatomy of a single species varies.

The thought summons the urge, so he walks over to the sink and whips it out for a quick wee.

But it's all just one piece in the grander puzzle, isn't it? What is the World As It IS and why is the Great Illusion coating it so mundane? Why does reality seem a vast public transit system and where is everyone fucking going? To work? Home for dinner with the family? Sure, those are the sort of answers you get when you whip out the small talk on your fellow commuters, but when you actually follow them – as his fellow Chroniclers often do – you find they never wind up anywhere.

There are no homes. No places of work beyond the transit system. It's all endless wandering, all naps on the train and gobbled fried foods. Every last one of the saps is forever waiting on the next transfer, the next express that will take them to some fabled destination.

What is happening?

Rondo shakes out the last droplets of piss and then turns the water on and off to wash it down the drain. He shifts his gear around and reaches into his cloak for his canteen. Takes a quick swig of lukewarm water.

Then, fuck it, another hit from the aspirator.

Just.

For.

Good.

Measure.

His mind jerks back to the three best spots to forage food in this portion of the train world.

• The tempura cart at Mantago Station. The seafood items are all actually vegetable. They're also reliquaries for a nature cult of some sort – Tet could tell you more – but the transubstantiation makes for good eats.

• The mold on the wall at Eight Points Station is actually an edible garden of some sort.

• Selected newspapers at Trollington Station are actually scrolls of meat or fruit leather. Read the opinion pages to decipher which is which.

He hears the door open and shut behind him. Bomb Tet.

The list drops out of his brain, back into the cognitive depths.

"I've got some new ones," Rondo spits, his lips moving just a little too fast as the drug reverberates through his brain. "Some real mind-bogglers."

He pulls out the sketchpad, but when he turns round he quite uncontrollably crumples its spine in his clinched fist.

The stranger before him wears a red policeman's uniform.

The face resembles everyone he's ever met. No one he's ever known. Just looking at it makes Rondo feel woozy. Somehow the wooziness shuts down the fear, locks down the impulse to flee.

The only exit is blocked.

Unless he can fit down one of the toilets.

Which alien life form has the largest bowel movements? Could he really do it? Could he flush himself to safety?

He reaches for the fuck gun under his coat, but the red cop lunges with inhuman speed and sends him flailing backwards. The gun fires an orgasmic pulse through the wall, skids across the tiles and underneath the toilet stalls.

Rondo lands hard, right on the bulk of the synesthesope. He feels it break and a sharp pain blasts through his ribs. The earbud crackles and whines. His vision blurs a little. Sounds leak into colors.

He scrambles up onto his side, then to his knees and looks up at the stranger. The uniform is red, the buttons and gloves are all red. The badge shaped like an inverted triangle.

Red. Red. Red.

Rondo screams and raises his arm to shield himself from the advancing cop, just as the damaged synesthesope flashes once more and Hellish moans flood his brain.

Red turns to black and a thing of chitinous plates and whip-like appendages looms over him. At least six arms uncoil, each terminating in cruel snapping beaks.

Rondo's scream bleeds out. Becomes a groan of breathless agony as the policeman in red reaches down to him with a human hand, as if to lay some blessed anointment on his skull.

Then Rondo's torso splits in half, erupting in a fountain of spewing gore, shattered bone and garlands of tattered entrails.

THE CAUSEWAY
ALIYA WHITELEY

I follow her along the upper level. We pass the Body Shop and Gap; perhaps she's heading for the car park, and my luck is out. There's no need for me to keep a distance. She wouldn't notice me if I trod on her cork wedge heels. She's in the grip of it, and she won't look round. Too much shiny on show.

She reaches the automatic doors and I think it's over, but then she veers right, down the long white corridor that leads to the toilets. I wait a few moments outside the door, then go in. It's empty; rows of basins and mirrors, too bright. I resist the temptation to examine my uninteresting reflection and instead look at the cubicles. All open, apart from the third.

I move the bin for used hand towels in front of the main door, and take up my place in the final cubicle, leaving the door ajar. From my backpack I take out the hypodermic needle, uncap it, check it, hold it ready.

'I know who you are,' she says.

I put one hand over my mouth. I'm not sure why. An instant reaction. She's still in her cubicle. I hear her tear off a handful of tissue paper from the dispenser, and then flush.

Maybe she was speaking on a phone. Or to herself.

'You,' she says. 'You've been following me all day.' There's the sound of the lock being drawn back, and her footsteps, and then the door I'm hiding behind is thrown open, and face to face she is taller, more real. She has amazing hair. It's straight out of a commercial, tawny layers arranged to frame her face. Highlights and lowlights, and nothing medium about it.

'Stay back,' I say. I make a stabbing motion with the needle towards her, which is fairly stupid but does the trick. She retreats until her back is against one of the sinks.

'I'm Gaylen,' she says. 'And you're…?'

'Doctor Parker.'

'It's unusual for a doctor to get involved in this war, isn't it?' she says, with a small smile. She seems so comfortable with this scenario, as if she had planned it.

'Not a GP. Economics Lecturer.'

'Ah. That makes more sense. Listen, can I ask you some questions before you…?' She gestures at the needle. 'I've never had the chance before.'

I have to admit I'm intrigued too. She's by no means my first target, but she's the only one to which I've seen the human side. She's not so different from me. Yes, the hair is better, and the shiny scarlet lips, of course. Apart from that, it's difficult to reconcile her with the threat she poses.

'What do you call us?' she asks. I feel the shock of realisation; she doesn't know what we do, how we plan, groups of us at long tables at the back of the UWE library, the lecturers and students discussing tactics in hushed voices.

'The Red,' I say.

She frowns. 'Why?'

'Because of the lipstick. You always have bright red lipstick.'

'Really?' She turns, looks at herself in the mirror. 'All of us?'

'We thought it was part of the uniform.'

'We all dress the same? We all look the same? Seriously? We look the same to you?' She seems amazed. 'But I got these shoes in a tiny little place in Clifton. One of a kind, the woman said. You can't tell me they all wear shoes like this.'

'You all wear one-off designer shoes. With heels.'

'Well, that's hardly our fault. We like to look good. Every woman likes to look…'

Her gaze falls on my flat slip-on shoes, and she stops talking.

'You're not exactly like the others,' I tell her, although I know I should stop talking. 'The others never wanted to have a conversation.'

'We've been fighting for so long. Maybe it's time for dialogue.'

She must be a leader. When I was first initiated into the Finders by my mother, I was told that someone had to be making the decisions. I never expected to see one of them. I didn't believe it, I suppose. The Red were brainless - drawn to the shops of the Causeway for the endless shopping opportunities, only intent on making themselves beautiful in order to work their magics. I never suspected higher thoughts: a grasp of the Friedman virus, or an appreciation of the global scale of the infection.

'Shall we arrange a meeting?' I say. 'Let's all sit down in a group and talk it through. Name a time and place.'

'Are you important enough in your organisation to make that kind of offer?'

'Are you?'

It occurs to me that there is no way to understand each other. I want a redistribution of global wealth to establish a new egalitarian model based on Hoxaist principles and she wants cheaper red lipstick.

'This isn't going to work,' I mutter.

'Wait,' she says, 'Parker. You're Francine Parker. Your mother was Doctor Norma Parker. She's a legend.'

I never thought I'd hear her name on the lips of a witch. I try not to let it distract me. 'Turn around,' I tell her. I'm not normally so squeamish about injecting them, but I find I don't want to look at her face.

She doesn't appear to hear my command. 'You have the nerve to accuse us of being brain-dead when you've turned into a little clone of your mother. Another Professor of Economics, repeating the same stupid ideas about how to make the world a better place, not realising that the only happiness a person should be responsible for is their own. And you can't even manage that, can you?'

'Is that making you happy? Dressing that way? Casting your spells over men with your promises of sex and marriage and babies and eternal life? I know the kind of glamours you cast.'

'Do you? What did she tell you? Did she say we all believe in God? That we allow suffering to happen because we think there'll be an afterlife to make everything equal?'

It's as if something inside me has started to unravel. I can't stop that suspicion that my determination is sliding away. The picture I had in my head is no longer complete.

'I've killed so many of you,' I say. 'You've all deserved it.'

'The question of who is deserving of what - surely that's a question for a philosopher, not an economist?'

I have injected them in the back of the neck, or in the buttocks if its summer and their floaty revealing dresses are thin. They've run away from me, to their cars, driven home, died later, perhaps in an armchair, perhaps in the bath. I pictured them floating away without complaint. Didn't they believe they were going to a better place?

'You have to be stopped. Tell me how I can stop you.'

The way Gaylen smiles at me sends a chill of understanding into my brain. I look towards the door; as if it has been waiting for my attention, it bursts open and the bin is sent flying across the room, the lid rolling, the blue hand towels flapping like birds set free. Three witches run at me. I don't see much but blonde hair and manicured nails as they wrestle me down and take the hypodermic needle from my fingers. There's a sudden pain in my skull; I manage to focus on Gaylen, standing over me, holding a small red tube, and then I lose the fight to stay conscious, and the world slips away from me, shrinking back into nothing but a blank space.

My mother would be aghast that I fell for such an obvious trap.

When I turned ten, my mother took me to church, a small one, in a village outside Wootton-under-edge, far enough from Bristol so that nobody we knew would see us. 'I want you to make your own decision about this,' she said. We walked around, past the wooden pews, up to the altar. Above us, the sunlight filtered through the stained glass window, depicting a woman in blue and white, her head covered, her eyes downcast. She was improbably beautiful. Perhaps she was the beginning of the images upon which the Finders had declared war - those unreal objects with their airbrushed bellies exposed to the camera, their glossy pouts.

'What do you think?' said my mother.

I pointed my thumbs down. I knew then that suffering through fashion - on crosses, in factories, nails in hands, worn fingers, had to be eradicated.

I dream of her. She's swathed in blue and white, her hands pressed together in prayer, and she floats around me, repeating phrases about dialectical materialism, never getting close enough for me to touch. She reaches the end of a long sentence about workers' rights, then turns into a stained-glass window and tells me to get up get up get up get up

So I do.

I'm alone in the toilets. My head is sore but not agonising. I make it to the mirror and cling on to the edge of the sink, expecting someone to jump me, to finish what I started. But there's nothing. I can't believe it, but as the minutes pass I have to face the fact that I've been spared. And I'm grateful for their mercy. I hate myself for feeling it, that gratitude. It's not an emotion I want to have.

And then I look in the mirror.

I have been changed.

My hair is loose and long, my complexion even. Something has been applied to my eyes to make the lashes look thicker, and a dab of green paint accentuates my hazel irises. My lips are plump and full and red.

I realise I'm dressed in a knee-high skirt and a tight white tee shirt, and I'm wearing brown leather boots with heels that show off my slim calves and tiny waist. My nails have been painted to match my lips. Magic has been done upon me, and I am beautiful. My reflection is smiling at me. I touch my mouth, and find I'm smiling back.

I walk out of the toilet and back into the causeway, past Gap, past the Body Shop. I don't know where to go. There are a group of three young men on a bench outside a Games Workshop. As I walk past, they look at me. I've never been looked at this way before.

'Are you okay?' one of them says. He is tall and handsome. He gets up and comes over to me. 'Do you need help?'

'Yes,' I say. 'Oh yes. I was attacked.

In the ladies.'

'Here, sit down, I'll call someone.' He takes my arm, and all of his attention is upon me. Without wanting to, without understanding how I did it, I have worked my first magic spell. And I realise I want to do more.

RED RIDING HOOD AT FIFTY
DAVID R. MORGAN

Forty years later, you come again...

along that path in the woods
to my grandmother's home,
planning to try us once more, and
knowing the woodcutter is
gone because the trees are gone.

Yes, forty years later, you come again...

but we have seen worse wolves
at the door since your occasion:
impending foreclosure, bad mortgage,
angina, chronic back pain, rotten molars,
my son caught with a shaggy hand in the till.

Yet your grey look is memorable to me.

Calling to Granny's ghost in the kitchen,
I laugh softly in your face. You just
stand there, not knowing whether to smile
or what to say. But yes, old friend:
I always knew who it was in that dress.

Come on in and have a drink.

BEFORE THIS HAPPENED
DAVID R. MORGAN

Before this happened, reality was within me, intimate as an internal organ.
Now far away, dark- mattered, booming, an earth dam I almost plug in dark nights on sleepless knees,
praying that pain won't balloon into death, that accidents will veer and swerve around, the vessels
in my loved ones won't rupture, my heart grow morose and tired, the wrong future confirmed.
All good tragedies are those of devotion, and therefore divinity, inside of us… yet still outside,
like dreams of dams bursting overhead, tornadoes
circling, sinister things rising from murky swamps, red eyed taloned, coming closer.

THE DESIRE OF THINGS
DAVID R. MORGAN

The white house is all black. The black house is all white. They dwell in the same fable. They naturally look alike.

He yanks open the tumble dryer, which feels violated and then guilty for enjoying it, dumps the hot, panting shirts and shorts into a basket, and heads back upstairs, carefully turning off the lights to avoid the lecture about electricity the woman will give him later if he doesn't.

He folds the clothes neatly and quickly, then smoothes each piece with his hand. It's hard to say who enjoys this the most–the shirts or the table he presses them upon–and then the woman is knocking on the kitchen door.

He opens it for her and she growls at him to stop locking her out when she is gardening; she leaves it unlocked for a reason.

The man is getting tired of this particular topic and instead of apologising snaps crisply that he has no memory of locking it, and indeed he hasn't.

The house just wanted a few more precious moments alone with him.

She stomps back outside, and he carefully checks that it is unlocked, even while muttering against the woman under his breath.

The door handle is sure it isn't its imagination that his hand lingers on the brass. It gloats.

The woman has tracked mud on the kitchen floor, which nearly faints with joy when he notices.

He looks closer at the cracked and peeling linoleum and forgoes the mop for a rag and brush. He mutters about how disgusting the floor is–how utterly, utterly filthy, as his nail digs at an especially difficult spot. Yes yes yes, squeaks the floor–who, like the braided cord over the washer, likes it rough.

Afterwards, he heads up the stairs (which groan loudly at the feel of his toes) to take his shower.

Despite its lascivious reputation, the shower couldn't care less about the man, even as it rains fat droplets down his chest and buttocks.

The bath, the sole dissenter in the house, yearns for the yielding fleshy rump of the woman. It hasn't felt it in ages, as it is summer and not time for long, hot baths.

The woman, cursing, fumbles with the kitchen door and has to find her key with dirt-encrusted fingers deep in her pockets.

She steps inside, notices the floor has been washed, and carefully removes her shoes, muttering that he'll probably want to be thanked now that he's done her annual unprompted housecleaning chore–then peers suspiciously down the stairs to be sure he hasn't left a light on in the cellar again.

She cleans out stubborn dirt from beneath fingernails, with a particularly indignant kitchen knife. Licks marmite from a razor sharp blade and kisses her cross with a tongue that knows no shame.

The midsummer sky is growing dim as she showers, unwittingly spurning the tub so far below, while the man brushes his teeth.

The orgiastic moaning of the toothbrush annoys the towel incredibly, because after all, who is it that gets to cradle his every last muscle rubbing rubbing rubbing and then contentedly wrap herself around the man's torso for a little post-pleasure snuggling?

It is too hot for even a tank top and the man lies flat on the sheet, staring up into the dark, and wonders how long it has been like this.

Just today? All year? Forever?

The woman, annoyed as she is with the man, sees the curve of his thigh in the light from the window and slides in next to him, giving it a tentative caress, reaching round between his legs.

She spent all morning with her eyes on the day time reality TV, grunting once non committaly and after lunch she had flat-out refused to dance with him when a slow waltz came on the radio.

She didn't feel like it, she said.

The ceiling fan stares down in utter loathing at the woman who sighs and moans away on top of the man.

If he was mine, thinks the fan, oh how I would waltz with him. Around and around and around, cutting her away.

In the kitchen drawer, the knives start to stir.

They naturally look alike. They dwell in the same fable. The black house is all white. The white house is all black.

I FORGET WHO WAS ON WHOSE SIDE
J. J. STEINFELD

First appeared in the poetry chapbook *Where War Finds You* (Canada)

A long-ago schoolyard game of war
a battlefield or battleground, rebuilt in recollection,
words even now carrying and constructing memory
I forget who was on whose side
what the objectives were
we being young and blood-thirsty
unaware of formal tactics and strategies
or a warlike nature in historical hearts and minds
belligerent and *combative*
words unknown to our childish artlessness
none of us had yet read *Lord of the Flies*
or *Nineteen Eighty-Four*
or *All Quiet on the Western Front*
looked through the lenses of disquieting authors
not a single poem by a forgiving or an unforgiving poet
or even dabbled in cynicism or worldly sorrow
we were kids playing the primordial, the language rudimentary,
too young to kill, too old to forgive

following the leader, falling into place,
I remember that
and I remember
one boy in particular
because someone thought
he was effeminate, aloof,
and another boy, as fierce as a movie warrior,
led a mid-morning raid
on the remarkable-bodied noncombatant
I yelled for them to stop
retreat, *surrender*,
unavailing adult words,

POLLUTO

and I was relieved that looks
were not knives
or I would have bled to death

that night I heard my father say
Europe is far away
and Hitler is dead
but my father did not sound safe

POLLUTO

THE ESPIONAGE AGENT
J. J. STEINFELD

First appeared in the poetry chapbook *Where War Finds You* (Canada)

You fill out the requisite form,
tell who and what you are:
where you were born, how you were born,
the code of your tears
when you were given a first slap by knowledge
when you began your refusals and your acquiescences
how you learned to read the death threats
how you swallowed the headlines and loneliness
how you make love with escapees without documents
with tales of close calls and enemies without magic,
especially the most recent, scarred and heroic.
If you need more space, attach additional sheets–
on an additional sheet, a sheaf of fine stationary,
you print in your agonized hand:
Before she leaves, dressing, she says:
'I imagine History a cunning little creature
a belching, blustering, conniving being,
saying, *I have something marvellous for you*,
and in your innocence or greed or confusion
you reach out your hand, seared or severed,
depends on the luck of the draw
the direction the smoke is drifting.'
Now is not the time for cynicism or foreboding
you hear yourself say
this sudden sex under worldly duress
has made you a cautious debater.
Your uniform is a disguise, she says,
despising the debate and the sound of warfare.
Your disguise is a uniform, you reply
polite as a man with a rope around his neck
such politeness I can do without
within my current confinement
stay, you beg,
and we will discuss plagues and secret calamities

POLLUTO

and the music of the deaf.
When will this warfare end? are her final words
as she flees your embrace and the room of your hiding.
You have espionage in your heart
which classroom lesson could have prepared you
for all this upheaval and folly
you open the envelope
not ripping it this time
you have learned neatness and patience
your orders within
no, not again, you scream
where you're born, how you're born
did not prepare you for this.

THE MEANING
NICOLE CUSHING

Entry in the *Encyclopedia of Obscure Video*

Witchfinders vs. The Evil Red (Unrated)
Year of Release: Unknown (Possibly early-1970s)
Country of Origin: Unknown

Introduction

As far as anyone can tell, *Witchfinders vs. The Evil Red* isn't even this unusual twelve-minute film's real name. It has no title or credits, and has been attributed to everyone from David Cronenberg to David Lynch.

A group of film historians estimated the year of *Witchfinders'* release based on the wear and tear evident on one of the surviving prints, as well as from the testimony of various Greenwich Village residents who recall seeing it as a short (shown before midnight screenings of Jodorowsky's *El Topo*). However, special effects professionals who have watched the film declare that its visual effects are state of the art, even by today's standards. The riddle of how such a technologically advanced piece of cinema could have been made so many years ago remains a significant motivating force behind the effort to identify the creative team behind this project.

Witchfinders vs. The Evil Red is just a name the underground film community has, apparently through consensus, given this short. If there's one single man or woman who originated the title, the identity of that person remains lost to the annals of cinematic history.

Plot synopsis (including spoilers):

The film opens with a panoramic shot of a raging river of blood. Viscera float in it, like seaweed. Crimson waves crash against a muddy, peninsular coastline.

A man rises up out of the muck of this muddy shore. A man *made* of mud. He doesn't so much walk as waddle. He makes an awkward march toward the river bank and takes a gander at the sanguinary tide. The soundtrack amplifies the squishy sound of mud separating from mud as his lips break away from one another to speak. He points to the river. "Sorcery!" he snarls. "Sorcery!"

The bloodwaves begin to break against the coastline more quickly, the tide rises, and before you know it the river's gotten to the level of the Mud Man's knees. He makes no effort to flee. "Sorcery! Sorcery!" he repeats, as though that's the only word he's ever learned. Eventually, the tide rushes into his mouth. But he continues on, gargling "Sorcery!" over and over until the bloodtide has its way with his body, until his head and neck and torso and appendages lose definition from all the erosion. Near the end we hear only the faintest wheezing of a residual pocket of air in the mud, then the loud crash of waves swallowing the Mud Man's body whole.

The final shot zooms in on a section of the muddy shore several yards inland from where the river's crested. A head (made of mud) erupts from the ground, like a molehill. Neck, shoulders and arms emerge. A new Mud Man struggles out of the muck and points to the red river. There's a squishy sound as his lips separate from each other to scream "Sorcery!" Then the screen fades to black.

Interpretations:

In his essay "Witchfinders at One with the Evil Red", American Buddhist scholar Ben Tillen suggested an interpretation founded on the Zen ideal of non-dualism. "The film is rife with images of opposites in confrontation. The individual against nature, life against death, river against coast. Ingeniously, it resolves these conflicts by revealing that they're all illusions. The individual is nature. Life is death. The river is in the coast, and the coast in the river."

Schopenhauer disciple Max Maxfield, Ph.D has instead focused on what he calls "the agony of repeated death and resurrection." According to Maxfield, "the image of the sentient being emerging from the muck must give one pause. I found myself yelling at my television, yelling at the poor Mud Fellow the way Burgess Meredith yelled at that boxer, Rocky Balboa – 'Stay Down,' I found myself yelling. 'Stay Down! Don't rise from the muck. There's no so-called sorcery to be found in the blood-ocean, or – if one is brutally honest with oneself – anywhere else!'"

But the most well-known commentary on the film comes from the Youtube video series "100 Ordinary People React to *Witchfinders vs. The Evil Red*"; specifically the now-infamous Video #58 ("The Woman from Kentucky"). Although Youtube removed the video due to inappropriate content, one could (as of the writing of this entry) still view it on other, more obscure websites.

A brief summary follows below for those who've not yet watched it.

The woman from Kentucky has bleached-blond hair, and a cigarette dangles out of her mouth. She has the burnt-brown look of a caucasian who visits the tanning bed far too often. For no apparent reason, she's sweating heavily.

We see her watching *Witchfinders vs. The Evil Red* on a television. She grins, stamps her cigarette out in the ashtray, and momentarily moves off-camera. When she returns, there's a razor blade in her hand.

She positions the blade vertically, so that the cut will run parallel to the vein (or, if she's lucky, actually strike it). She closes her eyes and digs the razor into her wrist, wincing when it makes contact but getting a good anchor a half-inch under the skin. She drags the blade upward, eviscerating dermis, vein, and muscle alike – all the way to the crook of her elbow.

Somehow, in the midst of this madness, the woman from Kentucky maintains the presence of mind to move the webcam so that we see a close-up of the wound. A tide of blood rises up from the slashed veins. We hear, over and over, the accusation – "Sorcery!" Most viewers assume this is coming from the television in the background. But a significant minority swear it's too loud and clear to be that. Those are the same people who insist they can see a tiny humanoid figure rising like a welt from the woman's dark, damp upper arm.

THE GREEN EYED BREATH-VAMPIRE
WITH THE CHEAP STRIPED TUXEDO AND MONOCLE TATTOO

MIKE ARONOVITZ

They shut him away up there because he'd become a bit of an embarrassment to tell the truth, and while Jordan didn't really want to come to terms with all this, he knew deep down she was right. Nowadays, if they didn't keep an eye on him he got into all kinds of mischief, putting napkins in the toaster, suitcases in the oven, clothes in the bath tub. Last week he'd opened up every conceivable threshold in the place, starting with the entrance door, the mud room storm door, and the screen door on the porch. Then he'd flipped up the lid on the basement meat freezer and opened the fridge doors in addition to all the cupboards and closets and every drawer in the place, that's right, the ones in the bedroom bureaus, the laundry room utility containers, the garage storage lockers, and the bathroom cabinets. Jenna thought it looked "ultra cool," like the house had sneezed, but Ann Marie wasn't having any of it. She'd been forcefully suggesting getting family support to put him in a rest home even before the wacked out shit he'd pulled *last* night, but Jordan hadn't caved even now. His father had been his idol too long for that noise, and he still saw him as the hunk of granite he'd grown up adoring, the king of the job site, betting man, and bar room philosopher. He saw it in his smile, in the flash that came into his eyes once in a blue moon. What he refused to acknowledge was the disoriented bone-bag living in the guest room at the far end of the upstairs hallway, gray hair thinned into that U-shape and greased behind the ears, forehead speckled with liver spots that spread to larger brown ovals along the top of his crown. Seems Jenna was the only one who understood his gibberish lately, and more and more Ann Marie was voicing her displeasure with the fact that an eighty-three year old man was so fascinated with an eight year old's dolls and jump ropes and Leggos and water colors.

Jenna called her grandpa "The Mountain Man," and sometimes her "Gorton's Fisherman." She liked to stroke his frizzy white beard, which had food in it more often than not, and Ann Marie was certainly no fan of that ritual. She'd had so many talks with the kid about "good touch and bad touch" lately, in fact, that Jordan was having trouble just laughing it off. Dad was no child molester. He was a hero, the guy who'd worked construction year round in the elements laying brick and tile, coring holes in concrete when he had to, taking on massive commercial restoration jobs where he'd balance himself out on rickety scaffolding hundreds of feet up in the air grinding out mortar joints, then bouncing on the weekends over at the Red Eye just to put his kids through school. He was the one who taught Jordan how to bury a linebacker on a straight run up the middle, how to avoid getting rinsed at the dealer by throwing the hood up yourself, how to shoulder failure, how to hit back.

What he *wasn't*, at least to Jordan Colella, was this wrinkled, withered old child-thing, always dressing in his red flannel and paint splattered overalls no matter how many times he or Ann Marie pointed out to him that there was a fresh pile of shirts and trousers there on his bedroom foot locker. He was not that shuffling sack of old meal, rolling and clacking his false teeth in his mouth like bad chewing tobacco, often staring with confused, tea-water eyes when you called to him, eyes that had once been hard flint.

Sometimes, he almost made it back, fooled you. Jordan would be sitting at the table with him, eating breakfast, bitching about how the Phillies couldn't buy a base hit, or how the new warehouse rat they hired at the tool place kept pulling the wrong caliber shots for the Ramset pins, or how much of a pain in the ass it was to keep up with the virtual orders coming in by the boatload when contractors used to just use a God damned telephone if they ran out of a box of sleeve anchors, or carbide saw blades, or three inch coarse threaded drywall screws, or how Frankie (his oldest, freshman at Widener) would only call for money or to complain about all the reading they didn't prepare him for in his high school classes. And old Aldo would listen to it all, legs crossed, hands folded. He'd say "Uh huh" once in a while, nod his head in the right places. Then out of the blue he'd ask Jordan in a spidery whine if the Russians were coming, or if the aliens from Planet Krypton had landed and taken over Route 476. And he'd started to refer to Ann Marie as the "scary nurse," seemingly unaware that she was right there in the pantry looking for a bottle of Clorox, or coming down the hall stairs, or bringing in two bags of groceries, close enough to hear the spitty little stage whispers.

The real trouble, however, started earlier in the week, when Dr. Shilingher suggested a combination of Aricept and Namenda, claiming it wouldn't "cure" Aldo, but rather, "keep him steady, like he was in a parking lot for awhile." This, of course, irritated Ann Marie to no end. Steady? Are you kidding me? But Jordan was hopeful. Maybe it would make a couple of subtle differences, take off the edge. It was just plaque in the brain after all. They could put a man on the moon, right?

Aldo wouldn't swallow the pills even when coaxed to do so with Mountain Dew, his favorite, so Ann Marie mixed them into some peanut butter. Three days passed, and then Aldo had come down into the living room that fourth evening wearing a white dress shirt and blue work pants, both wrinkled to holy hell. He slowly crossed the space, said "Excuse" when he temporarily blocked Jordan's view of the flat screen, and sat beside Ann Marie on the sofa, conservative neighbors, a plush pillow apiece. She'd been reading an exercise magazine, and hadn't looked up.

"Pop-pop, now this is our TV time. After dinner you can help Jenna with her puppet project as long as Jordie doesn't mind monitoring."

He turned his head slightly, eyebrows forking a bit.

"It's my birthday."

Now, she was looking. So was Jordan. Aldo met their stares one at a time.

"It's my birthday," he said, "and I want ice cream. Mint chocolate chip with syrup. And a cup cake with a candle in it."

Ann Marie put down the magazine and ran her thumb and index finger down along the corners of her lips. It was a battle preparation Jordan was well used to, and he cut her off before she could scold Aldo for giving her orders.

"Babe, I got this." He kicked down the foot rest on the Lazy-Boy, walked over, and took his father by the elbow. "Let's see what we can rustle up in here, Dad." He guided him into the kitchen, sat him down, and made him settle for vanilla bean. He even sang "Happy Birthday," and the overly hearty sound of his off-key voice ringing and then dying on the walls kicked off an anger in him that seemed to come from a thousand places at once. Why wasn't Ann Marie in here with him, celebrating this red letter moment, this sign that the doctors were wrong, that you could reverse this thing, that Dad had made a clothing choice and voiced a sober demand, that he'd come leaps and bounds in a matter of days? Hello? And why hadn't Jenna set the table yet? And why hadn't he gotten anything at work but cost of living in three years? And why the fuck did the end of his father's time here have to be marked and measured by random outbursts and fake-me-out birthdays?

Ann Marie was in the archway watching. She did get it, Jordan could see it in her expression, and his anger dissipated. The bride had always had that power over him, so pretty in her own no-nonsense neighborhood-girl kind of way, long ponytail tossed over a shoulder, big brown eyes, smoky campfire voice. Over the years Jordan had come to the conclusion that guys were angry on some level most of the time, and they often didn't even know the rhyme or the reason for it. It took a good woman to redirect that energy. He walked over and kissed her. She responded and their mouths opened. Aldo sat and ate his ice cream, and this was the way it was supposed to be. No scary nurses. No bumbling wanderers opening up all the drawers.

Dinner was ok, at least for a hot minute or so. Jenna moaned in dramatic agony when she realized she hadn't gotten ice cream before dinner like Pop-pop, but brightened considerably when she was promised two Klondike cookie bars after she finished her spaghetti. Jordan needled Ann Marie about having to fall asleep every night with the TV on, and she countered by claiming he had shirked cleaning the bathroom for so long that the sink had demanded an apology note. Then, in the middle of Jenna's rather scattered story about a girl at school who had thrown up in a trash can at recess, Aldo finished his glass of milk, sucking hard on the straw, causing that throaty, funneling, whooping sound.

From nowhere, Jenna burst into tears. Ann Marie was there immediately, scooping her up, switching places with her in the chair, rubbing her back saying, "There, there." Jordan looked at his hands and studied the nails, the cuticles. So much for a quiet dinner at the Colella's. Jenna had been complaining of depression, well, not in so many words, but for the last couple of weeks she'd been waking up with tears on her cheeks. If Jordan asked what was bothering her, she'd pout. If he pressed, she'd cry herself into the hiccups, blubber bubbles on her lips. Both Jordan and Ann Marie were mystified, especially since she was always fine after her shower and breakfast, ankles curled around the kitchen chair legs, coloring with the tip of her tongue poked out the side of her mouth, animated annoyance when asked to perform the slightest task, skipping in the halls, spinning in the living room until she fell down, the usual.

But morning depression? In an eight year old? And now the same shit kicked off by the sound of milk being sucked through a straw? Jordan just didn't get it. Maybe he was just cold or something, but being "sad" just wasn't quite tangible for him. Scared? Yeah, sure. Get mugged, fired, or pulled over, and you'd be scared plenty. Worn down? Yes sir. Working in the trades twenty years running would make anyone more than familiar. Desperate? You betcha. Just lay down a grand on the Eagles to cover and you'd cringe like the rest of us. But "melancholy?" Sounded just a bit too much like the excuse of some lit-geek, and it wasn't that Jordan was insensitive to his daughter's pain, he just didn't know the remedy.

"Hey honey," Ann Marie said, bouncing Jenna a bit. "What's wrong, baby, tell me."

It was muffled, because Jenna's face was buried in her mother's shoulder, but it sounded like she said that something was "stealing her happy." Of course, Jordan knew he'd been out of circulation for a good while by now, but you'd have to be living under a rock not to recognize the punch line from the Carrie Underwood single. So modern music represented the fall of western civilization after all. Would he next be consulting some therapist who'd claim his daughter was internalizing harmful pop lyrics and experiencing mood swings because she couldn't handle the more adult themes bombarding her from so many media outlets or some such lame shit? Was he supposed to take her clock radio? Give her ear muffs?

"Cheer up," Ann Marie said. "Tomorrow night's Dong Night, and all your friend's will be over."

Jenna pulled away a bit.

"Really?"

"M-hmm."

"Yay!" she shouted, sliding out of the embrace and down to the floor, then grabbing the table with both hands and jumping up and down. "I'm gonna go first, and I get the Justin Beamer song, and I want cheese popcorn, not just the plain Orville Redenbacker, and after, you promised next time we could make banana splits, and I don't want Margie Valelly to come over because last week she started calling me names!"

Jordan shook his head and smiled. Dong Night, women and their rituals, hell, he had better understood Frankie's klepto phase, his desire to play mud football, and the sleep overs where all the boys would sneak in Red Bull to chug down, because if you were the first one passed out you woke up with oatmeal in your shorts. But this girl stuff was really just out of his league; best to just play along (which he had learned to do quite well by the way).

"Dong Night" had become a monthly tradition with the Gregorio's, the Johnson's, the Valelly's, and the Pastalone's, all of whom they'd struck up friendships with through girl scouts and church. It was just plain idiocy for the sake of it. All the girls borrowed their mothers' makeup and hair spray and did themselves up like circus freaks: crazy multi colored applications of blush, eye shadow, and lip stick, big Scrunchie hair clips pointing out in all directions, and then braids all done up and tied to stand straight off the head. Then they would video tape themselves singing and crazy-dancing to their favorite pop songs, one at a time for a competition, and then all together for an all out dance party free for all. The parents stood around drinking heavily and applauding heartily. A night for no-minds. Just what the girl needed.

Aldo coughed and it sounded like phlegm came up from his chest. He rolled it around, bit through it a few times, swallowed lustily, and smacked his lips.

"Tastes good," he said. Jordan looked at the floor. Yeah. Baby steps. Ann Marie turned away and started cleaning up. Jenna helped. Jordan ambled off to the living room to catch the tail end of Comcast Daily News Live, and Jenna eventually took her grandfather over in the corner to try and teach him Monopoly. She was patient with him, praised him, didn't scold him for mixing the Community Chest Cards with the Chance cards or trying to eat the player's piece shaped like a top hat. Baby steps. Things were ok.

Until the next morning.

Jordan was always the first one up, and before he even made his way out of bed he sensed something. He'd dreamed badly, and couldn't remember. The air conditioner was making noise, like an airplane, then a smooth hum; had to get that freakin' thing fixed. He was cold and sweating. He swung his feet to the floor, rubbed his face, and got up. His Achilles tendons hurt like they always did, and he made his way to the bathroom.

One step in, he skidded and grabbed the doorjamb.

Something was stuck to his feet. He reached down and brushed at his heel. The bottom of his foot was covered with dots, pills, and for a second he thought that maybe Ann Marie had hit the Bolla too hard last night, gaining the common sense to down a few Bayers before sleep, then inadvertently knocking over the bottle. He looked closer at the floor and sucked his breath between his teeth.

It wasn't just the Bayer aspirin, and it was anything but a random spill. The entire medicine cabinet had been emptied, the CVS Rapid Reliefs, the Ambien, the Naproxen, the Sudafed, and a shitload of others Ann Marie had hoarded over the years, those that Jordan never really bothered looking at let alone pronouncing, all rearranged meticulously atop the black, gray, and white floor tiles, gel caps in the darker squares, tablets in the latter, all the oblongs in the "L" patterns, all the circulars in the squares. The heaviest concentration was by the toilet, and they spread to the outskirts of the room like planets and stars, as if some strange camera had caught the universe exploding. Jordan squinted and bent closer. Yes. Some of the flatter pills were stacked on top of each other four or five high, and the oval shaped capsules were all placed in uniform diagonals toward the window. It was strange, exacting work that must have taken hours.

Jordan smelled something. From the living room.

Bow legged, he hopped down the stairs two and three at a time, hair sticking up in the back, and when he reached the bottom, he stopped. To the left, he could see there was trouble in and around the fireplace area, and to the right, the open frame coat closet at the far edge of the living room had become a junkyard. There, right beneath the neat row of fall and winter coats, were their two rusty propane tanks stacked and stuffed amongst a hoard of other junk from the back yard shed, all weather spotted and floating with dust veils. He walked closer, not believing but believing it, his mud spattered half moon edger angled across the Scotts Speedy two-wheeled fertilizer dispenser. There was a Toro mower bag wearing its dark green beard of grass residue, and underneath it, a gallon of rock salt, a slew of paint varnish cans, the Christmas front lawn gingerbread men, and the weed wacker. An old length of kinked up garden hose was tied and screw-coiled around a Rubbermaid trash cover wedged in on a slant, and the 39 gallon recycling drum was stuffed in butt first, open maw crawling with water spiders.

       Jordan turned toward the fireplace. In front of it, the kitchen trash can lay on its side, the pokers propped across it on angles pointing back in toward the hearth. Inside, there was garbage, wet garbage from the can and the fridge. Up front sat a number of corner cut chicken quesadillas that Ann Marie had tried baking instead of grilling, on whole wheat tortilla wrappers no less, and Jenna had bitched and moaned, and Annie had chucked them. Two days ago. Jordan got to his knees, and bent in for a real look-see. Yep. The whole can had been emptied and rearranged in here. There was the deli roast beef from a week ago that had gone a bit greasy with age, now laid out strip by strip across the back edge of the dark space, along with empty Tortinos pizza boxes and Weight Watchers cartons stacked atop each other in pyramids. There was half a ham sandwich settled into a whitened puddle of bacon fat next to half an old cheese steak Jordan picked up at a lunch truck three days ago, and scoops of guacamole, browned now, placed as if decorator foliage at the front corners, smiley faces impressed into the surfaces by someone's delicate artistic touch. There were rumpled, damp paper towels placed at the edges like border flowers, and old, rank spaghetti snaked through all of it in "S" shapes and figure eights.

       Jordan angled in and looked up, first one side, then the other.

       Oh boy.

       He didn't.

       Oh, but he had.

       Somehow, Aldo had gotten the caulking gun, fitted it with a tube of the brick adhesive, and glued all of the exterior refrigerator stuff to the inner walls of the hearth. There was the photo of Ann Marie's autistic nephew, and the gorgeous print Jordan took last year of Jenna, hair in pigtails, sitting and reading a book on the iron bench outside Penn Wynn Elementary. The family portrait magnets that they got taken at Wendy Schulman's Bat Mitzvah last year were pasted in there, just like the poem Jenna did for homework a month ago, last year's Mother's Day poster with hearts on it, an archery award from the day camp, and a mini raft made out of popsicle sticks with Jenna's handprint in the center. Making up the rest of the three-sided mural was the stuff that rode the fridge side saddle, much of it old crap that he and Ann Marie had stuffed in a big mesh magnet basket for hasty convenience. There was an old Phillies schedule there and pages from an obsolete pocket calendar with Norman Rockwell prints on them. There was a Weight Watchers points slide, menus for pizza and Chinese delivery places, a Terminex contract, old receipts, a cable manual, and a voucher with Sears for a year's worth of free service on the gas range, all this amongst a litter of magnets from Kids First Pediatrician's, Blockbuster Video, Super Cuts, Lower Merion Tee Ball, and four or five real estate agencies. And all of it was placed meticulously, all of it so… *Aldo* for lack of a better word. Near the base he had set the larger, rectangular paraphernalia like bricks, the given layout course below its alternate, five rows in a neat horizontal stagger, and then as his fridge materials got smaller, more varied in size and shape, he adjusted his patterning to a strange mix of modular pin-wheeling and hopscotch modified, the lot of it interlocking like some madman's calico puzzle on top of the fire bricks beneath, a full "wall papering" that covered almost every square inch of space running three or four feet up the flue.

       Ann Marie hit the roof, and took

a day off from the hospital (they could find someone else to answer phones in the pulmonary lab for a shift, God damn it). She put all the shit back into the shed herself, took all the coats out for dry cleaning, and called Stanley Steamer to come scrub out the hearth, scour that closet, and shampoo the rugs. She paid one of them extra to chip the "mural" off the fire brick, and some of the bits and corners and pieces just wouldn't come loose. Aldo slept all day, snoring up there in his room, and he was still sawing wood when Jordan got home from the warehouse.

"He's got to go," she said. She was wearing green scrubs and a Phillies tee shirt, leaning into the sink, scrubbing a baking pan with a Brillo. Jordan was sitting at the table. His throat hurt on one side and his head was pounding. He'd been buried in returns all day, and one of the outside salesmen had ransacked the steel showroom cabinet in a rush to make a deadline. Jordan had spent his entire afternoon reorganizing drill bits, screw gun tips, and metric hole saws, and he wasn't in the mood.

"It's not as if he's using the washing machine for a toilet or anything," he said. "He's just confused." Ann Marie stopped scrubbing and turned the water off for effect. "Confused? Really? He's a child, Jordie. A dangerous child who turns into a night time maniac if you feed him a pill."

Jordan looked at his folded hands.

"Well that's one riddle solved. The medication might not be a good thing."

"You think?"

"Funny."

"Is it?" She tore a paper towel off the roll suspended on the side of the cabinet and dried her hands vigorously. "An eighty three year old man has adopted my daughter as his surrogate mother. I'm laughing."

"There's no harm."

"How do you know, Jordan? Are you there for every conversation?"

"She was happy this morning."

"For once."

Hands, eyes locked there. Psychology again, yeah, someone or some thing was stealing his daughter's good cheer and he was supposed to blame his own father. And he refused. And that wasn't really it either. What actually bothered Jordan was the fact that deep down, he wasn't sure if he kept defending Aldo for his own selfish kind of gain. For real, he wasn't quite positive that he didn't just accept his daughter as the baby sitter so he could have a moment of peace to watch Comcast once in awhile.

"I don't know why she cries, hon," he said, looking up. "I'm not a head shrinker, and I'm not about to go signing her up for one. It's a phase. It'll pass." Ann Marie had sat down across the table from him.

"There's not the same stigma as when me and you grew up, Jordie."

"No, I won't let it happen."

"You're being pig headed."

"I'm not."

He was. Absolutely. He was being pulled into strange waters here, he hadn't expected it, and it wasn't fair. This was supposed to be about Aldo. He tried to relax his face.

"She's got her Dong Night tonight, honey. That will cheer her up, I guarantee it."

"You sound like a car commercial."

"Guarantee."

They both smiled, and Jordan gave a sly look.

"The real question is whether or not you're going to invite the Valelly's."

Ann Marie pushed away from the table.

"I already did. Girls fight all the time. They'll be best friends by dinner, in fact, they probably made up already." Jordan grinned.

"See? I told you she didn't need a head-shrinker. A mom is every kid's best therapist."

"Hmm," Ann Marie answered. She hadn't pulled away from the edge of the table yet. She was standing there, arms folded now.

"The real question," she said, "is where we're going to put Aldo tonight."

"What do you mean?"

"Did I stutter?"

Jordan shook his head. "No," he said. "He's not an animal. You don't hide family away like some dog in a crate."

Ann Marie's hands were on her hips now.

"You do when that family member rolls his teeth, farts at will, wanders around, and talks about how good his lugers taste! Dottie Johnson Facebooks, and I'm not going to have my family moments broadcast all over the internet. She's still pissed that I showed her up at the beef and beer last month, wearing the black jeans and pumps, and she might smile in our faces, but I'm not giving her ammunition."

Jordan shrugged and screwed up his face.

"How the hell do you know she felt showed up?"

"*Everyone* felt showed up. She just takes it personally, trust me."

"You're just as bad as Jenna and the Valelly kid."

"Yeah, some things never change, get used to it." She turned to finish what was left in the sink. "We don't often have company, hon. I don't want my turn to host to be remembered as the miscarriage, ya know?"

Jordan stood.

"Ok," he said, "But I'm staying up there with him."

"Jenna will be crushed."

"She'll get over it. Besides, we're taping. We'll have more than a few family laughs over it."

He heard the laughter and the girls screaming in delight to the pounding music from downstairs, all in a tubular sort of a haunt, all hollow, the way his father heard life nowadays in its order and fanfare, marching away from him over the horizon. Jenna had understood, or maybe she did, it was hard to tell. She was ultimately distracted with Brittany getting to go to cheerleading camp this summer, and Colleen's current fascination with Christian rock, and Vicky's younger brothers who were totally *rude*, and mostly with borrowing Ann Marie's lady paint and hairspray and rubber bands and clips to make herself look like the bride of Frankenstein.

Dad was all tied up with a roll of aluminum foil Jordan had offered him, pressing square pieces to his face, making masks. He'd constructed twenty of them, and arranged them all around him in a rough circle on the guest bed he slept in. Jordan read a few Sports Illustrated magazines he saved for emergencies, and then moved on to a Sal Palentonio book he'd never finished. Ann Marie stopped up once to check on him, and toward the end of the evening, Jenna popped in her head to say she should have won, but Brittany cheated. It was all good, all so *normal*, especially since Dad had fallen asleep over an hour ago.

When Ann Marie came up the second time to let Jordan know the coast was clear, he convinced her that it was ok to clean up in the morning. She gave a half hearted plea that she'd just gotten everything professionally scoured, and he insisted that a few pop corn bowls and soda glasses wouldn't hurt anyone. He stood up and stretched. He had polished off a six of Coors Light himself and he was in no mood for playing house maid.

In the bedroom, Ann Marie rubbed her foot on his leg indicating that she wanted it, and he mumbled back that the morning was better. She didn't press. They fell asleep spooned, and Jordan came awake with a jolt a few hours later.

The air conditioner was on hum mode, and he thought he'd heard something, maybe in a dream or something. It sounded, or rather it felt like it might have come from Jenna's room, and it was doubtful he could have actually heard anything over this piece-of-crap air conditioner, but it was best to be sure. He threw off the covers and looked around the floor for his shorts. Ann Marie said something unintelligible in her sleep, and he made sure to close the door behind him once he was dressed.

Jenna was moaning, he could hear her from all the way down the hall. Her door was open, and there was someone standing over her, a shadow, a hulking figure.

Jordan limped into a run, passed through the archway, and flipped on the overhead.

It was Aldo, standing over Jenna, watching her with wide rolling eyes, rocking back and forth, drool coming off his bottom lip in a spindler. And he was a nightmare of make-up, lipstick drawn severe and clown-like over his lips, hot pink and purple blush smeared on his cheeks, eye shadow in blue sparkle and deep lavender and rust painted up over the eyebrows, and there were Scrunchies and hair clips hanging off the hair at the edge of his crown.

"Pop, what the fuck are you doing?" Jordan said, a bit too loud, but he was a bit freaked to say the least. Aldo looked at his own son with wide, unseeing eyes, and stammered,

"Ape…ape…ape!"

Jordan reached out and grabbed his father by the shirt. He shook him, shouted in his face,

"What the fuck are you doing in my daughter's room?" He shook him harder, the clownish face bobbing on its neck like some lunatic ball park figurine, and suddenly arms were around him gently pulling him off, and it was Ann Marie, and she was tight lipped and wide eyed with concern, but now that it was out in the open, she was on auto-pilot, and Jenna was up rubbing her eyes and crying, and when Jordan told his wife to take Aldo to the bathroom and clean him up, she obeyed. Jordan sat next to Jenna on her bed and she sat up straight. Jordan wasn't a big man, but he was "wiry strong" veins in his biceps always pronounced, and when he got to a certain point you didn't question him, didn't hold back, gave him what he wanted.

"Jenna," he said. "No bullshit, did your grandpa touch you?" She shook her head slowly, her eyes huge silver dollars.

"No Daddy."

"Not ever?"

"Never."

He took her hand in his.

"Look at me," he said. She already was looking at him, but she appeared to try to focus even harder. Breath came through Jordan's nose, and it was clear he was controlling his voice to stay even and calm. "Now listen," he continued. "You're gonna tell me what I want to know, and you're not gonna go having a hissy fit, understand?"

She nodded.

"Tell me why you cry some mornings. Tell me who's taking your happy."

"I'm scared."

"Tell me anyway."

Her bottom lip trembled, but she didn't burst into tears.

"It's the bad man," she said.

"What do you mean, the bad man. Tell me now, Jenna, it's important."

She scrunched up her face for a moment but she somehow managed to hold on.

"He comes at night," she said, "when I'm half asleep. He puts his hands on my shoulders and steals my breath."

Jordan was seeing nothing but deep, bright red, but he made sure to keep his voice aqua.

"What do you mean, he steals your breath."

"You're gonna be mad."

"I'm already mad, but not at you. Tell me."

"Can I whisper it?"

"Sure."

She reached and put her arms around her father's shoulders, her exhalations hot in his ear.

"He's creepy and mean and he wears a hat and a striped tuxedo, like the ones the clowns wear at the circus. He has white gloves with finger bones painted on them, and a tattoo on his face shaped like a pair of glasses cut in half, just over one eye with a black chain going down to his jaw like Germans wear in cartoons. He has bright green eyes, and rotten brown teeth, and his breath stinks like Cheetohs and fish."

She pulled off Jordan's shoulder, and looked at him with quiet sincerity.

"Then he puts his lips over mine and sucks in my breath. Steals my happy. Breathes back into me what's stinky and sad. After that he leaves, doing that tango dance by himself like we see all the time on Dancing With The Stars."

Jordan had let her go, and had the tip of his thumb in his mouth, biting down on it despite the cliché. It wasn't all that hard to decipher, at least most of the juicy parts. Aldo had had a construction site accident back in the seventies, when the abrasive wheel on a chop saw burst apart while he'd been cutting through some steel channel. It opened the right side of his face and left a scar going from the eye to the jaw, hence, the monocle tattoo. The Cheetoh breath was actually Nacho Cheese Doritos, those that Jordan had been sneaking to his father for more than a month as a kind of reward treat, and the fish aftertaste came from those disgusting canned sardines he'd grown fond of. The rotted brown teeth were the dentures he kept rolling around in there, and the sound of the straw sucking the milk down at dinner had kicked off the memory, plain and simple.

The son of a bitch.

Jordan took her in his arms, and whispered back to her,

"It's all right now, hon. Daddy will take care of it."

He stayed guard in Aldo's room all that night, eyes slitted and red in the dark, listening to his father roll around, moan nonsense, and make just about every disgusting gassy sound a body was capable of. Jordan was lucky he didn't kill him. Ann Marie had been right, and they'd have to get Jenna professional help after the weekend. Fuckin' A, she'd probably be on someone's couch clear through to her thirties now, and it was all Jordan's fault. He'd denied what was right out in front of his face all along, for the love of father, for pride. Well, he wasn't going to just sit around feeling sorry for everybody, last of all, himself. Tomorrow, he'd get the ball rolling, work day and night to get things right.

By 11:30 the next morning, they'd moved Aldo and his belongings over to Joey's place in Ardmore, hell, what were cousins for, anyway? Ann Marie called in a favor, and Dr. Silverstien pulled some fast strings, getting Aldo admitted to Dunwoody. Both Jordan and Ann Marie spent the weekend soothing their daughter, giving her extra attention, playing every board game in the house, giving her full charge of the TV. She woke up sad both mornings, clamming up, absolutely refusing to discuss it. Wasn't hard to figure out. She had "Grandpa-hangover." Made Jordan sick. They decided not to press charges. In a way, this made Jordan sicker, but he didn't want to drag this thing out, especially for Jenna. Move on, no wallowing.

Aldo Colella died two weeks later in the rest home lunch center, face down into a plate of meat loaf and mashed potatoes. At the service Jordan refused to give a eulogy and

Jenna cried her eyes out, some sort of glorious release or something, yeah, Jordan was psychoanalyzing everything nowadays and he was considering some couch time of his own. Jenna started her sessions a week later and was reported by the analyst to be rather non-communicative. Jordan said who could blame her, and there was almost a scene right there in the lobby.

Jenna missed her grandpa.

And she was still waking up each morning in tears.

Jordan pulled out the video camera. Where was the fucking cord for this thing? Where was the carry case? Where did Ann Marie hide the tripod?

Dong Night, over at the Johnsons. Great. Maybe it would cheer Jenna up, break her out of her funk. Lord knew the therapy didn't do squat. Jordan turned the camera over, their Canon Digital palm-corder. He'd originally wanted to buy the Panasonic, but Ann Marie had convinced him it was too bulky. He flipped open the small screen tab and turned the power knob, hoping the thing still had a charge. The screen came on electric blue, and he hit "Play" to get a point of reference. Nothing. It was at the end of the tape. Really? Jordan turned the camera around as if there was a button he'd missed. He sighed. They'd forgotten to monitor it last month after the dancing and had left it recording all night. He hit "Rewind" and watched the little white icons spin. After what seemed a logical amount of time, he hit "Play" and saw an image, slightly tilted, of the open bay closet he was currently standing in front of, the top shelf crammed with book bags, cases of Dr. Pepper, paper towels, and the beach coolers, the main area below occupied by the fall and winter coats, for all but about a foot and a half of empty space to the left.

He hit "Rewind" without hitting off "Play," so he could see the closet go backward in time and catch the last moment of dancing.

Something moved. On the tape. A blur right in front of the camera, and then something in the closet. Jordan stopped the tape and hit play. His spine went cold and beads of sweat burst out on his forehead.

The coats were now hanging to the left, with the one and a half feet of space to the right. There was no movement, no dancing shadows, just the dull illumination off-camera from the staircase light they always left on so Jenna could easily find her way to the bathroom upstairs. It was still the middle of the night.

Jordan gasped. There on the tape, the coats moved, all by themselves, from left to right, making the foot and a half of empty space switch places.

He hit "Rewind," then "Stop," and then played it again. No. There was no one in the closet hiding behind the coats playing a trick; the camera had a full view to the floor, and it would have shown his or her feet. He watched the coats start moving again, and hit "Stop" abruptly. Backed it up. Hit "Play," then tried to hit "Pause" at just the right moment. It took him three tries, but he got it. In regular time it appeared that something slipped to the edge of the leather aviator jacket all the way to the left of the bunch. It was a hand, connected to nothing, palming the coats and sliding them to the side like a shower curtain. A hand in a white glove with the finger bones painted in.

Jordan swallowed hard and let the footage play, back from the initial movement in the closet. There was the sneaky disconnected hand, the slide of the jackets across the coat bar, then nothing.

Suddenly, there was a burst into the middle of the camera, a face, close up and then gone, as if this "thing" had jumped through the air.

In live time it was but a blur, a flash,

nothing identifiable. Jordan fucked with the "Play" and "Pause" button seven times before he nailed it, there, dead center, a bit grainy, but mostly distinct, like the freeze frame on a bang-bang play at first base, where you see the given figure clearly, just accompanied by streaks and back trails.

This was not Aldo's face, though Jordan wasn't really expecting it to be at this point. This guy was younger, leaner, skull-like cheek to jaw, black tattoo circling the left eye, then drawn down like the dangling chain on the glassware pirates used, or that Colonel Klink character on the old Hogan's Heroes show. The eyes were bright green, piercing and inhuman.

And he was smiling, all teeth, all crooked, browned-up and rotten.

Jordan went shopping. He went to Sears and bought refrigerator magnets, blank photo sheets, construction paper, and a sheaf of loose leaf. He went to the photo department and purchased two digital recorders with tripod set-ups. Then he went to the Home Depot and bought a new caulking gun along with three tubes of brick adhesive. At the CVS, he purchased twenty containers of aspirin, five bottles of Omega Fatty Acid capsules, and ten boxes of Prilosec.

He convinced Ann Marie that it was ok he didn't go to Dong Night over the Johnson's. He made arrangements for Jenna to sleep there, and told Ann Marie to stay at her mother's. She didn't argue. You couldn't talk to Jordan nowadays, and she was clearly sick to death of fighting with him.

When mother and daughter finally left for their night away, Jordan set to work, first in the shed, then in the hearth, next in the kitchen trash, and last in the bathroom. The most difficult operation was in the fireplace, of course, not because Jordan had any trouble whatsoever duplicating the patterning his father had originally formed on the walls, after all he was a Colella and laying brick was in his blood, but more on account of the twisting and positioning of his body in this particular application. How the hell did Aldo do it? I mean, the guy was eighty three, and before the last tri-wall was fully "papered," Jordan's back was screaming.

It was 11:30 PM by the time Jordan had washed up and positioned all the cameras. The first one was placed outside the bathroom, floor speckled with carefully arranged pills, mostly around the toilet, all exploding outward, the flatter ones stacked on top of each other four or five high, and the oval shaped capsules in uniform diagonals toward the window. The second camera was down in the living room pointing at the fireplace, magnets and photo papers caulked to the inner brick facing, wet garbage arranged on the floor cement, trash can on its side, pokers leaning across and aiming in. The last camera was aimed like the original had been, at the open bay closet, but now the space was crammed at the bottom with propane tanks, trash can lids, gingerbread men and coils of garden hose, the recycling drum there on its side, this time crawling with stink bugs.

Jordan went up to his room, turned on the air conditioner, and waited. All night.

The next morning he trudged downstairs, cleaned the house, did the rugs with the steam cleaner and wet vac he'd borrowed from the shop, burned seven cans of Raid industrial duty bug killer, forced himself to be patient. Ann Marie called twice and he didn't pick up. He showered. Dressed. Gathered the cameras, and then watched the tapes.

The Breath Vampire first tried to enter through the closet, sliding the coats, yet unable to jump the blockade of outdoor shed paraphernalia. He was too tall, couldn't get his foot up and over, and he was slippery, only showing up in flashes and blips, covering more space in his patches of invisibility than you accounted for, but when he did sporadically "wink up" the frustration on his thin, mask-like face was more than evident.

The hearth was horrifying. The monster tried to pull a Santa Clause, but the caulked magnets and papers made him lose his palm pressure and slip down the flue; it seemed even representations of family togetherness defied him. The wet trash at the bottom made him go "whoopsie," on his butt like coming down off a playground slide, and the pokers propped on the trash can acted like Braveheart spears, impaling the son of a bitch through his inner thighs and privates, worms squirting out of the opened wounds. Then it exercised its own type of "Rewind" ability, and Jordan watched the thing make four fruitless and painful attempts before giving up and trying a bathroom entry.

That one was the strangest of all. Jordan had an excellent memory, honed from being in the construction trades so long and having to repeatedly retain the details of stocking and delivery orders on the fly, so his arrangement of the floor-pills was dead-balls accurate.

Aldo was a genius. The arrangement and its effect reminded Jordan of the Mission Impossible movies, where laser rays were set all over a room, guaranteeing failure of mobility. The capsules and tablets were set in some kind of diabolical mathematical perfection, and when the beast snaked out of the toilet, feet first, body curved and shooting, like liquid being pushed through a curved see-through science tube, his thin toed boots couldn't find purchase as he took fuller form. He made six attempts, each time doing his little flamenco, trying different angles, always slipping, hitching and pitching, then retreating through the pipes backward, upside down, and head first.

Ann Marie came home an hour and a half later without announcement, I mean, enough was enough already, and Jordan was still in the living room, watching the recordings, pausing, rewinding, over and again. He looked at his wife in the doorway, his eyes red and dull.

"What?" she said.

He cleared his throat.

"Jenna, go play a video game."

"Okay, Daddy," she said, prancing over to the "entertainment corner." He took Ann Marie's hand.

"Upstairs," he said.

He closed the bedroom door and showed her the tapes. Her hand remained up at her mouth, and after the viewing she wordlessly followed her husband out to the garage where he piggy backed the small black tape canisters to a small yet weighty decorator brick he had in a pile left over from when they had the walkway done. He wrapped the bunch with duct tape, drove out to the reservoir, and dropped it off the pedestrian walking bridge into what fishermen and occasional swimmers called "The Deep Run."

They stayed at Joey's for awhile, and Jordan put the house up for sale at tens of thousands below the neighborhood asking price. Soon, they moved back to South Philly, 10th and Morris, two streets down from where Jordan grew up, and they got Jenna placed in a magnet school. She had started waking up with a smile the minute they left Wynnewood.

Jordan Colella kept on at the tool house, often driving home in mute frustration, like when they closed the service end of the shop on account of the economy and stuck him with farming out repairs, or that time the ladders didn't get over to Liberty II on time, or when shipping sent out old cartridges with hardened epoxy crammed in the ports, and Jordan had to hear about it from everyone and their mother because he was the "inside man" in charge of the fun house. Ann Marie continued answering phones at the hospital, and last year when they didn't give her a raise, they gave her a title. Frankie failed English 102, dropped out without telling anyone, and took a job at the Navy Yard.

Life went on.

They discussed the possibility of putting Jenna in therapy, but Jordan insisted she'd get over it. And besides, what was there to uncover? A monster in the pipes? A fiend up the flue? Who would believe it? Any idiot could foresee the blame ending up right back on Aldo somehow. Ann Marie hinted that maybe that wouldn't be such a bad thing, like erasing the unexplained and putting it in a place Jenna could process or some such shit, and they fought about it.

In the end, there was no therapy. Jenna did get over it, but Ann Marie developed her own backward strategy of streamlining the unexplained by giving signals here and there that Aldo was indeed wrapped up in the dark time her family went through, somehow, some way. She'd seen things change the minute he crossed their doorstep, there was no denying it. Jordan argued a bit at first, then deflected it, and allowed the frequency to die out over time. He moved on.

But deep inside, he never let his father's true legacy dwindle to fumes that could simply blow off on the wind. He always remembered that Aldo had pleaded with them at the last moment with his "Ape…ape…ape," which was really, "Tape…tape…tape," mispronounced because his teeth were out, and the cold hard fact that his father, his hero, utterly gave himself up in that freaked out "Dong" get-up, standing guard over his grand daughter, ready to go painted face to painted face and toe to toe with the monster, the one only he could see in glorious Technicolor continuity somehow, because of a little plaque on the brain.

In Ann Marie's eyes, Aldo Colella would forever be known as the family monster no matter what she had seen on those tapes in the bedroom.

Jordan still goes to the grave site once a week to apologize for this, and to whisper to his dear father a more deserving and proper goodbye.

SOMNAMBULIST – SOUTHSIDE
CHRIS KELSO

Jerry looked in the mirror. He used to be a movie star.

His face was long and drawn like a starving reptile and Jerry's absent stare suggested all the traumas of a man who'd just fallen soul first into a river of leeches…

He had a beard of shaving foam which leaked from his chin. Living in the Southside of Hell was actually working out ok for Jerry. He moved there when L.A lost its edge and just never looked back. Sure, you get a lot of demons and monsters and people you really hated when you were alive roaming around on the sidewalks outside, but it still beat the killer responsibility of having a pulse.

Unlike most people who wind up here, Jerry came to Hell of his own accord. It's easier than you might think. You just gotta find an apartment, get a job and you're good to go. It really was that simple for him.

Jerry began popping his knuckles. He placed a finger and thumb on his neck then on the limp of his wrist just to check he really was still dead – *nothing* – thank god!

The phone rang from the living room, he let it go straight to voicemail. A hysterical woman spoke, shrill, indignant, thoroughly pissed off. Could've been his mother, his sister, his girl or any fuckin' strange woman Jerry come into contact with – that's a broad canvas of strange women in Jerry's case.

He did well in Hell. Demon girls could see in his eyes the awful places he'd been and they found this an alluring quality of his.

Jerry dragged the razor blade through the cloud of foam until the colours changed from bright white to dark red. Outside a train hurtled past, shaking the whole apartment. He'd missed his ride to work. It meant he'd have to jump a thorny tailed dragon across the lake of fire. Jerry made ends meet by clipping recently deceased Wall Street yuppies' cigars for them in a high rise downtown – but like I said, he used to be an actor, so he kissed ass convincingly.

Jerry matted a layer of shaving cream into his chest hair and lathered it into foam. He took his razor, poised it and dragged the blade against the grain until blood bubbled through. The cut from his cheek continued to bleed, dripped onto the bathroom tiles. The slash across his chest wept like Mary, a reservoir of blood forming neatly at his feet. Jerry unbuckled his pants and let them fall to his ankles. He squirted a dollop of shaving cream into his hands and mixed it into the wiry shrub of his pubic hair. He picked up the razor – took a breath – and dragged it across the base of his penis.

Jerry had completely changed his image, he had to. He was so sick of everyone watching him ALL THE TIME. After filming the Box office bomb "Too Cruel for School", he packed up his things and came Southside. Jerry's hair had been bleached by the burning sphere which hung over Hell's terrain, but it used to be black when he walked amongst the living. Jerry tried every mask he could until he finally found one which fit just right – ditching the peck implants helped. He was able to form a gut, a turkeys wattle, sores and acne scarring and a true sense of himself.

He'd also gone by a different name, but no-one could remember what it used to be.

This was fine as long as they stopped watching him…

GIVE 'EM THE FINGER
STEVE CONOBOY

People used to use something called 'money', according to Aidan's Dad. There were coins of small denominations, and notes of higher values, and there were plastic cards too. The concept still baffled him. Each person had a different amount, and this 'money' was used to pay for services and objects, and the bit that really confused him was that the same object could cost a different amount in different places. Dad had made a few attempts to explain it to him, but Aidan could never truly grasp it.

He found this strange time before the Witches came to be amusing and alien and scary. There were a lot of strange practices and notions in that other world, so it seemed to Aidan, who couldn't stop asking his Dad to re-tell these bizarre fairy tales. He would sit on the beautiful blue rug woven by Old Maid Davenport from up the road, and Dad would sit in his sweetly creaking chair, nailed together by Toothy Harry who lived next door, and Dad's smile was worn thin as if he was remembering a painful love long past. He would talk about such things!

'We had talk show hosts shouting at people to get jobs when there were no jobs to get.'

'Tell me again how jobs worked in *their* world,' said Aidan, shuffling a little closer to the dimming fire.

'For a start, not everyone had one. A select few chose never to work if they could help it, and they were reviled. There were those with disabilities of one type or another, much like we have, although I dare say we take better care of our own than those people ever did, with all their suspicion and jealousy. There were events called interviews, meetings with your prospective employer, wherein you had to convince them you were better than anyone else for that job, even if you didn't want the job, even if you were only there for the money to afford rent and clothing and food and…'

'*Food?*'

Dad chuckled; a dry, wooden, splintery thing. 'Yes. Everyone had to pay. Everyone.'

'Didn't they have enough to go round?'

'They did, in fact. Incidentally, their richest nation was also the fattest…' Tangents were common place in these talks with Dad. He was armed with hundreds of them. Aidan asked him once how comes he flitted from one subject to the next. Dad told him that it was because there were so many things that were wrong back then, and all these wrong things were all linked together to make one great big mess and so it was no wonder that their talks were messy as well.

On this night, with Dad in his creaking chair and Aidan in front of the fire, they talked their messy talk for a while longer until Aidan squirmed and couldn't wait and had to get an answer. 'Dad…'

'Go on, son. If you've got a question,

ask it.'

'Yeah, but every time I ask it I get told it's not for me to worry about, and my thirteenth isn't that far off so I think I should be worrying about it now.'

The tiny stump where many, many years ago there had been a little finger wiggled on Dad's left hand. It always wiggled when he was concentrating or agitated. 'Ah. That question. What do they do with all the fingers, right?'

'Right.'

'The truth is son, I don't really know. I don't suppose anyone does, except for the witches themselves. Don't look disappointed, I'm giving you the only answer anyone can or will. The thing to remember is that we don't have anything to worry about, do we? Whatever those fingers are for, those witches take care of us. We've got everything we need, everyone gets their fair share and works a fair amount. We're safe, we have no wars, crime is negligible. There is education and a health service for all. There is food and shelter for all, because everyone has something to give. I think that's enough to be going on with, don't you?'

Aidan could hear the sense in this. For a twelve year old boy, however, enough is never enough. It was good to know that they as a people were well looked after. But all those fingers… *Maybe Saul can tell me next week*, Aidan thought. *When they take his finger on his birthday, I'll tell him to keep his eyes open. Saul's my friend, he'll tell me what it's all about.*

Dad's tales whirled around in Aidan's head as he surrounded himself with blankets at night. Things like the internet, which Dad said eventually turned into the world wide web of lies, which made Aidan think of a ginormous spider looming over it all, pulling here and tweaking there and Dad said that, by the end, that wasn't very far from the truth. Once upon a time it was a free platform for all the voices in that world, but then the voices began to drown each other out, and they didn't hear the dark whispers of the Man coming to shut them all up. Things like newspapers that should have been papers full of the news but were nothing but gossip and distractions. Things like bonuses that important people paid themselves even when they were not any good at those 'jobs' they had. Things like 'politicians', people who made promises in return for perks, people who wanted to run the country not for the common good but for prestige.

What a crazy bunch they were, those other-worlders! Didn't they realise that witches are so much better than politicians?

Witches whose only want was pinkies.

He did not see Saul again until the boy's birthday, an event that summoned everyone in the village to the celebration on the Green. As always at these occasions there was more food and drink and music and games than anyone could completely consume, and getting to Saul was nearly impossible. Often Aidan could only get a glimpse of his blonde thatch of hair inbetween all the adults patting him on the back and telling him what an honour it was to make this contribution to society. Saul's mother was soothing him in that unstoppable way of hers, saying that everything was going to be alright and the pain was something he'd soon forget.

Saul did not look like a boy who thought that everything was going to be alright.

The music and shouting and games all stopped as a steam-carriage pulled up. One witch poured out of the bubble-shaped body. Aidan caught a glimpse of three other witches inside, hunched over a heavy-looking container, a sick-green light spilling out of it. One of them was stirring with a long metal ladle that looked to Aidan like it was melting.

Aidan's heart lunged for his ribcage. He had never experienced such a thrill.

A witch eased out of her seat, flowed from the steam-carriage, each footstep poised, graceful. There was an aching prettiness to her face, but it seemed to Aidan that it might be melting like that ladle, melting so slowly, millimetres over the ages. The slightest hint of a wrongness to the gentle curve of her cheek, the almond shape of her eyes, the alabaster tint of her skin, the amused tilt of her bowed mouth. She flowed over to the crowd in her shimmering black robes, stopped before them, held out a beckoning hand to Saul. The boy was given a light shove in the back by his impatient father, a man who wanted to get back to the business of drinking. Saul reached out for that slender hand, looking to Aidan for all the world like a boy who didn't want to. Her fingers folded lightly around Saul's, and she led him back to the steam-carriage, she floating, he plodding. Into the main bubble of the steam-carriage they climbed, with the witches and the cauldron and the sick-green light and the slow-melting ladle.

And then Saul was gone.

There are some places that aren't safe from certain twelve year olds, and there are some twelve year olds who can get into any place at all, and Aidan was one of those boys. He couldn't wait for Saul to come back with whatever meagre report he may have to offer. He could not summon that amount of patience.

He slipped away from the crowd as it turned away from Saul and the witches to congratulate themselves on sending off another one, and he hung off the back of the steam-carriage, careful to keep away from the sulphurous steam belching out of a tailpipe. They travelled for hours, leaving the village far behind, travelling past field after field, coming to the Dead City, populated only by the metallic revenants of a broken civilisation. Aidan had never been here. There'd never been a reason to come, except curiosity, and Dad felt that a boy's curiosity was a long distance away from good reason.

There was plenty to see, and seeing it did nothing to satisfy his curiosity and only made it swell.

He had seen a car before. George the Pig-man kept one in his shed across the way and let Aidan help him with fixing it up which was lots of fun and disapproved of by Dad. There were thousands of them in Dead City, though. Thousands. Every single street was full of them. It looked like they'd all been pushed to the sides of these streets, out of the middle of the road, as if a giant pair of hands had parted the way. The steam carriage was able to travel unimpeded, dwarfed by the enormous constructions around them. These must be the skyscrapers Dad had described in their messy talks, and Aidan couldn't help but think about how apt the term was. How did they remain standing? How didn't they topple and crash together and fall like concrete dominoes? His thoughts turned to dark musings. They called this place Dead City, and was that because these skyscrapers were filled with bodies that were festering and rotting and bloated with maggots? Had the dead been waiting for him to come and were gathering now at the windows, leering at him hungrily? A starving horde, slathering.

Every inch of him was goosebumpy.

He tried to concentrate on all the other newnesses this journey showed him. There were signs everywhere, absolutely everywhere. Some with names of places and arrows and numbers. Other larger ones in which people were displaying exotic objects and looking happy about it. Given the size of these and their amazing proliferation, they had to be more important than the place names and arrows, although Aidan couldn't quite grasp the point of them. Long poles at regular intervals with large bulbs at the top. He guessed these functioned in a similar way to the oil lanterns they had back home. But there were so many of them. So much of everything.

He was very far from home. Far from the smallness of the village, the safety of that smallness. No skyscrapers full of the drooling dead in the village.

'Don't think about that,' he whispered to himself, 'just don't.' He did, though. He thought about it until finally the steam carriage pulled up outside a building called a museum and true horror tensed his heart. There was no telling what the witches would do if they saw their uninvited hitch-hiker. Aidan thought that they would show him what his insides looked like. He scrunched himself up as small as he could, pressing up against the rear of the steam carriage. The only sound he heard was the door opening. He felt the weight inside the carriage lessen. That was the only clue he had that the witches and Saul had exited the vehicle. They could be walking up to the museum-place. They could be coming round to the back of the carriage to see if they had any taggers-along. They could be waiting for him to show his face.

Curiosity frazzled behind his eyes. He had to look.

Two witches were on either side of Saul, floating him into the grand front entrance of the museum-place. Floating. No graceful walking this time. They were almost a foot in the air, robes not even touching the ground. Aidan waited until they were inside and out of sight because if he couldn't see them then they couldn't see him either, and he followed with quick, pattering footsteps.

A small room was first with a desk and seats and racks full of printed leaflets and then through more doors and into an enormous hall that stretched forward and to his left and his right and up as well. Forward and left and right and up and up to a glass domed ceiling that showed a sky turning to night. Small flames flickered into life above head-height, flames without wick or candle beneath them. *Witch-work*, he thought. So many of them, like those poles in Dead City. The difference was that these flames worked. There was plenty of light by which to see the wonders of the museum-place. There were so many huge animals in here. He'd seen these in the books that Dad kept in his trunk. The giraffe, the mammoth, the whale, the dinosaur with a head the size of the car in George's shed. The witches and Saul had floated right down the middle of all this and had reached the doors at the back of the room. Aidan waited for them to go through, then scampered after them. If he paused too long to take in all these wonders he might lose the witches.

Perhaps he could come back another time.

He almost did lose them. It was a flicker of a shadow that showed him the way. They were heading downstairs, into the basement. There were signs down here, some of those less important ones that weren't dynamic people with interesting objects, that were only words and those words said *No admittance to the general public* and *Exhibit storage* and other things he didn't bother to read. There were lots of boxes of differing sizes and row upon row of benches littered with interesting things that would have to wait because he was getting left behind.

Into the next room he went and his courage gave up. Total blackness. If not for the sensation of the floor beneath his feet he would have thought himself to be falling into a bottomless pit. Such a pit would have spikes at the bottom, big fat ones to punch out his stomach and rip out his guts.

'Another boy. A fresh, fresh boy,' whispered a gluttonous voice.

Aidan whimpered. These witches weren't the forces of good that Dad thought them to be. They were going to snatch him up, sharpen their knives, chop him into bloody portions and drop them in the pot, smacking their lips as they stirred up his blood and meat and gristle.

Two dozen flames without candles fizzed into being, hovering above the semi-circle of witches before him. Saul was sat at a mahogany desk in the middle, the almost-pretty witch from the party kneeling next to him, a soothing arm around his shoulder, a hint of a serene smile on her forever-melting face. 'Forgive Greta,' she said to Aidan. 'She teases. Her fun is wicked.'

It might be fun for Greta, but Aidan didn't like wicked. No, he didn't like wicked at all. It made his heart feel cold.

Greta cackled. '*Hee hee hee, fun is right at a ceremony, fresh boy!*'

'Hush now, Greta,' said the almost-pretty witch. 'What are we to do with him? He should not be here.' Her tone was admonishing, but her eyes glittered. He thought it was with amusement. He hoped it was amusement.

He didn't want to end up in the pot. If he didn't use his voice now he never would again. 'I came to see, I only came to see. I just wanted to know what will happen to Saul's finger because nobody knows or nobody tells me and it doesn't matter which because it all comes to the same thing.'

'A curious boy,' mused the witch as she stroked nervous Saul's hair. 'Shall we satisfy him?' This received a warm, gentle round of applause. 'Then stay, curious boy, and hope that there's steel in your stomach.' She kissed Saul lightly on the forehead, whispered a tender something in his ear, then drew a knife from the folds of her robes.

Aidan had anticipated the finger-removal would be quick. Saul had no doubt hoped for the same. It was not. It was more hacking than cutting. The serene smile, the glitter, it all fell away from the almost-pretty witch's face, leaving an emotionless void as she raised the razor-sharp knife high and slammed it down on the extended pinky. Aidan jumped with the impact. Saul screamed, screamed like his soul had been ripped from his chest. He passed out, head smashing into the desk. It took a second for the blood to come, and when it came it poured. Nausea splashed over Aidan in hot waves and he couldn't stop watching. Another knife-strike, harder, and the noise was like stamping on a length of wood to snap it in half. Aidan threw up a little in his mouth and, unable to swallow it down, spat it on the floor in front of him. More strikes, more snapping. Then sawing, through the shattered bone, then the last strips of flesh and skin.

The table was awash with blood. It seeped towards the edges and dripped off.

The witch used a thick handkerchief to pick up the severed finger and hold it aloft to rousing cheers. 'A pity,' she said, 'that young Saul has slept through his sacrifice for the greater good. Like so many before him, Saul has given, and so he shall also receive!' More applause and hearty agreement. 'Our uninvited visitor is made of stern fibre. He still stands.'

'*A sturdy freshling,*' said Greta, who got some laughs for her efforts.

The almost-pretty witch withered Greta with a glance, then turned her attention to Aidan. 'It is a symbol of self-sacrifice,' she told him, 'and symbols hold great power. Like words on a page. Like instructions on a sign.'

'Symbols,' said Aidan, and because Dad had taught him the virtue of thinking, he thought. He thought about what he'd seen, what he'd heard and everything he hadn't been told. 'Symbols that make up your spells, right? The spells are good for us because our land is peaceful and we have everything we need and we're happy and all for the smallest of prices. If the spells are good for us, they must be bad for someone else.'

The almost-pretty witch smiled in her

serene way. 'Your birthday. When?'

The gathered witches waited in an expectant hush.

'Soon,' said Aidan.

'So soon as to make little difference.' She stated this as fact. She knew when his birthday was. She knew all the birthdays. 'A mature boy, this freshling, to come all this way alone for answers, to stand firm for his friend's sacrifice. Perhaps a boy who is ready to do his part?'

'Miss Witch, what do you have to gain from all this?'

That smile, it knew so much, more than just birthdays. 'Pleasure.'

Aidan thought it over, and he said: 'If I give another finger, what does that get me?'

HECATE
CLAIRE T. FEILD

Her black wings tease the light
into what she lovingly calls
a wide shawl. Her hedonism
seems to prevail, for the light
flickers, but like a hedgehog
rolls into a ball and spikes
the heinous hag.
Horror emaciates Hecate's
face, her wings limp from
deserved pain, and as for the
light? She's Tinseltown
visiting the Pan Alley to be
transformed, the prickly
heat she let Hecate feel
a distant memory: she's
too busy twirling rainbows
in the faces of the lethargic,
challenging them to be
creative, the hee-haws from
these headless catastrophes
just pantomimes of Hecate's
heckling voice.

HOST
CLAIRE T. FEILD

Although Lemanda had an independent
streak as peculiar as a diagonal, some thought
she was moving toward the norm to fit the
personality she had worn with the carefree
nature of a baby's bootie.
Since Lemanda was too agreeable, a foreign
entity as sneaky as a bacterial thread had to
be crawling through her system.
When her once lovely brown face resembled
a hairy coconut shell, the ciphony she
transmitted made her closest enemies think
they had won, and they had beat her down,
for the immaculate society they had
formulated fit over her like a purple hood,
their disease as wicked as crown gall,
Lemanda having been taken hostage by the
plants she had worshiped since childhood,
the ones turned cancerous in the pliable
hands of the contingent in power.

THE EDGE OF DARKNESS
CLAIRE T. FEILD

Pond water flickering, I turn my face
toward the holes in tree bark.
The gleaming drink I hold—
I stare at briefly before crushing its glass
into witch shards.
As dusk moves across me like a flotilla
of kites,
I am once again alone with the
dominoes I let fall.

WILD ROSE
CLAIRE T. FEILD

She wears a steel cloak when she rides a rough-hewn thoroughbred, the shadows she manufactures close to the hip. She moves fast through the wind's rattling coughs as she has no sick leave for one on the run from the law. A cacophony of gunshots scares her, for the sounds strike as close to her chest as the groups of tattoos shaped like sets of bowling ball pins cross her neck. But she will not leave her horse to die, his carcass food for side street flies. Instead, she plows forward, her horse's hooves making rows from mud almost rivaling the density of concrete. After her heartbeats sound like her horse's heartbeats, a stabilization between beast and burden occurs, and they fly past the moon, completely unhinged from the world's impertinent laws of nature and the humans who use diamond-studded vipers to sere sensory details from their prisoners.

WRAITHS
CLAIRE T. FEILD

The gnarly elderly woman, known
for her worm's-eye, swears she
sees ghosts picking cotton near
the mansion she calls a kickshaw
to get a laugh from her wealthy,
languid friends, the ones who
mistakenly think hogans a
disgrace to the land in the
Unites States of America.
Like a dew worm, the woman
crawls through her fields one
night to throw nectarines at
whatever resembles a specter.
After a male ghost deviates from
a wraith's script to destroy the
other ghosts before burying
them in a hole, she becomes
a chivalrous nomad of the night,
kissing the helpful ghost on
the cheek. Yet he forever
disappears, and with him
swindles her art in the field
of necromancy.

PROFESSOR DINGLEBERRY AND THE PERIPATETIC COXCOMB ABODE

MARSHALL PAYNE

As Bary puttered around his front yard, dealing with his dubious state of incorporeality the best he could, a familiar passerby came up the road. It had been a year since the gentleman's last visit, yet it seemed like an eon… or no time at all.

The red house jaunted up the dirt road before coming to a complete stop. As the dust from the road settled, the rooster legs conveying the peculiar edifice bowed slightly, as though grateful for the respite. And then the house swung down, presenting to Bary the small portico where its lone occupant sat.

"Hello, Bary," Professor Devereaux Dingleberry said. He was a distinguished-looking man with a pair of long, waxed mustachios.

"Hello, Professor," Bary replied in his reedy spectral voice. "It's good to see you. I'd nearly forgotten that it's that time of year."

Clad in only a thin overcoat, the professor, casting his eyes about to the chilled air, said, "Likewise, my boy. And no quips from me this time about how you'll catch your death of cold." He chuckled spiritedly.

Bary, dressed in his summer attire of light trousers and cotton shirt, rubbed his arms in a futile gesture. "Wish I could feel it," he said.

"Perhaps you can," Professor Dingleberry said, as he maintained his balance on the downward-tilting porch. "You know, Bary, I've given much thought to your situation since our last encounter. There's a reason I've chosen this route that's so far off the beaten path." He gazed down with concern.

"There is?" The half-haint boy had always wondered why this pitchman of elixirs and magical potions had frequented this isolated route. Bary's house was the only one for miles around.

"Yes indeed! Perhaps I should've listened to that scrying woman long ago and accepted that fate would lead me to this day, but no matter. That day has come! Bary, would you like to feel the breeze nip at your cheeks once again? Would you like to explore the real world like a normal boy? I'm in need of an apprentice and that person would right likely be you!"

"Me?" Bary asked. "But how is that possible? In the past you've referred to me as... a half-haint."

"Yes, I have. Which means that there's still hope."

"Hope? But what about my family? Ma, Pa, and sis?"

"Sorry, but there's not much I can do about them, seeing as they've already passed on to a state of full hainthood, as it were. But..."

They both glanced at Bary's porch, a dilapidated structure of rotting wood choked with weeds. His mother, father, and sister Aleen stood there, already waving goodbye, blank expressions on their spectral faces. Bary hadn't been close with them for years now, as with each day they faded even more into memories of the past. Were they giving him their blessing or merely glad to see him go? Didn't matter. Behind him stood only the bleakness of his unfortunate past. Above him lay his future.

"How do I climb aboard?" Bary asked.

At the Professor's command, the rooster legs squatted, allowing the pitchman to grasp, just barely, Bary's hand and tug him aboard. As they trotted off down the road, the boy looked back out of respect, but his ghost family on the porch had faded once again.

*

How many years had it been since Bary had not heeded his mother and sought to relieve himself by urinating in the backyard? A wizards war had been brewing for some time, and when a stray missile of dark magic had struck his home, he'd been spared from the direct blast. After the crimson smoke had cleared, he found his house still intact, his parents utterly etherealized, and himself half the boy he'd once been.

"I always felt so guilty," Bary said now as they strutted down the road on rooster legs.

"Why?" said Professor Dingleberry. "Because you only halfway departed this mortal coil and your folks were well on their way to the full journey? Don't be. And don't fret. I've seen the way they regarded you. Haints are weird creatures. I'm sure they still and always will love you on some level. But to them, you were no longer one of their own. Smartest thing you ever did, my boy, not listening to your mother. Pissing in the backyard that day saved your life."

Bary giggled. First time he'd laughed in ages. "So, can you really make me a real boy again?"

"Shouldn't be a problem. You sit here and enjoy the journey and I'll be right back." The professor stood and went into the house.

As Bary waited, he imagined what an odd sight they must be to those who'd never seen the strutting red house, plopping along on two legs, now with two occupants on the porch with its red coxcomb on top. They'd only encountered a few people on the road so far and received a few waves, a couple of dropped jaws, and a knitted brow or two. More people than Bary had seen in years, and they were still in the lowly populated hinterlands. What would it be like in the towns and cities where they were most likely headed?

Soon the professor returned with a steaming concoction in a pewter cup. Seating himself again on the stoop, he said, "Drink this, my boy. It'll put hair on your chest."

Bary took the cup. "Hair on my chest?"

"It'll make you corporeal again. In fact, it will put hair on your chest in time. Before you indulge you must consider that you will now grow old. You do understand that, don't you?"

"And someday die?"

"Yes, there is that. Does that trouble you?"

Without answering, Bary drank the potion. He was tired of being a half-haint.

The potion tasted nasty, but he'd expected as much. As a warmth suffused his body, he began to glow, to coalesce, to become substantial. Soon he felt the nip in the air. He'd forgotten what it was like to feel... anything.

*

They didn't make it to civilization that evening, and when dusk came Professor Dingleberry parked the coxcomb abode and showed Bary the interior of his home. One wall was full of books, while the other housed the professor's potions and herbs and other ingredients to make his magical elixirs. All of them secured so as not to be displaced by the sometimes jostling ride.

As the professor made them supper, Bary asked, "When will you start teaching me to be your apprentice, Professor? *How will you?*"

"Soon, Bary. And by osmosis. You'll be surprised how much an observant lad can learn in a short period to time. How to work the crowds at my medicine shows, how to make the magical elixirs we're to peddle, how not to wipe your ass. Did your mother teach you how to wipe your ass years ago?"

"She did."

"Well, you'll have to unlearn that." The professor chuckled. Seeing the confused look on Bary's face, he said, "All in good time, Bary. All in good time."

Suddenly the house began to rock, to sway. "What's that?" Bary asked.

"The house needs nourishment too. That's why I parked us in this grove of trees. Oak trees. The Coxcomb likes oak leaves and branches."

The interior walls of the house began to swell, to undergo a slight change in coloration as nourishment was passed. Bary realized he'd been riding in the creature's maw all day.

Soon the professor, cooking on a small stove in the corner, had supper ready for the two of them. A goulash of sorts made with meat and starchy vegetables. Bary didn't think he'd be hungry, but when the professor sat the steaming plate in front of him, he found himself ravenous. It'd been years since he'd eaten.

As they sat at the small dining room table eating, the professor said, "Is the food good, Bary?"

"Uh-huh," Bary said, feeling a bit embarrassed. His mother had always told him not to talk with his mouth full.

After dinner Professor Dingleberry saw fit to give Bary his first indoctrination to his apprenticeship, a lesson in life as it were. Or how Dingleberry saw life. "Bary, over the years I've developed three founding principles that are the cornerstones of my success. If you'll live by these three principles, then you'll achieve the same great success I have." He spread his arms to take in the coxcomb abode. "Do you think you can remember them?"

Bari knitted his brow. "I'll try."

"Do better than try. Remember. Remember these three. First, it's always *us* against *them*. It used to be me against the world, but since I've taken you on as my apprentice, you shall be privy to many things and that makes us a team. So, always remember that you and me and the Coxcomb come first. Can you remember that?"

"You and me and the Coxcomb always come first," Bary repeated with a nod.

"Very good. Second. Don't *ever* trust women. Don't trust anyone period, but remember that women, girls, ladies, matrons, noblewomen, gentlewomen, viragos, beldams, fishwives, harridans, chits, gamines, and milkmaids—they're all your enemy."

"What about my mother and my sister Aleen?" Bary asked, confused.

"All of them. Mothers, sisters, daughters, grandmothers, nieces, aunts, great-aunts, great-great-aunts, cousins of the female persuasion… They're all your enemy."

"Didn't you ever have a mother or a sister?" Bary asked, hoping he wasn't speaking out of turn.

"God did I ever. Had the most domineering mother you could ever imagine. And a houseful of bossy sisters, too. They ran my father off, that they did. Ran me off as well when I grew of age to make my own way in this world."

"I see," said Bary. They sat in silence before Bary finally asked, "I thought you said there were three rules or principles or whatever. May I ask what's the third?"

The mustachioed professor nodded, smiled, and twirled his waxed mustache. "Yes, you may. Professor Dingleberry's third founding principle for success is: Never, ever wipe your ass! Got that?"

Bary nodded. And with the goulash pushing its way through his gut, he figured he'd be testing principle number three soon.

*

"Step right up, folks, and witness firsthand the mysteries of the universe unlocked before your very eyes. I, the renowned Professor Devereaux Dingleberry, will show you how to cure your ails, increase your libido, improve your lot in life. Feeling physically under the weather? Financially down-at-heel? Does your paramour claim you're wanting for stamina? Does that special would-be beau not find you fetching enough? Then listen and learn! Your aspirations will be fulfilled. These products, distilled from rare ingredients gathered from the four corners of the globe, will fix what troubles you!"

Bary was well into his second month of apprenticeship, and he had to admit he'd learned a lot. At first he was bewildered by all the elixirs, the crowds, the uncanny ways the professor beguiled them, but he was slowly getting the hang of it.

Today they were in the modestly sized municipality of Quar, a town as bustling as any he'd ever seen. The crowd before him was full of miners, crofters, caravaners, drifters, all visiting to spend their wages. Locals, too, bankers, innkeepers, merchants, ladies of the evening who had perhaps not gone to bed yet as this was the first show on a fine crisp morning and there was money to be spent and made.

One of Professor Dingleberry's most popular products wasn't really an elixir at all but a perfume. Midnight Mystique, he called it. It seemed to make the ladies who purchased it more alluring, but as much as the professor loathed woman, Bary had his doubts about how effective it really was.

After the first show, and Bary had supplied the paying customers with their "every desire," the professor went off to deal with his muse in a nearby latrine. Soon a young gamine approached Bary, a pretty little street urchin, despite her dishwater-blond hair, hazel eyes, and overbite.

"You're very good with the people," she said.

"Have you been watching me?"

She gave him a rueful yet pert look. "It's all I can afford to do. You have such nice things to sell and I, unfortunately, have no money."

Over the next quarter hour while the professor was addressing his muse, Bary became quite enamored with Kate, as her name turned out to be. And when his mentor returned, Bary took him aside to ask a favor of the great Professor Dingleberry.

"You want to do *what?*" Dingleberry said, aghast.

"She won't be any trouble," Bary assured him. "She's really interested in what we're doing, and she could help us in the show. And we have to help her. She's alone in the world and doesn't have anyone."

"And now she's got you, is that the size of it?"

Bary nodded.

"I should say no, but you might actually learn something from this."

And so Kate came to travel with them.

She was a quick learner, the professor had to hand her that. She helped Bary sell the professor's wares while he coaxed the crowd. She might've made a good cook except that Dingleberry insisted on doing *all* the cooking himself. Bary wished he would let her take over some of the cooking chores. Not that the professor's cooking was bad–though it was a bit zesty and had odd aftereffects–just that it was the same thing meal after meal: goulash.

Two weeks into her journey with them Kate showed her true stripes. On the first night of the blue moon she transformed into her fiendish self before them in the Coxcomb. Her straight dishwater-blond hair frizzed out into a fiery red nightmare and her overbite bifurcated into vicious fangs.

"Woman-hater!" she seethed.

"And which succubus of iniquity sent you?" Dingleberry asked, so calmly he almost appeared bored.

"All the feminine souls who you have tainted with that foul potion of yours," she said, venom in her now crimson eyes. She looked at Bary. "Do you really believe that perfume you are helping him peddle is making women more alluring? Yes, it does for a short while, but by the time you two are down the road and on your merry way, its actual effect takes hold. Its olfactory appeal turns to a deep insidious despair that makes the wearer loathe her very existence. Makes her so miserable that death by her own hand is the only possible solution."

Bary looked up at his mentor. "Is that true, Professor?"

He shrugged. "But the despair and self-loathing are never the same on any two women." He chuckled.

"It's *not* funny," Kate said. "And now you will forfeit your miserable life as consequence of your actions." Fingernails morphing into talons, she lunged at him. But Dingleberry was ready. He pulled one of his special elixirs from his left coat pocket and doused her.

As she disintegrated before their eyes, Bary stood there horrified, gazing upon the goopy mess she had become on the floor of the Coxcomb.

Dingleberry shook his head and sighed. "See what I told you about women, Bary? This is the lesson I wanted you to learn."

"But... But..."

*

As time passed, Bary grew to realize that the great Professor Dingleberry was not so great a man after all. He'd thought about leaving him, but where would he go? And the professor had restored him to corporeality, so as much as he despised the man's tactics, he owed him.

One evening after leaving the village of Orth, the skies grew dim and the clouds descended to drench the roadway, turning it into a soupy mess. Though it was only a flash rainstorm that passed quickly, it ensured they weren't going any further that evening.

"Best we turn in and see if we can get an early start tomorrow," Dingleberry said as they stood outside the Coxcomb, surveying the marshy mess of the land around them.

"I have to pee first," Bary said.

"So do I," said Dingleberry. "But not here. Remember what I told you about not leaving one's spoor too close to the Coxcomb?"

Bary did, barely. The professor had so many additional rules and specific ways of doing things, they were sometimes a jumble in his young mind.

"This way," the mustachioed man said. "Not too muddy over there beyond those trees."

As they were giving the earth an additional watering it didn't need behind the stand, the horrible occurred. Golem-like figures of muck rose from the ground.

"Oh my!" Bary said.

"Oh my, is right," said Dingleberry.

"What *are* they?"

"Mudzombies. Quick, we must get back to the Coxcomb."

Their way back was cut off by the dreadful creatures, however, so they had to circle around. Yet every path they took more mudzombies emerged from the earth to form an army of muck monsters. Though lithe and not terribly tall or large, there was a plenitude of them.

"They're all women, Professor," Bary said, noting their loamy breasts and supple curves.

"Figures."

"What are we gonna do?" Bary asked, his voice clutched by fear.

"Only one thing we can do. Stand and fight."

They found two fallen trees in which to make their stand. It wasn't much of a defense, but it was all they had.

"But what chance do we have?" Bary asked. "We don't have any weapons."

"Ah, yes we do!" The professor then proceeded to pull down his trousers, and then his underwear. Then Bary learned how the great man came by his name, as he proceeded to pick the dark fruit from his ass.

Dingleberry didn't waste any time as he flung the small pellets at the approaching mudzombies. "See, Bary? See? What did I tell you about women? They're all our enemy!"

As each dingleberry connected with its target, each muck monster was rendered once again to inert dirt, or mud as the case happened to be. Bary wondered how this was possible, and in between volleys the professor explained it was the goulash.

Ah, thought Bary, that explains why my stool has been glowing in the dark. He'd thought about bringing it up before, but didn't know how to broach such a delicate subject. Instead he'd washed it from his mind.

Soon, however, the professor's arsenal was depleted and the mudzombies still kept coming.

"Your turn, Bary. Quick! Doff your drawers."

"I–I–" Bary's mouth was cotton.

"Boy, are you trying to tell me what I think you're trying to tell me?"

It was true. Bary had not adhered to principle number three. He had wiped his ass. And the mudzombies kept coming, their evil intent imminent. They were about to die and it would be all Bary's fault.

"We've gotta run!" Bary said, but there was no place to run to. As the mudzombies converged, however, they didn't seem to pay any attention to Bary, only the professor. Dingleberry tried to fight them off, but all he could do was flounder in the mud, his suit now a grimy mess. Several mudzombies held the great man down while the others sacrificed their bodies, entering his mouth and drowning him in a river of mud.

When Professor Dingleberry had released his last gurgle and died, one of the mudzombies, apparently their leader, turned her slim, full-breasted form to address Bary. "I'm unsure whether we have any grievance with you, young man. So tell me. Why do you follow this wicked man? Are you a hater of women as well?"

"No, ma'am," Bary said, hoping his sincerity gleamed in his eyes. "I like women. A lot!"

"I believe you," she said, finally. "But that's not enough." She had a directive for Bary, which she related to him before returning to the Mother Earth.

*

It was a bright fresh morning and Bary sat upon the porch of the Coxcomb as it strutted down the road. He still had a lot of work to do to retool Professor Dingleberry's elixirs to where they'd be an agent of good, but he had time to work on that. He was young.

He was founding his own set of principles as well. The first one would be to learn altruism and not be too self-serving, though he certainly didn't plan on going through life as a naive schmuck. As to the second, he'd never held the professor's queer notions about women, so he looked forward to making their acquaintance without mistrust. The third principle came easy enough as he'd never unlearned what his mother had taught him to do, though he was grateful he'd never listened to her about peeing in the backyard.

Up ahead he saw a coarse, hunchbacked harridan marching up the road with a burden on her back. He would've preferred a young maid with blond hair, hazel eyes, and a slight overbite for riding company, but he probably wasn't deserving of such good fortune yet.

He commanded the Coxcomb to halt. "Excuse me, good woman. May I offer you a ride?"

DISSEMBLANCE
DOUGLAS THOMPSON

The early Dupliportation experiments went badly wrong. Things had seemed fine with fruit flies and white lab rats. A quantum-entangled mouse lifted up by a human hand in California would magically levitate inside its glass cage in Oxfordshire. One fighting with a rival over a block of cheese, would creepily interact with nothing, on the other side of the Atlantic. So NASA raced ahead into trying the first human, an eager science student looking for extra money, made sure he had few family, made him sign the forms. They thought they botched the first Entanglement, then the second, so kept going, but all had worked, just not predictably.

By the time they stopped, the experiment in disarray, they had created eleven versions of Guy Lecaux, all of varying quality and stability, distributed across the planet's surface.

At first, Guy could only inhabit one body at once, and pass instantly between them, his mind teleporting only upon falling asleep or fainting. But the situation deteriorated over time. Simultaneity, disparity, dissolution and disintegration took hold.

In New York, his face was mostly gone. A field of grey static, flickering, pixels rearranging, in flux, like digital interference. He kept out of sight, in raincoats and broad-rimmed hats, found himself disassembling in rain showers, interacting with the lights on Broadway and Times Square, during long evening walks. Nearly lost his left arm to a cathode-ray tube, sucked into the electron storm in an old TV repair shop in Queens, had to go stand on Three Mile Island to re-build his hands.

In Tokyo he was raped by modem. –Split open three-way with his semblances in Brussels and Lima. Dangerous singularity meshing him with traffic noise. He remembered his girlfriend and went to find her, all three bodies boarding different planes to London. Stopped at customs, only one got through, by dissolving through several walls and an aircraft hull. Emergency landing at Paris Charles de Gaulle, screaming tourist pointing to white electro-ghost slipping along the aisle floor like luminous piss. Bled into the Autopilot and phoned himself to Surrey. Inhabited the network for six years before downloading in a disused railway siding in Swindon, from an accretion of stolen mobile phones connected up in parallel, electromagnetic meltdown of social networks, texting of DNA.

He lived again and hid himself in a Teflon suit, kept cover of darkness. Found Amy at last in East Croydon, but his legs were gone from the knees down. Imperfect translation, Berlin semblance was resonating with him, his movements being taken over remotely like a deranged Pinocchio operated by distant hands. Taken into hospital as suspected epilepsy patient, escaped through an oscilloscope, ECG heart beat trace like Morse code, digitised street to street through webcams. Found her again in Greenwich Park but dissolved among the pigeons and ducks as she looked on, screaming. Energy haloes breaking up, feathers and flutter of wings, each bird taking a different part of him up into the skies and stars, over to the trees and down into the autumn leaves.

He became the essence of London, remembered days, trampled underfoot. Amy smelled him everywhere, in rain-damp mornings and late afternoons of exhausted, exalted light. He was neon, lipstick, magazine stands, all ephemera, gesture, glances, lost moments, fragments of touch, overheard snippets of music at Saturday morning markets. She could find him only when alone and despairing, on long walks two-hours-in, in the light on clouds, burning cigarette butts discarded at bus stops by people moved on, in cooling coffee cups left behind at lonely café tables in unprofitable thoroughfares.

She turned to prostitution then drug addiction, every form of annihilation and loss. In the needle's winking eye at last, she downloaded or uploaded herself or him, what's the difference. At the moment of orgasm with a stranger, she found she could disassociate herself, disengage briefly from the physical as Guy had done permanently, and in that fleeting window of non-being touch the horizon, kiss the sky, circumnavigate the globe and find him again as she cried her little death, crucified on the winds of time. The strangers always seemed to leave with something of Guy invisibly smeared over them, cross-meshed into their fabric, implanted by osmosis. She thought for a while she might be bringing him back to life a little with every fuck. Guy and Amy.

Their faces and souls became billboard images moving in Trafalgar Square, cryptic giants etched over city maps, shapes in fog, refugees in peripheral vision, posters of the missing, dead police files, smiling girls, models in magazine adverts twenty years out of date, stained by rain and semen.

Meanwhile in Berlin, the action moved on. His missing legs after walking alone at night for a year, downloaded two fragmented semblances from Warsaw and Rome. Completed himself, but never quite stable. Lived in subways and detuned radios, white noise, EVP. The CIA were on his trail now, agents in all the target cities. One of them, a woman Gina F, found him in Rome and followed him to Turin. They met and embraced on the banks of the Po in early February, swirling in chill fog. She followed him through the dreaming arcades of Nietzsche and De Chirico, one eye on the Alps and the Basilica of Superga, white snow-like dream of innocence and peace, unattainable, found he broke up at city boundaries, her arm reaching right through him, a prisoner of the grid, of human static. Every power-cut he died a little, his essence bleeding out towards elemental nothing, the ultimate terror of human silence. The collective unconscious was keeping him going, like WiFi, Infrared, afraid of being undreamt. He needed her, his open file, on-going, a story, any story.

In a hotel room in Milan they attempted sex, but he meshed with her and became her, screaming. The startled maids understood nothing. He began a new life as her, but her old colleagues tracked her down, suspicious.

Years went by. Her body died in public, heart failure on the marble floor of the Galleria, within sight of the Duomo, passersby coming to her rescue. His ghost emerged, disengaging to startled gasps. Late afternoon light thrown through muted glass, filigree pattern across him, he became Milanese shadows for three decades, plaguing tourist photographs and shortwave radio.

The space programme had moved

on, the technology mastered. His semblances in Detroit and Buenos Aires had been quietly consolidating, one a tramp, the other a serial killer. Both fused through a police file in Mexico City, the face unstable, liable to contraflow with another dying fragment in Moscow that blew through streets as torn newspapers.

Finally they caught up with Lecaux in Los Angeles. He had wandered Sunset Boulevard for decades, cross-contaminating with celluloid re-masterings, Hitchcock, Humphrey Bogart, decayed films from military installations, Roswell, the 1950's, wind blowing through empty film sets. At the desert's edge, he would tremble like flimsy Drywall, on the threshold of dissolution as dusk approached, gazing up at the stars.

They found him in a derelict apartment, limboed between developments, one boom and the next, construction and demolition. Four agents with back-up on the way, encapsulated and sterilised, condensed him into a foot-square steel box of electro-mesh, after a brief maelstrom involving swirling curtains and frayed electrical wires, blue flashes, two agents electrocuted, minor burns and an epileptic fit followed by four years of psychotic episodes.

They had found Lecaux watching television in the empty room, amid the pools of rain and turned-up carpets, rotting detritus of abandoned construction work. No power, the television was wired to his wrist, feeding on his own ebbing life force, a century in the dying.

The screen was showing the arrival of the first probe-spores on Gliese 581d, the eager astronauts reporting to the Nevada Telepdrome for upload and Dupliport, pacing the shining polygonal corridors in their safety suits and pig-masks, glass chamber doors springing open in futuristic ease, antiseptic anticipation. He hoped they would make it, intact. He had paid the price for their ambiguous journeys, to walk on distant worlds, twenty light years distant.

He would be a footnote in history he knew, scrubbed out, as he awaited the stealthy steps in the corridor outside his ruinous apartment, a state secret obliterated, a man who never was, the cost of progress. Not fully alive, how could he ever die now? Detuned radios, malfunctioning televisions, schizophrenic's day-mares, would forevermore be suspect. But like Marilyn or Kennedy, he would be data-safe, culture-encoded, bound, stitched, integration-encrypted, irresolvable left-over fraction, non-divisible, residual, background radiation. He smiled, as he pressed the remote control and the picture faded, as the door was burst open, dissolving himself in silver static.

NOTHING WILL BE GOOD ENOUGH FOR YOU

KIIK ARAKI-KAWAGUCHI

Nothing will be good enough for you
I fed eel to you straight off the metal grate
Straight off the rocks throbbing in red fire
You took my finger up to the knuckle
It waggled on your tongue making accusations
Until you chomped and the scummed seas puffed
from your cheeks like an apparition

The witch brought you bread wrapped in her hair
She pulled the bundle out from under her cloak
How she'd held it there while walking I don't know
You ate and became as self-righteous as a whore
Saying you gave more than you took

But you took the witch's scalp
To dangle as a black jellyfish in your window
It glowed like oil riding the night-colored seas
Your skin cured by the window
You whisked away the salt
And I kneeled down to polish it in snow

There is no amount of polish you say is right
There is only an amount of polish that exists nearby you
The meat droops over your teeth
like a flummoxed oyster
At least it is not my tongue
and my voice on the line
It is your tongue rotting in the sun
Your voice chewed upon in the breeze

TODAY, PARADISE
KHK ARAKI-KAWAGUCHI

I want that seed been dropped from the horse's tongue
Seed gone packt under thousand years hoof and weathered heel
Seed pressed a mile from nearest flickering daylight
Seed strangled from a parched breath

And moth-eaten
Moth-rag fed down its throat

Seed been separated from a speck of earth lathered by moisture
To rattle the sides of winter casket
And pierce the root and bone-slept dust
And the snow wept by animals clambering beneath ax and rifle

And the mud gagged by rain and piss and tears
To shout for all of paradise would part
And throw itself prostrate for what the seed has become –

An enormous, terrifying bud
And ruffle loose the slick, dog-eared petals
For the bees to guzzle at

Where the bees to drink and become massive and immortal
Where they to lose their wings and begin scurrying through fields like rats

The whorled corolla piping ceaselessly from its wig of pollen
Where the pollen touching the birds – the birds fell asleep
And that amnesia gone out for every winged creature to forget their flight

And the colossal leaf to rise to rise over the earth and take all the sun
And for the sun to elope with the heavens –
Grown too plain for what our lone paradise has become

POLLUTO

WHAT WE CALL THE NIGHT
KIIK ARAKI-KAWAGUCHI

The hands are done with this silence
They have endured a black snow, shivering

Now silence falls to the floor,
flickering like a dead moth rolled
out of a forgotten blanket

The voice has awoken from starvation
Wrapped in the bone clutching
bone stretched the anger of the hands
over the four-lipped hulls
the pale stones

Anger has carried it this far
The voice is still there

Like a damp oil rag
Ready to be funneled, cast
into suffocating snow

And strike the ash been sleeping
under carpets been clinging
under boot soles

Strike the knot held like an apple
to the lips of any creature
strung up by its voice

And feed them the hot sky
past their strangulation

And catch the dry ribbon of a next voice
until we change what we call the night

THE BALLAD OF THE BULLET HOLES

ERIK T. JOHNSON

I. THE BULLET HOLE

"The bullet hole," the headless panhandler's head said, "looks full of dark moving life, but also motionless, like a cluster of ants on a gumdrop looks still as it does swarming."

II. WHY NORMAL PEOPLE LAUGH

Martin Box, struggling private investigator, had demonstrated no sense of humor his entire 40-years of existence. Somehow, he had always known this but it took his partner ten years of acquaintance to confirm the diagnosis for him. They were sitting together at their usual spot on top of the hill, under the flagless pole in the park, eating their usual shitty sandwiches and Denny Zynowiak drinking his beer through a straw and Martin sipping coffee with baby formula that had accidentally been delivered to his house. Dennis stretched out his sandaled feet and farted loudly. Martin took a bite of his sandwich and slowly chewed.

"You know what, Marty? I think you've got no sense of humor."

"How do you know?"

"Because I'm a detective, man. I detect."

Martin kept chewing. There was a kid running after a ball that was going into the street. It would be easy for him to get hit and die or worse.

Dennis sighed.

"Because, man, normal people laugh at things that happen, just because they are funny. I've seen you laugh at a joke, but jokes are like amusement park rides. You get prepared for them, and you're ready to scream when you drop down the rollercoaster. Jokes are like that, only laughs instead of screams. But you don't find things funny unless they are supposed to be, not ever. You don't see how funny things can be. And I don't mean laughing at jokes *designed* to make you laugh."

"You mean farts."

"Farts are freedom, man. Laughing at a joke's like praying in church."

No, Denny is just talking shit, the way he talks to his lost-boy friends–dopers, musicians, poets and circus freaks, Martin reflected, looking at a mole on Denny's face and thinking, for the last ten years, every minute I look at him, I want to ask Dennis if that mole on his face is cancer or if he has checked to find out. It could get worse, fast. Things usually did.

Lunch over, they got up and dusted

the bits of yellowed grass from their pants. Martin straightened his black tie. Walking down the hill, past a boy throwing a ball to his friends, Martin said:

"You know, I think you're right. I think I might have no sense of humor. After all, we're broke, can't land a case. So I am not laughing. This seems like Hell to me. And while we're at it, I'm afraid of dying, I guess. But I have to die, right?"

"Don't do that, man. Without you I'd be dead last in the phone book–Zynowiak Detective Agency? Then I'd really be poor."

Martin watched the ball arc between small hands like a water drop burst from an exploding boiler.

"You know I'm kidding, right?" Dennis said. "Marty?"

Martin was not paying attention. He felt like he had eyes on the back of his brain, straining to see the gloom in the giggly sunlight.

III. MR. TICKLER WEEPS

Later that week, Dennis landed a case. It was a weird one.

Martin entered the Box and Zynowiak Detective Agency office to find a hunched, quivering figure dressed black as a grackle sitting across the desk from Dennis. He wore a black top hat emblazoned with white stars and crescent moons. He clutched a spectacular solid gold suitcase on his lap. The man was built like a sapling Martin had seen trying to grow out from the crumbling spaces of old chimney bricks. He was crying, softly. There was a welt shaped like the outline of a donut left in the rain on one cheek. His nails were long and dirty and his sparse hair unwashed. He reeked of bladder failure.

"Mr. Tickler, this is my partner, Martin Box. Marty, Mr. Tickler has a problem."

Martin sat down in a chair next to Mr. Ticker. The man's oyster-gray eyes turned to the grotesque chattering teeth chomping down on a skunk joint on Denny's swirly-doodle-obscured desk calendar.

"What is the problem?" Martin asked.

"I've seen a terrible thing," Tickler said, blowing demon-green snot into the middle of a pentagram-embroidered tissue. "I saw a homeless guy get murdered and I want you to find the guy who did it."

"Who do you think did it?"

"Me. I need you to find me. Can you help?"

Martin leaned over to Dennis.

"This isn't one of your I'm-the-Zen-Master-Teaching-Marty-About-Life things is it? Is this supposed to be funny? I mean, even his name…"

"No, man. Seriously. He wants us to find him."

"Mr. Tickler," Marty said. "I appreciate your situation. But what are you willing to pay us if we can track you down?"

"I have $2 million cash in this briefcase," he said.

That was extremely unlikely. Martin leaned over the desk again.

"Is this true? And did you have him sign the contract?"

Denny nodded, smiling like a killer.

"Take a look, Marty," he said.

Martin took the heavy briefcase from Mr. Tickler, opened it and checked the contents.

"Mr. Tickler, I'm happy to report we have solved your case. There you are."

IV. QUOTHING NEVERMORE

It was too easy, and that bothered Martin.

He lay awake one night, thinking about Elias Tickler's story, thinking he needed to check it out even though it was crazy.

Why? Because Martin had learned well on the job that people can only be crazy if they share enough sanity with you to communicate their madness clearly. And in that sane space they share with you, there is reality on the level of two hands that can interlock fingers, which is about as real as it gets. And just like holding hands with a complete stranger, talking to a nutjob is unpleasant but you don't forget it too quickly. And you tend to remember important things and forget useless things. So maybe that crazy-talk was important.

And he couldn't sleep and he was rich but he didn't feel rich and that made him think that the feeling lay on the other side of a mystery and he'd like to feel rich, all right. So he got out of bed and drove to the abandoned building where Tickler said the murder had taken place, where he and Denny had not bothered to look because they had a cool $2 million in pocket and Tickler was clearly insane and just needed some convincing that the case was closed (passing him the joint in the chattering teeth also helped).

The building was not on the wrong side of town. It was not on any side; it was deep in the borough in a neighborhood that detective Box had never known before, which was strange since he had chased people and paper trails all across Brooklyn.

The address Tickler gave was an old, wood-framed farmhouse stuck between two vacant lots overrun with weeds and teeming with rats the size of bus drivers. Nearby was a housing project, full of lighted windows. Martin noted that no silhouettes ever passed the windows, as though it was empty. But housing projects are never empty; if anything they're too full. The night was silent. There was no broken glass on the street and no graffiti on the house and no openings cut in the wire fences holding in the parking lots.

It was as if nobody had ever done anything bad there. Except build a farmhouse on a concrete field.

Martin walked up to the house and found the door hanging by one rusty hinge. Taking out a flashlight and holding his breath, he pushed the door aside and it gently fell back the way it had been. He swept the dark room with an electric ray. It illuminated a bullwhip, a smashed bottle of whiskey, and a wet Gideon's Bible on the floor near a small enamel-topped table.

There were also spattered bloodstains on the floor.

And then he found it. While the street had been quiet as a broken clock, a headless body lay atop a huge fireplace mantle like some bloody raven quothing "nevermore" the whole damn time.

It was the body of a middle-aged man. His chest was welted in what looked like a giant tentacle's oval sucker-marks. He had an outie for a belly button. Blood had run down from the corpse to the fireplace below and doused what appeared to have been burning planks of wood, probably extinguishing a recently-lit flame.

Martin walked closer and stepped on something out-of-place. He flew forward into the wall and put his palms out just in time to save his face from hitting the ground. The flashlight rolled away and was shining into a head with Martin's size-10 shoeprint running from the forehead to the tip of the chin. The face was missing a nose.

Martin picked up the flashlight and walked toward the head when the beam struck what was unmistakably a bullet hole in the wall. Lacking projectile expansion, it had been fired from within the room.

"The bullet hole, Martin said out loud, surprising himself, "looks full of dark moving life, but also motionless, like a cluster of ants on a gumdrop looks still as it does swarming."

He thought: what the hell was that? But a situation like this can make anyone say, do weird things. Keep calm or things could get worse. They usually do. He turned the flashlight back toward the head.

It was gone. Martin tried not to shake as he searched the room carefully. Where did it go? He looked for the shell from the recently-fired gunshot. Nothing.

Martin went outside and around the back of the house, to find the bullet's exit hole. There were no marks, not even the smallest puncture in the flimsy wood siding. There was a large, open and empty animal cage– recently used, judging by the smell–but nothing else of interest.

He went back inside and examined the hole again. He tried to put his finger in it, but he kept missing somehow. It was a bit like trying to read the last tiny line of type in an eye-exam. It was like how you can't touch a shadow but a shadow can touch you. The murdered man was still there, thank God. But it seemed the body had shifted position a little bit. Martin decided he'd had enough of this house.

As he got into the car, he thought he heard crunching noises and groaning, as though a rat the size of a bus driver was biting into someone's skull. But a situation like this can make anyone think, imagine weird things and he just drove home. He wouldn't call the cops. How could he? Things would just get worse, real fast.

V. SOMETHING THAT SMELLS

They were sitting on the hill, eating lunch. Martin had real milk in his coffee and Dennis was drinking a bottle of 1907 Heidsieck champagne.

"There's a nose on your shoe," Denny said.

"What?"

Dennis was right. He started laughing hysterically in Martin's face.

"You stepped in something that smells, man."

Martin scraped the nose off with a twig and held it up in the sunlight. It was pocked. A twig was picking its nostril. But it was a good nose, sturdy, smooth like a rudder. It deserved better.

"Come on, you don't think that's funny?" Denny said.

"Where did you find that Mr. Tickler, again?"

"Where did you find that nose?" Denny said, suddenly watching it like it was that guy at an art gallery that keeps looking at the same paintings at the same pace and direction as you, to the point where you feel you should talk but it doesn't quite make sense to do so.

"My question first," Martin said, putting the nose down, where some ants investigated.

"It's like I told you, man. This guy just walks into the office with a gold briefcase. He was off his rocker, you saw. He had a few million that I am sure weren't his. That's really it. My question's turn," Denny said, finishing off the champagne in one swig.

Martin told him about the farmhouse in the concrete field and all that happened. He didn't feel like talking about it, but it spoke through him anyway. When he finished Denny was pretty pale and he kept looking in his champagne bottle to see if he'd missed a drop.

"I'm going home early," Martin said, "to change my shoes."

VI. THE BULLET HOLE

"The bullet hole," the associate professor of astronomy said, searching for his arms, "looks full of dark moving life, but also motionless, like a cluster of ants on a gumdrop looks still as it does swarming."

VII. THE FIRST BEGINNING TO THIS STORY

Back at his apartment, Martin took off his shoes and decided to run himself a hot bath.

But the water was cold and Kashmir brown. He loosened his tie and sat in front of the TV. It was off and he could see his bored reflection staring at him from the screen. That made sense. But behind him, a man-sized shape hovered.

"What now . . ." Martin said.

"Iff N. Quid, Mr. Box, at my service."

Martin looked over his shoulder and got an eyeful of fist. The blow knocked a lateral incisor from his mouth and his face clattered into pasta-soiled dishes on the floor.

"I'm missing my gun, Mr. Box. Know anything about it?"

"Can't help you there."

Martin rolled away quickly as a boot came down where his groin had been, snatched a black panther-shaped lamp from the coffee table and swung it up toward Quid's jaw–Quid heaved back his arm to strike–the lamp went past the face raging above Martin, his arms curved over his head and he smashed the lamp on the back of his neck.

Iff N. Quid laughed: "Astounding, I did not know that would happen!"

"Everyone thinks everything is damned funny," Martin said, spitting blood and moldy gnocchi.

The intruder was tall, draped in dusty black cloth like something stored and forgotten in an attic between a phonograph and an incomplete set of encyclopedias. His face was long, worn but strong, eyes of blue gas flame that amaze children and warn adults, hair like dirty ice, mouth too tight to bellow, the face of a bad priest, a good sniper, some schoolboy's worst nightmare.

Quid went to hit again with a huge fist; Martin held up the broken lamp and Quid's knuckles struck glass shards. Quid grunted; Martin ran behind the television and held up his hands surrender-style.

"Let's talk," he panted. "I'm a detective . . . I don't have your gun, I swear. But I can help you find it if you'd just explain."

Quid considered Martin with one eye while the other examined the glass shards sticking out from his fist. Martin felt double-screwed, like a stigmatic hemophiliac.

"Astounding, I did not see this coming," Quid said. "Let's do it this way. I am thirsty. If you have my favorite beverage on hand, we'll speak. If not, I'll split your face with these improvised panther claws."

"Care for water? It's brown."

"I enjoy nothing more than a tall glass of baby formula. I have found it is both delicious and extremely nourishing to my kind. But seeing this place, my guess is you do not have–"

"–Straight or on the rocks?"

Martin got a bottle of Similac Sensitive for his guest and two cold beers for himself.

"I did not see this happening–absolutely beyond my control," Quid said, oddly pleased. "Where would you like me to start?"

"At the beginning."

"There are a few beginnings to this story."

"Pick one," Martin said, sitting down next to Quid on the couch, putting one beer behind his neck while the other washed the blood down his throat.

"I come from somewhere very, very far away, Mr. Box. As far away as the middle of your brain, a place you will never be able to visit. You would likely call it another dimension. In my world, there is what you would call 'magic'–within each one of my kind, there is an identity between will and existence. In other words, whatever we think 'really' does 'happen', to use your terminology. We control our reality. We call this process 'glamour.'

"Recently, I grew tired of making glamours. I wanted to see your world–what we call the Human's Enchanted Land, or Hel. They all said the humans were worthless but

I was not so interested in humans specifically as much as anything that changes from one thing into another without being able to pick what it will become, like wood into ashes or fire into smoke–things under an enchantment beyond their control. I dreamed of being tangled up with all… *this*," Quid said, waving his hand at a pile of unwashed laundry on the floor, next to the dirty dishes.

"Since I was a boy, I had been told that a strange state of affairs existed in the Human's Enchanted Land. It was supposed to be ruled by an inviolable force called the Past. The Past resembled a spell but I was not sure if it truly was one or not. The Past was to the human's Physical World what Belief was to the human's Mind. In any given moment a human is just "there" and that is it, no story or anything to tell. But because you believe things, you imagine there is more to them than there is and each person imagines something a little different. But unlike my kind, when you imagine something it does not 'come true' or do anything. Under the enchantment you live under, Mr. Box, thoughts and actions are not equal. But even so, you suppose belief does affect reality, and act in accordance with your beliefs.

"I will tell you a secret: The Past is the Belief of your Universe. Consider, for example, this panther-shaped lamp which you broke on your neck. At each moment, the lamp is just sitting there and that is it, no story to it. But when you tried to clobber me and smashed it, in the next moment there were shards of glass because the Universe believes that by hitting your neck with the lamp you did something to it and so the Universe makes sure it is still all broken for the moments that come after the breaking. Then you, as well, perceive the lamp and believe that you broke it. Therefore the Universe and the human both share, and are victims of, Belief. Since I was small, I wondered what it must be like to feel such a constant *weight* press from the inside and out."

Coolly professional, as though Iff was simply a woman relating how her husband was cheating on her, Martin said:

"And the gun?"

"The second beginning to this story, about my first trip to Hel. It involved a singular incident."

VIII. THE SECOND BEGINNING TO THIS STORY

Elias Tickler was juggling a gun, a bible, and a full bottle of whiskey.

"Whichever hits the floor last is the path I'll take," he said.

"I know you're an honest-to-god circus clown, man, but be careful, man," Dennis Zynowiak said, lighting a North Carolina Blue Cheese spliff.

"That's not the point, Denny. Look, I appreciate my friends asking you to come by and talk me out of doing something… clownish, haha. But what will be will be you know?"

"Friends of friends, actually."

"Just my point. My own good pals don't care enough to check on me. I'm losing my worth; I can see myself disappearing day by day, the less I look in the mirror."

"Well, somebody cares about you. Bongzo the Magician lent you his clothes and his partner Throngzo the Tiger-Tamer is letting you stay here in his old house. That gun isn't loaded?"

"Is the bottle of Jack full?"

"How long have you been juggling those?"

"All day. I'll get tired soon and drop something. Shouldn't you be working?"

"Too busy to work, man."

The bottle fell in slow motion and shattered at high speed.

"That's good. Drinking's no good for you," Denny said.

The Bible fell next, Jonah and the whale plunging into Jack Daniels.

"It's the gun, then. I can't say I'm disappointed," Tickler said.

"You're not gonna hurt someone?"

"Not someone, but nobody."

Tickler kept the gun in the air juggling between both hands. Then he missed it by a fraction. It twirled barrel over handle like lumber over Niagara Falls, about to descend, when a man's long-fingered hand appeared out of the air and grabbed it before it could strike the floor. The hand retracted back into invisibility and Denny said:

"I gotta go."

He ran out and left Tickler shaking in a puddle of whiskey, peering and peeing into the space before him.

As the loose door rattled closed on its single hinge behind Zynowiak, the hand rematerialized with the gun, followed by the body of Iff N. Quid.

"This gun… is enchanted, causes change, makes things become what they did not plan to be," he said. "But I have a few questions. Would you mind answering them? I understand exchange is required in Hel and I can give you something in return."

"Is this Hell?" Tickler asked, feeling far sicker than a dead man.

"Yes, of course. Now, what would you take in return for tutoring me about this gun?"

"But I didn't do it. How could I be in Hell? Or did I? Have I been in Hell all along?"

"Of course. Name your price, please."

"Anything? Two million dollars, I guess."

"Certainly," Iff said, plunged a hand into deep air, and pulled back a gold briefcase from his world (where thought and existence were the same). "Incidentally, I am Mr. Iff. N. Quid."

Tickler examined the money from beyond.

"Okay," he said, afraid but going with it. "What do you want to know?"

"I will know what questions I have after a demonstration. Show me an example of how it works."

Tickler took a lump of gnawed American cheese from the fridge and smooshed it into the wall about head-high. He stepped eleven feet away and lifted the revolver, cocked the hammer back, and, with arm shaky from juggling and fear, took aim at the cheese blob. Iff N. Quid watched from beside him with patient interest.

The gun felt light as a bug-bone, which was odd since Tickler's arm was tired and the gun loaded. It was as if the brief touch of Iff's hand had drained the density from it. As the clown squeezed the trigger, the blob of cheese began to spread into the head of a man and a naked body descended from that head. The cheese turned into flesh and the flesh turned into the recognizable face of Whiskers, a local homeless panhandler who Tickler knew quite well. By the time Tickler realized what was happening the bullet had fired silently from the barrel and pierced the wall just a few inches from Whiskers' head.

Tickler jumped, felt his breath freeze solid in his lungs and hoped he would explode. Whiskers, looking merely disoriented, rubbed his temples and squinted at the two men facing him.

"You missed," Quid said.

"I don't know what you did to that gun, but that's a human be–"

Tickler was cut short by an impossibly large tentacle that launched out from the bullet hole and slapped his cheek. It retracted and joined more tentacles pouring out of the hole as they wrapped around Whiskers and promptly popped his head off.

"Astounding!" Quid said. "I didn't know that would happen, in the least."

The tentacles withdrew into the bullet hole. Quid lifted the body and placed it sitting upright on a chair to examine the sucker marks, which he repeatedly traced with long fingers as though playing the rims of crystal glasses.

When he turned around, Tickler was gone and he had taken the money and the gun with him.

A tourist in this world, Iff was surprised at that, too.

IX. THE BULLET HOLE

"The bullet hole," the hedge fund manager said, digging in his viscera with diamond-ringed fingers, "looks full of dark moving life, but also motionless, like a cluster of ants on a gumdrop looks still as it does swarming."

X. JUST A BIG MISUNDERSTANDING

Leaving Mr. Quid at his apartment (who promised to leave the place messy as he found it), Martin went to Denny's and knocked on his door.

"Denny, open up. It's me."

He could hear someone blubbering and Denny alternating between frustration and reassurance.

Martin pushed the door. It opened on Tickler curled up like a broken fist, sobbing on Denny's floor. Denny was standing over him, drinking a bottle of champagne and smoking a cigarette. The gold suitcase sat underneath a statue of Avalokitesvara, the many-armed Bodhisattva of Compassion. Martin noticed that the mole on Denny's face, that might be cancer, looked like it had changed shape a little.

"Mind if I join the fun?"

"Marty… you know Mr. Tickler."

"I've met with Iff N. Quid."

Tickler uncurled, whimpered "No, not him… don't say that."

"Man, I can explain man."

"You'd better. Quid is dangerous. And there's a certain, special gun I'm looking for, and I believe that Tickler here has it."

"No… I dropped it when I ran."

"Where?"

"Near the house where the homeless guy… Whiskers…"

"What's going on here, Denny?"

Denny took Martin into his bedroom. They sat on his futon and in the liquid glow of orange and purple lava lamps, Denny blurted it all out.

Through the rambling smoke of his hippie-on-the-edge discourse, Martin was able to gather that Tickler was a friend of a fire-eater friend who'd asked Denny to check in on Tickler, a very depressed clown. The fire-eater asked Denny because he was the only "professional" he knew. After Tickler inadvertently murdered Whiskers by unleashing other-dimensional tentacles through the bullet hole left by an enchanted gun, Tickler went from sad to nanners. He sought out Denny for advice, claiming they were all living in Hell. Denny spied a business opportunity. He told Tickler that everything would be all right if he would just give the money over to Denny, that it was magic money and that he'd be absolved of the murder after it was all spent, but Tickler couldn't be the one to spend it. But, Denny said, he didn't want to leave his old partner Martin out of the deal, so he set it up with Tickler to act like he was hiring them for an easy case. Now Tickler was weeping in the living room because he had nowhere to go and didn't know what to do, and that was really the whole story, man, you gotta believe me.

Some of this didn't sit well with Martin. There were probably a few lies in Denny's explanation and he didn't know what to believe. Then again, nothing sat well with Martin lately. But even accepting Denny's story at face value, there was one big problem: where was the gun?

"So it could still be outside that farm in the concrete field," Martin said. "I'm going to go check that area out again."

Martin passed the quivering form of Tickler, and opened the door to the hall. As he was about to leave, Denny said:

"Marty, I'm sorry."

Martin nodded, and turned to face a headless body lacerated by tentacles. It neck-butted him and he went flying across the room, tumbling over Tickler and hitting his head on a sharp petal of the Buddhist statue's bronze lotus flower.

When he cleared the stinging blood from his eyes, it was to witness the headless body tearing out clumps of Tickler's hair, and the noseless, bodyless face of Whiskers gnawing at his Achilles tendon. Martin would have recognized that face but didn't have time to register it because a dead man in a "Space is Really Cool" T-shirt with telescopes uselessly stuck where his arms should be was blocking the doorway, and through his legs, another corpse had flung its intestines into the room, looped them around one of Avalokitesvara's limbs and was hauling itself forward with one hand, sliding on viscous guts.

In its other hand was a gun.

Denny was stuck to the spot in terror. The cigarette was almost out and burning his lip. He was trying to say something, his mouth opening and closing like a fish drowning in air.

"Spit it out!" Whiskers' head shouted.

"It's just a big misunderstanding, man," he said.

"What is going on?" Martin said, getting up and walking slowly backwards, dizzy, seeing red and bright white spots everywhere, thinking this must be Hell.

"You don't know what it's like," Whiskers' head said.

"We know what it's like," the man with telescope arms said, gazing out the window, straining dead eyes for stars.

"Whiskers fired the gun twice, pulled us to the bullet holes, the things came out and changed us. Now we know what it's like," the intestine-climber said.

"I wish I'd studied anatomy," the dead astronomer said, gazing down at the astrolabe where his foot should be. "Now I know what it's like."

Tickler grew quiet and stayed quiet.

"I don't like this one bit," Denny stuttered.

The man with the gun raised it and pointed it toward Denny.

"I do," he said.

The silent bullet struck Martin right between the eyes. Everything went from dazzling white to black the color of the inside of a forgotten time-capsule. He vaguely saw a woman who lived down the hall appearing near the coffee table, was slightly pleased to get to see her naked, felt his head splitting, heard many screams, the sound of sleek things whisking along shag carpet, crunching, wet frog dropped in a coffee grinder kinds of noises. He passed out into very darkness, where not even pain could reach him.

XI. THE BULLET HOLE

Iff N. Quid entered the Box Detective Agency.

"There you are. You have found my gun?"

"I've got it right here," Martin said, and passed it over the desk to him.

"Thank you. I understand that exchange is required in your world. I can give you something in return. Is there anything you'd like?"

"No," Martin said, "I don't need anything. I feel rich."

"Astounding, what has happened," Iff said. "I could not have predicted it. Your eyes look full of dark moving life, but also motionless, like a cluster of ants on a gumdrop looks still as it does swarming."

"Wait, there is one thing," Martin said. "Was that mole on Denny's face really cancer?"

"Yes," Iff said.

Martin laughed so hard his tentacles flew up in the air.

DAGGI COMES ASHORE

J. MICHAEL SHELL

THE LURID ADVENTURES OF DAGGI SCHLONGSTALKING
EPISODE 1

A hundred years prior to the psychedelia of the 1960's, a newly respectable, war profiteering pirate built himself a villa near the once-again-Union city of Charleston. Captain Lars Schlongstalking was a thoroughly seafaring gent—enamoured of all things nautical—and so built his villa to resemble a ship's stacked forecastle. A dizzying array of catwalk-sills and widow walks connected and bisected the skyward rambling structure. "Villa Fullacoca," the Captain declared it, referencing a habit he'd acquired while privateering in the southern Caribbean.

Though something of an eyesore to those lacking nautically eccentric sensibilities, Villa Fullacoca was well built and structurally sound. Captain Lars passed it on, along with his pirating skills, to his son, who similarly willed it to *his* son, and so on and so forth, until it became the property in 1945 of Seaman First Class Stig Schlongstalking.

Stig had made his fortune during World War Two as a Navy black-marketeer, and at war's end purchased a fine sailing ship with which to tour the Caribbean and South Atlantic. Along with Villa Fullacoca, Stig had inherited an enduring love of the sea, extra-legal activity, and the extract product of the coca plant. Combining these qualities, Schlongstalking continued to grow his fortune captaining his ship in the smuggling trade.

Somewhere in the West Indies, Stig took a wife who bore him a daughter and expired from the effort. After naming his little girl Dagmar O'Stig Schlongstalking, the Captain went on a three day drunk. On the third day of his binge, in memory of his voodoo priestess wife, he had a cute little dragon tattooed on his arse. The year was 1950. During the eighteen years that followed, Captain Stig, his swashbuckling crew, and daughter Daggi sailed the ocean blue, became fabulously wealthy, and occasionally stopped in Charleston to spend a few landlubbing weeks at Villa Fullacoca.

Daggi Schlongstalking quickly grew through tomboyish childhood into exotic adolescence. The budding of puberty came for her more like a bursting, which, combined with her mocha-silk skin, flaming red hair and dragon green eyes, inspired in many of her father's crew salty dreams and sticky awakenings.

On one occasion, a sailor named Bluto Parks cornered young Daggi in an aft hold. A mischievous sprite, Dagmar had noticed Bluto's eyeing attention, and allowed him to follow her into that dark and empty place. What transpired there took all of one hour, and left Seaman Bluto empty of blood, which had apparently escaped through a newly acquired ear-to-ear slit in his throat. Dreams among the crew persisted (Daggi was intensely beautiful), but no further plays for her affection were ever initiated. Though she wore the red mane of her Schlongstalking ancestry, Daggi was truly her mother's daughter. She was fond of saying that her Mama was ever looking up from the Hot Place, watching over her and granting protection.

In the spring of 1968, Captain Stig and Daughter Dagmar were concluding a stint of R and R at the family estate of Villa Fullacoca. On that clear and beautiful morning, the Captain announced over a plate of Daggi's Crawdad Pancakes, "Pack yer duffel, Darlin', we set sail again at ten this morn."

"How do you like your pancakes?" Daggi replied.

"You know they're my favorite, Darlin', though I'm also fond of yer oyster biscuits."

"Well, here's the recipes for both," Daggi told him, holding out a scrap of paper. "I've decided to stay on at Villa Fullacoca."

"I'll miss ya, Darlin'," Stig said, wiping his mouth on his sleeve.

"You'll get over it," Daggi told him.

"Aye," he agreed. "Well, I've always taught ya to do as ya please. Glad to see yer takin' my teachin' ta heart."

"Always, Daddy-O," she smiled.

"Just be careful, girl. Yer far too good-lookin' fer most men's own good. There've been times when I've been tempted to take ya myself, were ya not my own daughter."

"Why *didn't* you?" Daggi asked, cocking her pretty head. "Haven't you always told me, 'Morality is the redoubt of immoral men'?"

"Aye," the Captain smiled. "And it is. But whenever I was so tempted, a picture came to mind of my old mate Bluto Parks."

Daggi smiled wickedly, and a cute little sparkle shined in her eye.

"It *was* you, then, wasn't it, you little scamp?"

"A lady doesn't kiss and tell," Daggi replied, feigning a shy look.

"Well then," Stig said, rising from his seat. "I'll leave ya a sack o' cash and another of coke—in case ya run through the money or run out of coffee."

"I'm sure I'll do both."

"Aye, yer Daddy's little girl," Stig smiled.

"And my mother's daughter. So watch your arse, old man," Daggi grinned.

"I always do, lass, and she's always smilin' back at me."

The first thing Daggi did, once Daddy was gone, was paint the trim around Villa Fullacoca's doors and windows a bright, electric blue. "That'll keep the hoodoo's out," she said to the hideous little dog that had followed her home from the paint store. "If you can get past these wards," she told him, indicating her paint job, "you can live with me in Villa Fullacoca. If not, I'm afraid I'll have to wring your neck."

The nasty little dog cocked his head, then trotted past the electric blue trim and in through the villa's open door. "Good enough," Daggi smiled. "I think I'll call you Lord Assface, on account of your outstanding good looks."

"Woof," the dog agreed, looking out at her from the villa foyer.

"You're free to do as you please," Daggi informed him. "But if you shit on the floor, you're a goner."

"Woof."

Charleston, South Carolina, during the late sixties, was old and staid and pretty much touristy. Dagmar, for the most part, shunned the place, instead frequenting the more wild and dangerous town of North Charleston. In that raucous burg, immigrant Jamaicans were forming posses, importing all manner of drugs, and generally engaging themselves in the great American pastime of making lots of money any way you can.

Daggi liked to cruise around North Charleston on her new Ducati motorbike, looking for fun and maybe a soul to steal. One night, in a bar called *Rascal's*, she chanced upon a white-boy wearing his hair in dreads. Instructing the bartender to bring the boy another Red Stripe, Daggi sidled up beside him and said, "You'd look familiar if you weren't so white."

"Actually, I'm half, though I seem to have gotten my skin from my mother's side," he told her.

"What's your name?" Daggi asked, her eyes narrowed to slits.

"Harry Parks," he told her.

"Was your father a sailor?" Daggi asked, her eyes widened with surprise.

"Still is, I suppose, though I haven't seen him in years. How did you know that?"

"You look a lot like old Bluto," Daggi told him. "Except for the skin, of course. You've got his eyes. Have you anything *else* of his? Anything *large*?" she grinned.

Through a grin of his own, Harry asked, "Where did you meet my father? He didn't exactly hang out in respectable circles."

"No, he didn't," Daggi agreed. "He trapped me once in a cargo hold, and had his way with me."

"I'm sorry," Harry told her, taking a nervous pull from his Red Stripe Beer.

"Oh, don't be sorry, Harry!" Daggi told him. "I didn't let him have anything I didn't want him to have, though I *did* give him a little something extra for his trouble."

"What was that?" Harry asked.

"A second smile, which he wore for the rest of his life."

"Are you saying he's dead?"

"Would it matter if he was?" Daggi asked.

"Not to me," Harry assured her.

"Oh, pooh," Daggi pouted. "Then I'll say no more. Shall we buy a bottle of rum and go back to my villa?"

"Villa?" Harry laughed.

"Villa Fullacoca," Daggi said, ignoring his laughter.

"Is it?" Harry asked.

"Is it what?"

"Fulla coca?"

"Oh! Yes! I have a big sack of money, a big sack of coke, and a hideous mongrel named Lord Assface. You're welcome to the dog, but if you try to take my money or my coke, I'll break both your arms and put a tire iron up your ass," she smiled.

Through a strained little chuckle, Harry said, "You probably could, too, couldn't you?"

"Oh, I can and I will," Daggi assured him. "I'm as fun loving a filly as you'll ever meet. You ridin' or walkin', sailor?"

"My bike's outside."

"Barkeep! Hand over a fifth of rum," Daggi called, slapping a fifty-dollar bill on the bar. "And *you*," she said to Harry. "Follow me. I'll be the one on the Ducati with a bottle of rum. By the way, you don't by any chance have a girlfriend, do you?"

"Would it matter if I did?" Harry asked.

"Well, they say three's a crowd, but I *love* a crowd," Daggi crowed.

"I could call some friends if you want to get up a party," Harry told her.

"Just *girl* friends," Daggi said. "I've been at sea with nothing but men for *years*. Besides, don't you want to be the only cock in the roost?"

"Absolutely," Harry enthused. "Let's head to your villa and I'll make a couple of calls."

"Barkeep! Two more bottles of rum," Daggi insisted. "It looks like it's going to be a long night."

Daggi entered Villa Fullacoca and encountered a foul odor, which she immediately recognized. Following her nose, she found on her coffee table a nicely sculptured pile of shit. Turning to Harry, who'd followed her in, she said, "I should have been more specific."

Then she picked the coffee table up by one leg as if it were made of balsa and air, carried it to the door without spilling its odorous contents, and pitched it into the yard.

"Damn, you're *strong*!" Harry exclaimed.

"No, that's the dog shit," Daggi told him.

"I mean..."

"I know what you mean. Find the phone and make some calls. No more than two, though, I'm getting drunk." Then she yelled into the house, "*Lord Assface!*"

The nasty little animal came running in and sat quite primly at Daggi's feet. "If you shit in the house again," she told him, "*anywhere* in the house, I'll boil you. Are we clear on this now?"

"Woof."

"Then get out of my sight. You're hideous."

Lord Assface scampered out of the room, and Harry scampered in. "I got Roxanne and Sally. They're on their way."

"Did you give them good directions?" Daggi asked.

"Good enough. All they have to do is get within sight of this wacko castle and they'll recognize it."

"Wacko castle? Is that what you told them?"

"Actually," Harry replied, "I think I said Loony-Tunes barn. They'll find it."

"Time for a drink," Daggi said, turning on her heels and heading for the kitchen. "You want Coke with your rum?" she called back to Harry.

"You mean coke or cola?" he asked her.

"Either, both, name your poison."

"Then I'll have some of everything," Harry told her.

"That's just what you're going to get," Daggi said under her breath.

By the time Dagmar handed Harry his rum and cola, the three orange microdots of LSD she'd dropped into it had completely dissolved. Smiling as he took a belt, Daggi said, "C'mon, let me give you the tour before your friends arrive."

"What about the coke?" Harry asked.

"We'll do some lines on the roof. It's a beautiful view from up there."

"I don't know, I'm a little afraid of heights," Harry told her.

"So have another belt of courage, sailor!" Daggi insisted. "Are you a man or a pussy? And, anyway, there's very sturdy catwalks on this Loony-Tunes barn. Now c'mon or I'll have to tell your girlfriends what a cheese-dick you are."

"You should watch your mouth," Harry said in a warning tone.

"Come up on the roof and I'll tongue your noodle," Daggi said through a sexy grin.

"That's better," Harry smiled. "Let's go."

Though it took some coaxing and a premature line of coke, Daggi finally got Harry out the window and onto the maze of widow-walks and sills that latticed the overhead of Villa Fullacoca. Shortly thereafter, the LSD he'd swallowed with his rum took a shine to his ass and started whipping it. Standing on a wobbly, four-inch-wide plank, Harry said in a freaked out voice, "I'm gonna fall!"

"So, sit down," Daggi told him.

Shakily, Harry managed to seat himself on the catwalk. The metal roofing below him sank away at a dizzying and violent pitch. As Harry watched, Daggi daintily danced over the catwalks and sills toward the window from which they'd emerged. "Where are you going?" Harry called to her frantically.

"Why, I'm going to greet our guests, of course. I'll tell them you're indisposed."

As she closed and locked the window, Daggi waved to Harry who was clutching the catwalk for dearest life. "Even if he doesn't fall," she said to herself, "he'll never be quite the same."

When Roxanne and Sally arrived, Daggi opened the door and said, "Welcome to my Loony-Tunes barn!"

"Naw," Roxanne said. "Harry's nuts! This place is the tits! Where is that asshole, anyway?"

"I'm afraid his plans became suddenly up in the air," Daggi smiled. "Perhaps he'll drop in later. Now tell me, who is Roxanne and who is Sally?"

"Call me Roxy," Roxanne told her.

"I'm Sally," said Sally, who was a little bit shy and blushed.

"Well, I'm Daggi, and I've got rum for Sally's blush and coke for Roxy's rush! Welcome to Villa Fullacoca!"

"You're a trip!" Roxy giggled.

"Hell, girl, I'm a roundtrip ticket!" Daggi exclaimed.

After much imbibing, Sally lost her blush, Roxy shushed her rush, and Daggi entertained them both in her big, round bed. As the girls played, Harry managed somehow to balance himself in a fetal position on that four-inch plank high above Villa Fullacoca. Daggi had been right, he would never be the same.

When finally she'd kissed, licked and caressed her guests into submissive slumber, Daggi huffed up a fat line of coke and began a search for the keys to her Ducati. After only a minute of looking, Lord Assface trotted into her presence with the keys dangling from his mouth. "What a good boy," Daggi said as he dropped the keys into her palm. "But I'm afraid you're still quite hideous."

"Woof?" Lord Assface asked her.

"Out," she replied.

"Woof?" he pressed.

"I want to go get a tattoo," she sighed. "Is that alright with you?"

Satisfied with her answer, Lord Assface scampered away and disappeared into the labyrinth that was Villa Fullacoca.

At the Catawba Castaways Go-Go Bar and Tattoo Parlor, Daggi looked through the tattoo artist's catalogue of designs. When she came to the cartoon-ish image of a little girl with bright red pigtails, Daggi squealed, "This one!"

"Where ya want her, honey?" the enormous lady tattoo artist asked.

"Just above my snatch," Daggi smiled.

"A Pippi on your pee-pee?" the gigantic woman laughed.

"Unless you'd prefer my ass," Daggi offered.

"Either way, I'll probably have to put a finger or two in to hold you still," the fat lady sang.

"Then take your pick," Daggi told her. "It's your finger, after all."

SALT AND PEPPER

JACOB EDWARDS

For most people it is merely a nightmarish half-remembrance – twelve hours of madness that the New World rode fitfully, never fully to understand. Brisbane convulsed. The fever spread. And yet, there were those who managed to free themselves from the tangled bedclothes and act on our behalf, embarking on a quest as peculiar as it was pressing. Darkness dawned, the sun burnt cold. From a world pulped with possibilities, this is their story:

Part One – from the Memoirs of Imperial Agent Lucius Sextus Domitianus:

It was only when my lucidity was threatened that I came scuttling out from under my rock.

The evening of June 23 was cold. While trees bent their boughs to a wind high on bluster, swarms of bloated raindrops hurled themselves sporadically against the window panes. I sat at my piano and gazed out over the Brisbane River.

Even from the heights of Hamilton I couldn't see much. Suburbia lay huddled against the rain and in the distance skyscrapers blurred and wavered like the dying flames of a campfire. The music room was closeted and still. Only the sudden pressure-sealing and release of the windows hinted at the tumult outside. Banshees shrieked as they were sucked headlong through the maze of old houses up there on the hill. I played *The Ants Go Marching Two By Two* and watched as the city was lashed.

I'd just opened one of the windows when a triumphant sluice of rain cut through the breach, wetting my face. I blinked water from my eyes and squinted at the luminous dials on my wristwatch. The roads outside were empty and dark, save for whatever light ventured out beyond the hazy line of street lamps. Rain held sway over Brisbane and even Kingsford Smith Drive's intestinal thoroughfare had been flushed clean. There was nobody in sight.

At 7:06pm the shooting stars fell.

They appeared as if in response to the click of divine fingers. One second there was nothing, then they were there, dropping straight down. They seemed neither to burn through the cloud-cover nor pierce the atmosphere at any sort of angle. I happened to be peering at the sky and I saw that there were two of them, fused together and spinning like a coin. One was pale white, the other dark. They clung together like Yin and Yang.

As the meteorites tumbled towards Brisbane, a jagged thunderbolt lanced toward the ground, yet did not strike. Instead, it was pulled sideways halfway across town, whereupon it intercepted and was absorbed into the spinning black and white mass of the shooting stars. The lights in my piano room were purloined in similar fashion and the whole city went suddenly dark.

Although this gave me pause, it would have remained little more than a curiosity if not for a second event, which followed so closely upon the flaming heels of the first that I felt compelled to reveal myself. According to my mission brief, nothing short of an apocalypse should have induced me to break cover. But what do they mean by an apocalypse? The movie Apocalypse Now recently re-premiered at Cannes, but there's no clear definition and so I felt entitled to exercise some discretion. Thirty years of anonymity ended that night.

For on June 23, at just before twelve, the Emperor Vespasian was murdered.

Now this was not totally at odds with past history. The original Titus Flavius Vespasianus was born in the year 9. He ascended to the Imperium in 69 and ruled Rome until his death ten years later. History in all three instances has, more or less, repeated itself; and in fact, Vespasian died for the first time on exactly the same date – June 23 – after a nasty piece of intestinal inflammation.

But the New World is possessed of far greater a medical sophistication than was Ancient Rome, and the Emperor certainly had no wish to die for a second time. I saw Titus Junior interviewed a few years back, saying, "I shan't succeed my father until well after the Flavian Amphitheatre is completed. *The Mule* will cling stubbornly to his second life." And that quite accurately portrayed Vespasian's mindset. He ruled the Here, Then and Now with an augur at his left hand and a gastrointestinal specialist at his right.

Anybody who has experienced the Here, Then and Now knows that it is an unusual time and place in which to live. Back in the year 2000 the Gregorian Calendar was digested and excreted by a large millennium bug within the Rubikon $Super$String$ computer at the Quantum University of Timesharing (as it subsequently became). Brisbane emerged as capital of the New World and every century of history was pulped together into an apoplectic, two-digit framework.

The year is now merely '79. It's been almost a decade since Lucian spoke for a second time against fatalism; ten years since the New Suffrage Association landed a woman on the moon. We of the New World are no strangers to bizarre happenings and anachronistic juxtapositions; but whereas these invariably are the product of chrono-historical amalgamation, the shooting stars' descent was entirely without precedent.

History versus New History. Predetermination versus free will. Lucian, Heidegger & Co. would have a field day but I don't much concern myself with philosophising. Whether or not Vespasian had to die again on June 23, the fact is that he did, and his inglorious departure from the New World occurred within hours of the meteorites' spectacular arrival. I closed the lid on my piano and trudged up to the Emperor's Palace.

Superficially, the Imperial residence resembled a stirred-up ants nest.

In actual fact, ants are purposeful and highly organised during times of emergency, whereas what I saw at the palace was more akin to an Easter egg hunt conducted by headless chickens. Servants skittered around with flaming torches while police detectives scribbled and the Praetorian Guard seethed. The only people not moving about aimlessly were Vespasian, who was dead, and young Titus, who had alighted like a misplaced gargoyle on the bottom step of a blood-smattered staircase.

The heir apparent glanced up and gave me a resigned wave as I threaded my way through unravelling loops of police tape. "You must be one of the Claws of Claudius," he greeted me. "I've been expecting you."

A smart young man, that Titus. I nodded and sat down between him and his late father. "Lucius Sextus Domitianus,"

I confirmed. "This is a nasty business…" Which under the circumstances was one of my more understated remarks.

Pieces of Vespasian lay strewn about like knucklebones.

The Emperor's first passing had been a messy affair; but this was something else entirely. His torso sat with us on the cold marble steps. His raggedly severed head lay askance on a Corinthian bust-stand. This was death painted without a canvas, the grandiose blood spatters striving for artistic recognition. It was as if Jackson Pollock had been let loose with a scythe.

"Can you fix this?" Titus asked, the words clinging momentarily to his lips before dropping like hapless mountaineers. On the surface of things, an absurd question, but in two short lifetimes the Emperor's firstborn had proven anything but fanciful. Born originally in 39, Titus Flavius Vespasianus served as his father's hatchet-man in Jerusalem before succeeding to the throne in 79. Despite fire in Rome and the eruption of Vesuvius, he built onwards and upwards, completing the first Flavian Amphitheatre before his death in 81. This was a man who got things done.

It is hard not to be traumatised by the violent death of a family member – indeed, one might ask where young Domitian was at this juncture? – but Titus clearly was neither gore-struck nor in any way *non compos mentis*. In fact, the only Latin of any real bearing was now smudged upon the weeping wall behind Vespasian's head. Two words had been inscribed there using the Emperor's blood-tipped femur bone as a quill:

IMPERATOR SUM

I am Emperor, written in blood and in the highly possessive tense? Titus had seen enough in both his times to recognise that somebody with a curdled coconut had just pulled the throne out from under him. Now, a serious man, when cast centre-stage in a minefield, keeps himself very still. He thinks things through. What he doesn't do – particularly if he tasted early death in his first life – is run blindly or stamp his feet in defiance.

"I've sent my wife to the country," Titus continued, "as I did once before upon my father's death. I do not fear an ending to my own life, but nor do I covet it, and there is much that I would do in the Here, Then and Now. So I ask you again, Lucius Sextus Domitianus: can you fix this?"

It is difficult to live your life as a sleeper, especially when the night is long and the dream far from realised. For years I stayed holed-up in my unit, perfecting my skills, playing my piano. I looked out over Brisbane but never really lived there, emerging only once a fortnight to pay the rent and buy groceries. I became convinced that my existence was pointless and my new life wasted. But now, in that drawn-out moment of uncertainty between death and succession, my purpose finally was revealed. Unfolding slowly at the knees, I rose to my feet and patted Titus on the shoulder. "Give me twenty-four hours."

So saying, I took leave of the future Emperor and threaded my way carefully past what remained of his father. I turned when I felt eyes upon me, yet Titus remained lost in his own musings and the police and the Praetorians were snuffling around like truffle hogs. The only one paying me any attention at all was Vespasian, whose sightless gaze followed me like that of the Mona Lisa.

I nodded once and took my leave.

Part Two – from the Field Notes of Agent Lloyd da Vinci, GAFFE Squad:

It began with a knock on the door.

Knock. Knock-*knock*. On the one hand it was commonplace mundane, yet on the other it rang false. We are a top-secret organisation. No visitors; ergo, no knocks. Anybody who needs to be here knows how to get in. And yet, the knock came again, louder.

Knock. Knock-*knock*. Everybody had stopped what they were doing, and a dusty stillness lay draped across the room. This was a smoky, pool-hall moment, illuminated only by whatever light could penetrate the dirty window atop Sloth's loft. The scene was grey and unreal. I was closest to the door, damned by proximity. All eyes were upon me as the knock repeated.

Knock. Knock-*knock*. Apart from the slight increase in volume, the sound was exactly the same each time. I pulled open the door.

An old man stepped past me. "My name is Lucius Sextus Domitianus," he announced. "Take me to Odin."

Our guest was short and balding but with bushy eyebrows and long arms. He wore a toga. He smelt of rain. He had a cleft chin, Buddy Holly glasses, and carried a metal baseball bat loosely in one hand. *A nursing home vigilante in sandals*, I thought as I pushed the door closed again.

Before the old man could take more than a couple of steps forward, Agent R had pantomime-danced across the room and set the tip of an out-thrust rapier quivering against his galliformed throat. "Whoa, stranger!" René began, lifting his own chin in heroic defiance and arching one pencil eyebrow towards the velvet underside of his soft-brimmed hat. "What brings-"

Quicker than you can say 'prestidigitation', the old man did something with his free hand and sent the rapier somersaulting over René's head, impaling his hat as it spun. It landed point-down in the floorboards, whereupon the old man punched René on the nose and repeated, "Take me to Odin, please."

So we did. Shelley and I escorted the stranger to Nimrod, who then led him off into the Inner Sanctum. They returned after five minutes and Nimrod announced, "This is Agent LSD, on secondment. He is a Claw of Claudius. Do anything he says." Emotionless, perfunctory, like a mortician moonlighting as a cosmetics salesman. I always feel that Agent N is holding something back. Evolution, perhaps. He turned now and walked stiffly away, leaving us alone with the old man.

"I know all about the GAFFE Squad," Agent LSD told us. "I've been watching you for some time. Now I have need of you. Take me to the device."

We didn't stop to wonder how he knew about it. The Claws of Claudius were legendary in our profession, and – as Agent R would now attest – carried the reputation of the Silver Shields and the Delphic Oracle combined: good to know; better to avoid; best not to ask questions of. We led Agent LSD down to the armoury and pushed open the door to storeroom one.

The object lay on an upturned Styrofoam box that once had been filled with grapes. It was a diamond-framed, charcoal-black crucifix, made of wire but hard and cold like petrified wood. This was no talisman by which tawdry, unwashed warrior kings could ward off the worm-infested prophecies of their own bloody entrails. Delicate and strangely beautiful, this was a shield for gods. This was magic.

René gasped and looked up beyond the ceiling, crossing himself and murmuring something wholly unintelligible. Reverence or profanation? It was difficult to tell. The undistilled beauty of the object might well incite one to rapture, but in stark counterbalance was the sight of Jonathan 'Jack' Frost, known to some unfortunate of us as 'Jaybird'. Clad only in boxer shorts, he lay like a mechanic beneath the device, pushing with greasy fingers against its blackened frame and by all appearances trying to tame it with his body odour. Sweat, flesh, an overwhelming dose of corpulence. I had to look away.

"Forged in hell!" Jack spat as he looked up. "Arsed-up trinket's still *je ne sais quoied*… Who's the buzzard?"

Say what you like about Jack Frost as a homo sapien, but when it comes to making things work, well, he really is the man. Even if he's not seen it before, has no grasp of its underlying principles, doesn't know so much as what it's supposed to do; somehow, instinctively, Agent J can fix it. He can turn it on, tune it up, make it sing. Within seconds he'll have it dancing a fandango. A horse-fly to people but a horse-whisperer to anything that runs on power, Agent Jaybird has never failed to have an impact.

Except on this occasion.

And none amongst us doubted that the object was in need of Jack's attention. From the moment we retrieved it from the smoking crater in the middle of Queen Street Mall, it was clear to everyone that 'something' was wrong. 'Something' was missing; that indefinable spark of life, the twinkling ripple that separates lake from swamp. The device, quite simply, was not working.

"My name is Lucius Sextus Domitianus," the old man replied. "Bring it upstairs. Lloyd," he said to me, "gather together all available field operatives. We leave in half an hour."

And so we assembled on the floor just inside the front door: Brian Gator; Reginald Arthur de là Fantayzee; Peter Robert Mann; Jack Frost; Janet 'Shelley' Beach and Sloth. I stood as an unofficial two-eye-see beside Agent LSD while Nimrod looked on from the wings, his eyebrows crouched in ambush alongside hedge-like sideburns thick with disapproval. Agent J held the crucifix in one podgy hand as if it were a stick for toasting marshmallows. Agent LSD addressed us:

"We are powerless," the old man observed. "Quite literally, without power."

"Like all the king's horses and all the king's men at the world jigsaw championship," I agreed.

"And we are not alone," LSD continued, floating serenely over my helpful wave of emphasis. "The New World has powered down. Batteries are dead. Electricity dissipates within seconds of being generated. Even the sun is fading. Reality," the old man said, "is hanging by a thread."

"Like the Sword of Damoc-"

"Coinciding with this threat to our existence, we have the extra-terrestrial arrival of two objects. One-" he gestured to Jack Frost, "is in our possession. The other, I have good reason to believe, was used last night to murder the Emperor Vespasian."

This news broke like a ruptured abacus, rattling us with its chaotic implications. LSD held up one hand. "I am a Claw of Claudius. I have devoted my new life to the Emperor and the New World. You, too, are pledged to serve. We must go in search of the second device." He paused and stared at each of us in turn, his gaze acutely penetrating. After a few moments, he lowered his hand and nodded. "Let's ride."

The old man led us from the building and suddenly I realised that he meant this spur quite literally. The New World was bereft of power. Combustion engines no longer were combusting. Civilisation had been stripped of its upholstery and we were forced to fall back on mankind's greatest invention: the wheel. "Spank my Wankel engine!" Jack Frost spat as we stepped outside. "Bicycles!"

Sure enough, Agent F had cobbled together six decidedly rickety old bikes, including a lowrider, a pink bmx, a slack-chained tandem and a wretchedly fangled penny-farthing. "Alas!" René exclaimed as we stood and gazed upon those rusty steeds. "Not even a horse! Are we to save the world upon these contraptions? The sanctity of our quest is tarnished, no? It is a miscarriage!"

"Would you rather walk?" Agent LSD asked serenely, gliding away with an enviable grace and humming something classical. I think it was from Swan Lake.

Shelley chose a yellow bike with a carry-basket for Sloth and pushed off after the old man, leaving the rest of us to wobble along in their wake. Brian Gator perched himself like a circus elephant atop the penny-farthing while Pedro and I clambered bravely onto the pear-shaped seats of the tandem. René crossed himself and mounted the low-rider. Jack Frost heaved himself onto the bmx and promptly fell off. All in all we were a crisis of geese, oscillating uncertainly between gaggle and skein.

The streets of Brisbane were deserted save for a few tai chi extremists wearing 'Mr. Ed – RIP' t-shirts. We cycled around fallen branches and abandoned cars, past a lonely billboard depicting Kermit the Frog and Fozzie Bear in a Studebaker coupé. At one point I thought I caught a glimpse of Patty Hearst, her M1 carbine raised to the memory of Louis Napoléon as she ducked behind a phone booth; but I could have been mistaken. The city was eerily silent and there was a coldness in the air, a fearful expectation that last night's storm and the subsequent power drain were merely the prelude to some sort of doomsday event. The tai chi faithful moved as if in slow motion. The entire population held its breath.

"This is the way the New World ends…" I observed, under my wheezing breath and in time to the protesting turn of pedal and wheel. "This is the way the New World ends… This is the way the New World ends… Not with a bang!"

We struggled up an on-ramp and onto the South-East Freeway, headed inbound towards the city centre. The desolation was more profuse here. Cars lay like corpses on the prairie, macabre and portentous. We trundled along in dreary silence except for Jack Frost, who periodically felt compelled to thumb the jarringly shrill bell on his left handlebar. This usually preceded a juggling of the crucifix and a precipitous loss of control, whereupon he would overbalance and go tumbling from his bike like a punch-drunk budgie.

Just as we came to the Captain Cook Bridge the air was rent by a bestial howl that rippled out from the city centre, knocking us from our bicycles. *I am*, it seemed to shriek. *It is mine*! We struggled to our feet, fighting against the echoing aftershocks. The air seemed notably colder now, the sky darker, as if the sun were dipping towards a polar night. And yet that very same sun remained high above us. "We don't have much time," the old man observed.

Urgently, we pedalled across the bridge, crouched low upon our bicycles, racing it would seem against the onset of the Apocalypse. The Brisbane River lapped beneath us and a few unfortunate souls punted upon its surface, jittery as if the muddy depths might conceal swamp rabbits. We passed QUT and were weaving around the husk of a blue council bus when Shelley braked to a halt. "Look!" she cried, pointing to the city skyline. "Monsieur Macérer!" The rest of us stopped and followed her gaze to the brooding skullcap of the State Law Building. Sloth opened one bleary eye and then went back to sleep.

Sure enough, there stood the dark figure of Monsieur Macérer, the New World's most deadly goth-martial nihilist and former right-hand man to the dastardly Baron Clobassi. He wore a beanie and a pair of black jeans, nothing else, and blood dripped from his right hand where he clasped the exposed blade of a long, serrated dagger. Pearl-white and oozing with stolen power, the jagged shard looked like nothing so much as a lightning bolt forged within the furnaces of a supernova. Monsieur Macérer held it aloft and roared out his challenge once again. *I am*, he thundered. *It is mine*!

At once the world grew darker still. In the cold silence that followed, all eyes turned upon Jack Frost.

Part Three – from the Diary of Agent Jonathan 'Jack' Frost, GAFFE Squad:

The business with the crucifix was a pain in the butt.

And in my case that's a big pain, my sizeable hindquarters stuck like a toffeed apple to the shaft of that infernal bike. I blame the French, what with their *derrières* and their *touchés*. They flood the New World with poofy-hat chefs and fine cuisine. Frog legs. *Foie gras*. They probably invented that *hors d'oeuvre* of a bicycle. *Tête-à-tête*. Bastards.

The problem with the crucifix was that I couldn't make it work. Quite seriously. There was power somewhere in there – more, perhaps, than the world has ever seen – but I couldn't coax it to life. I couldn't tap into that core and bring forth the essence. The magic was gone.

That had never happened to me; not once in my increasingly eventful second life. Making things work was my gift. From the cradle to the grave, they said, that would always make me special. It defined me and, of course, it ruined me. The Midas touch. Midas-well not bother! What need did I have of other skills when already I had this incredible talent? Mister Natural, they called me, Jack-all of most trades, master of one.

But then the New World started to end and I realised just how intangible my gift is. You grow up with something. You take it for granted. Next thing you know you're cycling *au contraire* on a girlie-pink bike and using a fuse-blown *object d'power* for a balancing stick.

I'd just fallen off for the fourth or fifth time when that tautologically crazed Frenchman got up on Gotham Tower and sent out his Wagnerian bat-signal, waving a lightning bolt around and screeching like a prima donna, sucking all the energy out of the universe. That's all I bloody-well needed.

The crucifix of course was lifeless as a stick of asparagus photographed in front of Loch Ness. So why were the others all looking at me? Did they think I could make everything better?

"Let them eat cake," I muttered.

The old man led us up the Elizabeth Street off-ramp and then left onto George Street, pedalling frantically. The sky was very dark now. We rode like Horsemen of the Apocalypse; particularly me, I suppose, with a crucifix on my handlebars. When finally we reached the State Law Building I crashed into the gutter and tumbled once again to the pavement. *End it now*, I thought, unable even to gasp out the words. *Somebody put me down*!

But death must be another French invention, like sautéed prawns in garlic butter or the much-fabled *ménage à trois*: it's never on offer when you feel like it.

My fellow agents bojangled from their bikes and dragged me to my feet, into the building and past the elevators. Brian yanked open the fire door and we took the stairs – lots of stairs – enthusiastically at first then with an increasing lack of energy. The stairwell was black like the cosmos. I heard metal upon concrete, ragged footfalls, the respiratory wheezing of my own punctured-lung zeppelin. *Step*, I counted, *step*, *step*, a con-stepual hall of mirrors stretching from bang to crunch.

At world's end we crashed through another fire door and staggered out onto the roof. Monsieur Macérer was waiting. He tilted his head back, lolled it slowly from left to right and then, without preamble, he leapt at us, spinning and whipping about, pulled forward by that serrated blade like a shark behind its own mawful bite.

And just like that it could have ended. *Fin*, as the French would say. *Parfait*.

Because this was real life – the Here, Then and Now – and our helter-skelter pilgrimage had left us but ill-prepared for any sort of confrontation. Pedro's magic was useless, as was Shelley's mathematical wizardry and Brian's fantastic strength. Lloyd was tongue-tied. Sloth looked ill. Even René seemed about as heroic as the outstretched kissing lips of a drowning camel. I was the one holding the crucifix but, of course, it wasn't working; and in any case, I was doubled over in pain and using that same crucifix as a crutch. Sad to say but at the end of the day – perhaps the end of all days – the GAFFE Squad was useless. Good men doing nothing.

Not so the old man. As Monsieur Macérer scythed towards us, the crazy old coot tapped his baseball bat once on the concrete and then stepped forward, muttering, "Bring it on, Sonny. I was re-born for this!" Reaching full pace after only a few steps, he dived at the Frenchman's bare feet, swung a line-drive at his knees and then rolled off to the side. Macérer jumped over the intended blow, pivoted and jagged away, sneering his approval.

What followed amidst doomsday shadows was the cut-and-thrust interplay of blade and bat; a surreal motion-blur airbrushed in wispy ink and hanging like frosted breath. Macérer lashed out in pursuit, whirling like a rogue dervish, that deadly white bolt cutting a void as it sliced through the grey air. The old man ducked and dodged, tumbled and ran, cavorting with death's murky silhouette. Still he counter-attacked, the baseball bat flashing down in search of an ankle, ricocheting up towards a low-flying wrist, ever-mindful of the serrated teeth that snapped all around.

Impressive though this was, there really could be only one outcome. Before we could even draw breath – let alone think of raising a hand – the old man slipped on some of his opponent's spittle and fell to the concrete, caught momentarily in the flapping folds of his own toga. Macérer howled in triumph and brushed aside the last vestige of resistance, swiping dismissively with the white blade; but as its wicked teeth tore through the old man's bat, the knowledge came to me. Genius? Intuition? Who knows. It just dropped with a splash into my bath, while – Hark! – the herald angels sang, tralalalala to a new-born epiphany. I smiled and raised my doubled chins to the night.

"Macérer!" I spat, dredging the accent from deep within my throat, coating it in phlegm.

The Frenchman inclined his head and turned slowly in my direction, a menacing about-face that allowed the old man to regain his feet and scuttle away. *Leave it to Mister Natural…* I hefted the crucifix into the air and held it out in front like a buccaneer's cutlass. To René's groaning dismay I then thrust out my *gluteus* and hawked, "*En garde!*"

This somewhat provocative gesture had much the desired effect. Monsieur Macérer – never the most balanced of personalities – plunged deeper into a foaming trough of madness, his ghoulish face contorted, his bloodshot eyes glowing red in the dark. He screamed like a tectonic plate and hurled himself at me. It was as if I'd just made rude gestures at his mother with a feather duster.

"*Imperator sum!*" he howled.

"*Impuissant êtes vous!*" I returned, holding my ground.

The way he swung that lightning bolt at me… Well, I might as well have been holding a duelling cactus. With an evil leer those rough-hewn, pearl-white teeth tore through the air, power-hungry and sharp enough to bite deep into the flesh of the universe itself. *This is the end!* the white blade taunted. *This is your final moment on a world grown cold!* And with darkness shrouding the midday sun, a stillborn crucifix at rest in my hand, it was hard to argue.

Time distorted. Doubt flash-flooded my synaptic canyons. What if I were mistaken?

But then the crucifix sparked; a single, flaring ember buried deep within that diamond-head frame; the faintest of twinkles in Prometheus' eye. There it was! And in that precious instant where energy is created, an infusive magic falls upon those who once were forsaken. With that spark comes light.

I knew from the glint of recognition in those mad, tortured eyes that Macérer had seen it too. His guttural howl changed tenor and with reflexive savagery he tried to pull out of the hacking down-thrust. He threw himself back but the blow itself could not be retracted. It was as if his pearl-white dagger had entered a gravity well, passing beyond the point of no return. Macérer's feet swung up, his back arching, but the white blade pulled his arms down until he hung sideways in mid-air, conceptually in full retreat but actually trapped in a *fait accompli*, just microseconds away from the killing blow.

I stood with crucifix raised while Monsier Macérer corkscrewed behind his pearl-white blade, unable to keep the genie from escaping its bottle. For the briefest of instants – the half-life of a thought, no more – Brisbane lay frozen in contemplation; then the crucifix flared fully to life and- *Voila! Bon voyage!*

The lightning bolt and the crucifix came together.

Equals reunited in opposition, the objects embraced fleetingly then spun back unto whence they'd come, sparking at the edges of understanding and belief, a sword and a shield in *folie à deux*. Everything was as I had intuited. The power of history, so gluttonously leached, poured back into the Here, Then and Now – a deluge that swept us away from darkness to enlightenment.

Swimming a river that no longer flowed, Monsier Macérer flapped and flopped and fell flat on his face, the stolen energy draining away and leaving him limp – a *poisson* spent. His thin lips twitched and his eyes bulged; even more so when I turned my hindquarters around and sat on him.

Unplanned. Unprophetic. Another triumph to Mister Natural – the goose that laid the golden egg.

I turned to the others and shrugged.

*

Thus Zeus struck out across the ages at Benjamin Franklin, ending perhaps the strangest quest in the ever-changing chronicles of New History. Fused together with barely a whisper, the lightning bolt and the kite vanished. Normalcy defaulted. We know nothing more of Agents LSD, da Vinci and Frost; only that they survived, as did we all, to breakfast once again upon the scrambled dawn of the Here, Then and Now. *Bon appétit*, as the French would say. With condiments. The New World turned.

FAVORS & GRUDGES: A TALE OF SISTER MERCILESS

GARRETT COOK

MOTHER

The whip is truth. The whip is salvation. Pain is might. Blood is the answer. The whip is truth. The whip is salvation. Pain is might. Blood is the answer. Grit teeth. Bite tongue. Goddess forsakes those who scream. Crack of whip against bare back is prayer. Mercyscream is heresy. The price quick death. Bite tongue. Grit teeth. Swallow blood. Don't spit. The Goddess' servants do not waste vital fluids. Mercyscream is heresy. Price quick death. In death, given over to the Hungering to elicit an eternity of screams. Crack of whip is prayer, the abbess' prayers loud and passionate, befitting one of her station and spiritual might.

"I'm impressed," the abbess purred, "you show potential."

The abbess took a scalpel in one of her four hands, made a series of cuts on the novice's buttocks. The novice was a big girl, well built, six and a half feet high, curvy and muscular. It would take effort to make this one fail, to trick this one into relinquishing her soul. The abbess appreciated, feared, resented and envied the girl's strength. Strong enough to be worth devouring, strong enough to be a rival for her favor from The Goddess. Strong enough perhaps to take the relic from her… couldn't let that be.

As she cut and lashed, she plunged her third hand into the novice's painmoistened sex. Her long spidery fingers weaved magic in there, masterful inveterate movements, the product of intensive pleasure training. Her fourth hand took hold of one of the girl's nipples from behind, squeezing and yanking. Fingering, yanking, cutting, lashing, a flood of conflicting sensations that brought all but the strongest novices to their knees. The girl's legs were shaking and her excitement was running down the front of them as the blood from the cuts on her generous ass ran down the back of her thighs. The lashes had made giant sores on the girl's back, but she had yet to scream.

"Surrender!" the impatient abbess shouted, "Scream like the weak, pathetic child that you are! You will give yourself to me! You will surrender your soul to The Hungering!"

The novice almost let out a "NO!" But knew that if she opened her bloodfilled mouth, a scream would surely follow. And a scream would be the end of it. Although she sensed the abbess wished for her to fail, she wanted more than anything to become a sister. The Sisters had killed the bastard that made her, an answer to her mother's prayers to The Goddess, and she would honor her mother by becoming one of them, no matter what it took, no matter what she would have to endure at the hands of the abbess, though it would not be much longer. The Sun would rise soon.

"Surrender!" the abbess screamed again. She stopped lashing, she stopped fingering, she stopped toying with the girl's nipple. She opened her mouth filled with the Goddess' investments, clamped it down hard on the girl's neck, took in the delectable taste of the girl's blood and...

Fell to the floor, howling in pain as smoke billowed out of her mouth. The blood burned. This could only mean one thing; as little as the abbess liked it, the Sun had risen and The Goddess had declared the girl fit for service. Never would the abbess be able to drain the novice of her strength. She would have to call her Sister and though she might have outranked her, she knew that Milk Of Creation flowed fickle and would do nothing to protect a weak abbess from the powergrab of a worthy Sister.

"Welcome," the abbess hissed, "Sister."

DRAUGR

She shouldn't have stared at him. If she hadn't, he wouldn't have had to teach her the "lesson" he taught her. If she hadn't cringed at the sight of his face, almost pure purple, more bruise than skin, its contours shaped by the fists of men who turned out even worse off, he wouldn't have made hers like it, pounding it into a shape too awful to recognize as a person's. If she hadn't been disgusted by the long, stringy hair that smelled and looked like strands of an ancient illused mop, he wouldn't have pulled out her long black tresses in big tufts until her head was all baldness and bumps. If she hadn't stared at the swastika on his t-shirt or worn the symbol of Parter Of Seas around her neck, he wouldn't have torn her clothes off and made a swastika on her belly with his clawed nails. His buff, buzzcut bandmates wouldn't be lining up to jerk off into the wound, their seed augmented by the Thunder of Glory to better mark and burn the blasphemer, rotten subhuman servant of Parter of Seas. If she survived this, she would be left with a raised pink swastika mark to remember this confrontation by.

She tried to pray to Parter of Seas, but her mouth had swollen shut. She hoped He knew she was praying and that she believed that there was a chance that maybe He would intervene against Thunder of Glory's minions, opening fire with the uzi hands of his prayerdriven mechasuit. He couldn't let this happen to her. She hadn't done anything to offend him and really hadn't done anything to provoke this seven foot tall cadaverman. The eye that wasn't swollen closed noticed that one of the entourage was looking at his watch. They might have somewhere to go. Parter of Seas would make them part.

"Yo, Varg," said the one looking at his watch, "we've gotta be at the show."

She thought this would be it, the thing that would save her. The last she would see of these thugs. It turned out to be the last thing she heard. The last thing she felt was something nobody should ever feel; the freakishly long overmuscled arm of the bruiseface thing sliding in and out of her, doing its damnedest to punch her in the uterus a dozen or so times. The bruisefaced thing didn't so much as look back at her corpse after getting on its motorcycle to head over to the gig.

A silence went over the beerhall as the bruisefaced thing and his cronies entered, took the stage. These guy had taken out many lesser bands and would react to a shove or a "fuck you" with extreme and often lethal prejudice, so everyone knew to stay silent until Varg started screaming. After that, there were shouts of Zieg Heil, beer bottles breaking over heads, loud propositions and drunks doing their best to sing along with the Old Norse obscenities Varg was "singing".

Out in the parking lot, a scorpion the size of a horse clicked its excitement. It smelled the coming carnage, knew its mistress would feed it the delicious carrion, the aftermath of the devastation she was going to inflict. There was a lot of noise inside, but the scorpion at its eagerest could make enough noise that someone inside would hear. Its mistress patted it on the back, whispered to it.

"Shhh! I'm excited too, but let's not let the whole neighborhood know, okay?"

It quietly clicked compliance. It loved her deeper than family.

"Good boy," she whispered.

Varg punched out some motherfuckers he didn't like. Varg came in the mouths of a half dozen groupies, left one of them hemorrhaging anally on the beerhall floor. He broke tables, cut himself with shattered mugs. He screamed, roared and exalted in the Thunder of Glory's possession of him. He spoke to the Thunder of Glory like a wicked queen before her loyal mirror.

"Who's the toughest motherfucking black metal band there is?"

"Lothdin, motherfucker!" the Thunder of Glory shouted back in Varg's battered, bruised egoenlarged head.

Varg and his entourage stepped outside, saw the woman waiting for them. Jaws dropped. Erections grew. Six foot eight, flaming red hair, bare breasts revealed by an open red nun's habit. They didn't notice or care about the gladius on her belt or the blood red chainsaw in her hand. Thunder of Glory had clearly sent this bitch as thanks for what they did to the heretic in his name.

"Varg Bloodaxe," she called out, "you're hot shit, huh? Draugr? Risen from the grave with the strength of ten men?"

"Ja," Varg shouted back, "Champion of the Thunder of Glory, slayer of Ulf Demonhand and Arinbjorn Blacksword, Corpseprince, Soulgrinder, Bruiseborn! And you?"

She revved up the chainsaw.

"Urban myth, Bloodrumor, Gutrender, Harbinger of Bedwetting."

Varg nodded, somewhat impressed.

"I've heard of you. You come to fight? I'm ten men in each arm. I count one of you. Get down on your knees, suck my cock and pledge loyalty to Thunder of Glory. I will let you live."

"Ten in each arm. Five at your back. And yet you're the one that's afraid."

Varg backed off.

"I won't dignify that with a reply. I'm not even going to soil my fists with your blood. My bandmates will tear you up and I will fuck your organs."

The bandmates advanced, took off their clothes. Muscles rippled and changed positions, fur grew over skin, claws grew out of their hands, heads widened and expanded. Where once there were five black metal thugs, there now stood five human/grizzly hybrids bigger even than Varg. Not quite as hideous, not quite as battlescarred, but bigger even than Varg. It worried Varg that the chainsaw wielding barebreasted nun did not seem at all frightened, but he was sure they would make short work of the bitch.

Until, that is, his drummer's arm came flying off. His other arm. His head. Bare breasts covered in bear's blood, she leapt at the bassist whose long claws and powerful paws where no match for red metal teeth. An arm, an arm, a head. There were three left after that, all trying to come at her at once. Two from the front, one from behind. One caught her in the stomach with his claws, made a real nasty gash. Would have disemboweled most people, but she was tough, knew how to take a hit and might have been protected by some kind of warding on the chainsaw. He paid for the fleshwound with his head. She turned before the one trying to sneak up on her could strike, plunged the chainsaw into his gut. What Varg and all the others expected to happen to her happened to this guy. As it did, her stomach wound closed, as if her body was thanking her for the length of werebear sausage lying at her feet. Wasn't too long before they were all dead.

Varg advanced, cracked his knuckles.

"Impressed. But a Draugr can only die honorably. Throw down your fancy weapon."

She made a face.

"Unarmed? Hardly fair."

Varg laughed.

"I do not make the rules. I do you a courtesy by telling you them. You're permitted a knife. I have one for you if you need it."

She reached into her right boot, pulled out a nice, sharp kukri.

"This do?"

"It's a knife."

Varg hit her with a surprisingly fast right jab. Smashed a couple of her ribs. Somebody less acquainted with pain would have crumpled, fallen down. She stood her ground, sliced his face. He bled something black and acrid that wasn't blood. But didn't so much as flinch. He threw a left that she just narrowly craned her head out of the way of. She punched him in the gut hard as she could manage. She had no delusions about it actually hurting him, but wanted to distract him so she could get in another swipe with the kukri, cutting a tendon in his right arm as he tried to get in a second jab at her with it. He backed off slightly. She backed off too. Kept backing off.

He leapt, tigerpouncing, long limbs covering a fair distance. He brought his left hand down, hoping to get hold of her neck and choke her to death. She caught his open strangling fingers, twisted hard, broke a couple. Right arm bleeding, many fingers on the left hand broken, the Draugr was stunned. He didn't expect this kind of brutality, this quick of a tactical mind. Neck slashed with kukri. Bled black, secondmouth opened in his neck. Reached into the flap of his opened throat with her left hand and pulled, hard, peeling it open. Much more blood. Would have screamed if vocal cords were intact. He staggered off her, trembling in terror and disbelief. Head bobbed up and down, barely anything to support it. Hurt him bad when she jumped to her feet, roundhouse kicked him in the face. Looked as if he were looking somewhere in the sky for Thunder of Glory, who seemed to have forsaken him. Snapped back further. Rolled onto the ground. Shoved the kukri into his severed head hard as she could, just in case. Pulled back. Shoved it into it a second time, just in case. Third time just for fun.

The eager scorpion cleaned up the delicious mess, absorbing body bits in acidic spittle before eating up the spoils of war. She hopped on its back, rode off.

THE MASTER OF ARMS

There was one man at the abbey and he was perfect. Tall, alabaster, a creature of lean, predatory muscle. He taught the sisters swordsmanship, how to match his grace and his strength. He endured their most vicious attacks to show them how to ruin a man's body. Milk of Creation favored him, so he healed quickly, whether it was from small cuts or lopped off limbs. He pleasured The Bloodbathed and took the worst of the Abbess' cruelties, and that was truly remarkable. She was nervous about becoming one of the Bloodbathed, but the Master of Arms made it easier on her.

She took great pleasure in fighting him, he was eager to do her harm, but was receptive to pain. Though lightning fast, he was not afraid to slow down to let her see how he executed the skillful kicks and the pinpoint arcs. And when he hurt her, he hurt her bad enough to teach, yet did so without malice. He was gifted and beautiful and she started to love him. She used her long strong legs and her natural skill to hurt him in ways he couldn't forget. She of course succeeded in doing this. Any who saw her performance at the tests, or the great many corpses she would one day leave in her wake wherever she went, would know that she, of all people, could accomplish this. And he didn't forget it.

He dropped hints in the strikes he inflicted. His pinching of intimate zones at speeds too fast to perceive could be seen by some to be an attempt to debilitate and break her, to give the abbey's healers something to test their powers. The grazing of fangs across vulnerable flesh could be seen as sadistic, as it was by many of the Sisters that had not understood the surprisingly chaste intentions of the Master's other beatings. But she knew better. Three days from the time when she was to be Bloodbathed, something that had to happen happened. Things that have to happen often turn out that way.

They came together in front of the impaled heads out in the skullgarden. There was something wonderfully thrilling about so flagrantly performing acts that they could never perform again, of tantalizing the dead with that which for all eternity they would thirst for. Though in defiance of the abbey's rules, they adhered to the spirit of them sublimely. A stunning spectacle, hands, teeth, passion, and she gave up that which she was to keep til bloodbathed. The Goddess would have to understand. Who better to bless the spilling of virgin blood? Who better to bask in furious erotic fervor? They decided, as sinners often tend to, that The Goddess not only understood, she would condone it. It was a union blessed by The Goddess…

But envious Abbess watched through hundreds of sockets. And although she could partake of the Master of Arms whenever she liked, she still felt as if she had it no better than one of the skulls. Of all the dead things that they teased with their erotic displays, she was the hungriest for contact and the most envious. She had already envied the favor The Goddess showed during the tests, the power Milk of Creation had given this giant shapely girl to resist the teasing and the violence alike. She envied the girl since she felt in her heart that Milk of Creation had given her all that she could get and this girl, as she rose through the ranks would get new gifts, stranger and stronger gifts…wings, a barbed stinger, hair full of snakes, a secret word that caused open sores on the bodies of her enemies…even…hmmm…The Abbess prayed to The Goddess for favor, in hopes that she could make a plan come into fruition to show the girl for being a warm thing full of potential that dared seek actual affections from her consort. And The Goddess agreed, for like The Abbess, she was ancient and bitter and possessed a wicked sense of humor.

THE HIGH PRIESTESS

Siegfried Carcassfucker was nervous. In his years building up power and making conquests for Thunder of Glory, he had not once been to the Schwartzkirsch. He had sworn that he would not do so until he had great power over his guitar and his voice, and great strength for swinging a battleaxe, and had raped and ruined a multitude of undesirables.

Unlike Varg, who had been impetuous, a big drinker, a party guy and a creature of changeable moods and random violence, Siegfried was a hard worker, loyal to the cause and eager to rise in the ranks and become something fabulously different. Most servants of Thunder of Glory were alright with taking the berserker route, striving for their fur and claws, but Siegfried had grand dreams. He wanted the strength of ten men in each arm and the eyes of the dead, detachment from mortal life and the lingering passion and emotion that kept him from being what he could be.

He entered the Schwartzkirsch, passing photos of the hundred year old handiwork in the camps in the days before Thunder of Glory ascended to godhood and sent forth messages from his divine kingdom, passing tapestries woven of flesh and the scarves of slain gypsies, passing werebears in chains undergoing their first transformation, passing trophycases of sacred weapons wielded by Reichspaladins of the past, battle axes, zweihanders, mausers, halberds… weapons that were great, but not needed by the elite ranks of the draugr. He basked in Thunder of Glory's prestigious and wicked history, excited that he was soon to be a part of it.

He came at last to the doors of the chamber of rituals, knocked thrice. The door opened for him, leading into a sumptuous chamber. The walls were crafted from millions of gold teeth; statues of bears, wolves and two headed eagles engaged in proud sexual congress faced the door, looking expectantly at any visitors and letting them know that they had better have a good reason for entering.

A similar look was on the face of the white goddess with the long blonde hair, the tiny waist and the impossibly large, impossibly pointy breasts bared without shame along with her faith, revealed by duct tape swastikas over her nipples. A similar look was on the face of her consort, a blonde smooth giant, all abs, decorated with swastika tattoos from his face all the way down to his sculpted abs. Siegfried was impressed that there was neither crease nor stain on his lilywhite trousers or perfect tennis shoes. He fell to his knees before the mighty Reichpriests Zyklon Barbie and Swastiken.

"Reichpriests, I am Siegfried Carcassfucker and I come bearing grim and unfortunate news…"

"You should've like come sooner, ya know?" said Zyklon Barbie, "you've done, like, some, ya know, amazing things, for like, the Reich, ya know?"

He had not expected her to speak like this. He found her somehow less intimidating because of this. But he found her more intimidating because her lips were not moving at all as she spoke.

"Yes, most beauteous valkyrie of the Reich, but I did not wish to come before you until I had killed many and sacrificed much in service of Thunder of Glory. I wished to come before you disciplined and strong, not weak and reckless as some had in the past."

He silently prayed that this would not be grounds for gassing. He had heard of many being gassed for less.

"Is this news like about one of these "weak and reckless" ones?"

He did not silently pray this time, deciding that he so loved Thunder of Glory that Thunder of Glory would not let him be gassed in the temple while presenting himself.

"Yes, priestess. I speak of Varg Bloodaxe."

Zyklon Barbie made no facial expression. It then occurred to him that she might not be able to, because he knew for sure she would have.

"Reckless ya know, but like weak? Don't think so. Strength of like ten men in each like limb, okay? What like happened?"

Worried that the rumors might be true, he did not feel good about reporting the next part.

"Most beauteous valkyrie, Varg and the rest of Lothdin were confronted outside a beerhall. I was told a giant scorpion was parked out there. The werebears in the band were dismembered and disemboweled, Varg, decapitated. The arms and legs of the werebears were never found for some reason, nor were any of their organs or intestines."

Swastiken raised an eyebrow. Everyone in the room was surprised he had. Zyklon Barbie uncrossed her legs, revealing only impenetrable inarticulate smoothness. Had Siegfried not seen the things he had seen in his life of service to Thunder of Glory, he would have vomited. He concluded that Swastiken, her lover, therefore must have had nothing inside those white cargo pants. The lack of a bulge confirmed this.

"This is like most like heinous, ya know? This is like not like that I like wanted to ya know hear today, ya know? I know the bitch that did that. I hate her and she will die for this. And you, Siegfried are going to make sure that she does."

Siegfried's heart jumped. He felt a warmth in his blood. This was what he'd been waiting for, eschewing the meager rewards and minor tasks of his brethren to seek a greater calling, one that he would surely be given the most precious of gifts to accomplish. His arms had seemed small to him no matter how much he built them up, for they lacked the strength of ten men. His cold judgment eyes and weary hateful heart had been close to being those of a dead man but had never felt close enough.

"Thank you, priestess!" He tried to show gratitude without something so juvenile as enthusiasm.

"I'm going to need, like, your testicles."

"Yes, priestess."

DO YOU KNOW WHY IT IS...

"...that I left nobody alive the last time I faced off with one of you pieces of shit?"

The lone, one-armed survivor of Sister Merciless' latest massacre of Thunder of Glory's men shook his head "no." He had heard rumors, rumors that had eluded the ever-cocky Varg, rumors that said there was a tall redhaired goddess wielding a magic chainsaw. She would come to temples and desanctify them. She would kill, torture, castrate and dismember anyone that did the will of the gods that had fucked with her. And anyone lucky enough to be left alive that dared to pray would suffer indignities that only a vengeful nun could conceive of. He wanted very badly to pray. Thunder of Glory was no angel of mercy but surely would not see one of his followers treated so shabbily by a woman who dedicated herself so completely to the cause of blasphemy.

But if he prayed, she would at least kill him. AT LEAST. So, praying would be a less than calculated risk. It would be sheer, unadulterated folly. It would be... an act of faith. True faith. To pray when prayer is safe and one's prayers will surely come to them, is nothing. To pray under duress when the prayer's results are uncertain is faith. The sort of faith which would lead to a martyr's death. And a martyr's death was rewarded richly. He would return to Earth in a golden panzerwagon, rolling over the servants of Parter of Seas and then grinding down the vicious cunt that killed him for his faith, let him die in a state of valor and grace in the eyes of Thunder of Glory. That would show her. Prayer would be the best course of action.

"No," he said. This was not a prayer. It was a poor cousin to a prayer by anyone's standards. Not the best way to die in a state of grace. He made the decision. Then he hesitated. He realized this. Perhaps Thunder of Glory would appreciate the thought and understand his predicament and that he was one of the faithful and knew that his faith would save him; he just hesitated this one time. Anybody might have done the same in the situation he was in. When he found the right time, he would pray, making sure his last words were in praise of Thunder of Glory.

"Because," she said, "I know that your kind are weak. I know that I can track down another one of you and break them and get the information I need at my leisure, so unless I simply wipe all of you out, which I wouldn't mind doing, I can always shake down somebody else. If you don't tell me where to find the Schwartzkirsch, someone else will."

How dare she! How dare the bitch say that Thunder of Glory's minions were weak and easy to break down! How dare she think that she could stand in the way of the glorious Thousand Year Reich! Thunder of Glory would show her the error of her ways when he rewarded his shining martyr with the glorious golden panzerwagon of justice. He wouldn't just run her down with the panzerwagon, no. He would make her get down on her knees and beg for her life with a mouthful of cock and then he would violate her every which way until she begged for death. And he would grant it to her under the treads of his divine tank.

"Thunder of Glory, let me be strong, grant me the golden panzerwagon to smite my…"

His prayer was drowned out by the sound of the saw chewing up his face, eating blood and essence as it ruined it completely. But he was filled with peace. He was dying in that state of grace to be delivered unto Thunder of Glory for his eternal rewards. And he was indeed delivered unto Thunder of Glory and found himself wishing that he had not been.

THREE DAYS EARLIER

The golem had beaten her into submission. Thrown her to the floor. Gutrender was three feet away and a powerful hand was wrapped around her throat. This was not the first time Sister Merciless had been in this position, but it was among the more demoralizing. Gutrender had gotten some chips of clay off it and had found a certain rudimentary lifeforce present in the clay guardian, yet there was no way to prepare for the kind of weight and force the golem could get behind it. So much for the thought that Parter of Seas would be an easy target in this town.

A middle aged man with a big braided beard walked into the room, pointed a shotgun at the prostrate nun.

"I know who you are. What you're here to do. You're here, at best, to desanctify my temple and kill me. I wouldn't mind being killed, I don't think. Not all that much. A bunch of drunken werebears took my daughter into an alley, used her, then ripped her head off last night. Even with my golem and my nice big arsenal of weapons, if I went out and tried to hunt them down, they'd kill me. I'd take a few of them with me, get myself killed and they'd take it out on hundreds of us. That's their way."

Sister Meciless tried to wiggle toward Gutrender. The golem stomped on her arm. The bearded man shook his head.

"However, seeing you here now makes me rethink dying. Presents me with possibilities. To kill you and gain great favor in the eyes of Parter of Seas. He wants you dead like all the gods do. He wants that thing sealed in a trunk at the center of the Earth. I wouldn't mind doin' that. But, right now, I'm thinkin' more about Thunder of Glory than Parter of Seas. Thinkin' maybe you don't want so much to be shot point blank with a locust gun or broken by a golem just to give a man whose daughter was killed by religious fanatics a little bit more pain. Thinkin' maybe you're smart enough to get the fuck out of my temple, live to carry on your fucked up crusade and bring some hurt down on a bunch of stone cold killers."

I BELIEVE, SAID THE MASTER OF ARMS...

"...that we are being watched." And she agreed.

The skulls in the skullgarden emitted an eerie sense of presence. There were no eyes in the sockets, but there were eyes upon them, old, baleful, angry eyes that disapproved vehemently of their tryst. The sweet, sweaty innocence, virtually unknown in the abbey, faded, and in its place, Sister Merciless felt a cold speculum prying into her. They could no longer meet in the garden. She could lose this. She could lose everything. She could choose to never see him again and never know his touch and never feel appreciated and loved for anything, like all the other sisters. She could wait until bloodbathing and take his affections ritually before the others as the bloodbathed did, becoming not a special sacred savored thing but another of his duties as consort. She did not wish to wait. She did not wish to lose it all. She needed to find a place where the abbess' eyes could not see them.

But where? The abbess was strong with vision and she had other sisters like Sister Envious that could watch and scry if need be. If not necessarily a panoptikon, that made the abbey damn close to one. Sister Merciless thought hard, but could think of no place that they could make use of. Until she heard the voice.

"The Reliquary," Milk of Creation whispered, "The Reliquary cannot be scried. If you have faith, Sister, I will open the way."

Sister Merciless' eyes widened with wonder.

"She has spoken to me and given me a message. She told me that she will open The Reliquary to us. She blesses our union and will protect us from the eyes of The Abbess."

The Master of Arms embraced her, and they basked in the glow of hope.

"Goddess be praised! The lady and pain of blood favors love!"

They came to The Reliquary, with its doors of burnished gold that opened for none and sure enough those doors opened for them, blessing them and their togetherness. Though they were surrounded by instruments of torture, whips, bladed things, death masks and the bones of sisters that had performed miracles in the name of Milk of Creation, they thought only of the love that was growing between them and the need to be in each other's arms, touching, caressing and consummating. And they did just that, taking greater joy in each other's bodies and souls knowing The Goddess had such love for them.

The whisper crept into her ear when she was at the height of her passion. It was soft but forceful and was not to be disobeyed, regardless of the position she was in both literally and figuratively.

"Let go of him," said the whisper, "I have need of you. It is a simple task and when you are done with it, you will be free to love him with impunity."

She slid off of her lover without a word, waiting for more instructions from Milk of Creation.

"It is, as I said, a simple task. You need only open the red chest in the corner of the room and take that which you find inside."

"Yes," said a second voice, this one lower, gruffer, almost a growl, "take me! TAKE ME!"

The second voice frightened her. It was desperate and loud and cruel. It seemed impatient and like something that would do her harm. She told herself that she could trust in Milk of Creation and she would be alright. Their love would be alright. She walked to the red chest. She opened it. Found the red, bloodcaked chainsaw inside. Mean looking thing from its jagged teeth down to its handle, an inverted cross with a little upside down man suffering on it.

She picked it up. It did not take long for her to see it was a bad idea. HUNGRY! HUNGRY! Sprang to life in her hand, buzzing, growling through her head. HUNGRY! FEED! Milk of Creation and the saw pushed her forward, toward The Master of Arms, sucked the thoughts from her, fed her "HUNGRY! FEED!" All that she had wanted was gone and replaced by what it and what The Goddess wanted and what they wanted was for her to feed The Master of Arms to the saw, ravenous Gutrender, ancient, everthirsting, sharp, deadly Gutrender, it screamed its name and its intentions.

The Master of Arms had not earned his position solely by being handsome. He knew how to react to someone with a weapon in their hand, particularly a mystical artifact that could cut the gods themselves. He knew of Gutrender and he knew it would not stop and she could not stop it from taking the essence from anything close enough to cut. There were plenty of weapons in the reliquary possessing powerful enchantments, poison coated poniards, machetes that burst into flame at their owner's command, a broadsword that spread AIDS, a rapier that induced projectile vomiting. But, he loved her and would not choose such a wicked thing to subdue her. He selected a gladius off the wall, a sharp, quick shortsword, something with which he hoped to cut her badly enough to get the implacable Gutrender away from her and back in the chest.

He dashed around her, slicing quickly, attempting to kick the legs out from under her, to make a knockout punch to the side of her head, but she was damn quick, welltrained and indefatigable. Each time she nicked him with the saw, one of the cuts with which he hoped to get her to collapse from bloodloss vanished. And each time, he felt tired and deprived. He felt less like saving her, less like fighting for her. Soon, it cut him deeper, took a nice chunk of him. He got slow. He got tired. He got cut. He bled more. He got cut. He bled. He faded. He died.

YOU ARE ALL INSIGNIFICANT

…in the eyes of Thunder of Glory, you have all done nothing to bring honor to yourselves," Zyklon Barbie began, inspecting the troops, leatherjacketed, wifebeatered, tattooed, drunk, trackmarked, stinking shavenheaded beerhall refuse, "but you are not without hope or potential. I think you are more than disgusting chaff that dishonors your splendid and perfect master. You have it in you to be werebears, to perhaps be draugr and most importantly, to honor the Reich."

Ears perked up, though eyes were mostly averted, unsettled by Zyklon Barbie's lack of facial movement.

"A woman in red is coming. You can try to fight her. Thunder of Glory admires valor. But, really, know that the moment you see her face, you look upon death. But, she will let one of you live to extract information from you…"

"I would never!" a leatherjacketed skinhead interrupted.

Zyklon Barbie held out her hand, which released a thin mist. The skinhead's ears began to bleed, his body developed a multitude of big pink sores, which he scratched at until they bled profusely. He screamed. He cried blood, which rapidly congealed, sealing his eyelids shut. As he suffered at death's door, Zyklon Barbie continued.

"If she tries to extract this information. Tell her everything. Tell her exactly where to find the Schwarzkirsch."

All went according to Zyklon Barbie's plans. Siegfried Carcassfucker reaped the rewards of sacrificing his balls. All but one of these men were killed. One of them revealed the location of the Schwarzkirsch. Sister Merciless showed up.

THE BLACK CHURCH

Sister Merciless got off the scorpion, advanced toward the ruined building that now served as the temple of the Reich. It still bore the cryptic sign it once had, two words that didn't really go together at all. "Holocaust Museum". Framing a fire? Encapsulating a conflagration? Freezing death in time? She would never know what it was supposed to mean. Even the clerics now occupying it did not comprehend this. It would be lost to the ages.

Trap. Sneak around the back see if there were guards posted there? No. Sister Merciless hated ambushes. So much so that she was willing to barrel into them Gutrender throbbing and hungry. Kicked down the door. Six werebears waiting. The derivative, unpopular band known as Hellberd, a pun that barely made sense, but they'd attained werebear status for their brawling, not for their music. Though for werebears, their brawling was not all that welldeveloped. With six grizzlysized mangiants coming at her at once, somebody should have disemboweled her or at the very least scratched her before Gutrender started cutting through their ranks. They didn't. Three were bleeding profusely, losing strings of bear tripe before so much as laying a paw on her. As hands, an arm and one poor werebear's nose flew through the air, three more of them rushed the entrance, the power trio known as Svartalfheim. Somewhat more inspired musically, somewhat better adapted to the use of tooth and claw than Hellberd was. While Hellberd was bleeding to death, the more valiant warriors of Svartalfheim showed her the sting of an angry bear's claws. And the girlbears from Angrbroda were coming in for backup. It wasn't more than she could handle or more than she expected, but it was more than she wanted to.

Parting the crowd by putting an end to Svartalfheim's lead singer, she caught a glimpse of what lay in wait inside. Fuck. Smiles on decayed, pale faces. Swastikas carved on bared muscular dead chests. Three. Waiting patiently. Taking pleasure in the licks each of their werebear kindred was getting in and each of them that fell alike. Gutrender was taking in plenty of blood and essence, but she was taking a lot of hits and even when dealing with seven werebears, there was only so much to go around. Sister Merciless was starting to really regret doing this favor. She was two teeth short, spitting blood, body still covered in scratches Gutrender had not yet managed to fix up by the time the last of the werebears was dispatched.

She cursed quietly as she threw down Gutrender and drew the kukri, knowing three ritual combats were about to occur. She gathered her breath as she walked through the bear sludge to approach the first in the line of Draugr.

"Urban myth, Bloodrumor, Gutrender, Harbinger of Bedwetting."

The Draugr replied with a casual nod.

"Cuntshredder, Manpanzer, Walker After Death. I am Fritz Grimjaws Ravensnake, Guitarmeister of Hauptmann Hellstorm."

Sister Merciless had been through enough that she did not mock this man's convoluted and frankly hilarious title. She rushed him, a little slower, worse for wear than she was when she came into the Schwarzkirsch, knowing that she was probably going to take a punch before she could cut him. It would be handy, a way of knowing just how capable he would be of breaking her. He did not punch her, instead choosing to take her by the throat and lift her up. It would be only seconds before the Draugr crushed her windpipe.

Since the Draugr could quickly strangle her to death, he felt that victory was inevitable. While he did not directly order Sister Merciless to shove the knife into the side of his head, he might as well have. Three, four, five, six, seven times she stabbed him before he let go of her throat and died a second time, groundbeef red greymatter leaking out of his head.

Second in line Reichshammer, Heartbiter, Limbtaker. Two broken ribs. A shoulder she had to pop back into place. Castrated him. Cut open two veins as he tried to grab her. Rolled under his legs, came up, thrust the kukri up his ass. Third in line Steelcock, Wolffast, Skullfucker, Dragonssperm. Pain blurring eyes. Punch that should have shut down her kidneys. Caved in his ball sack with a kick. Knife through the left cheek. Sidle around, knife through the right. Up through the chin. Tendons in each foot cut. Spill of curdled corpseblood. Collapse. Legs barely supporting her. Something sharp embedded itself in her back.

She focused, clearing herself of the pain so her eyes could catch sight of the Aryan posterboy tossing patches of tattooed swastika flesh like flying shuriken. Reichpriest Swastiken. Blonde perfection, yuppie cargopants, marked all over by Thunder of Glory, flesh growing back, tattooed as before, each time he tore some out. Not quite quick enough to dodge, she was cut a few times before she got close enough to take a swing, and Swastiken was fast enough to jump out of the way as she did it. She charged at him, missed him again, got another tattoo embedded in her side, wondered how much more of this she could take.

Merciless realized she could use her obvious proximity to death to her advantage. Rallied her breaking body, begged it to let her keep going until she could get Gutrender back in her hands and fix it back up. He did not anticipate a jumpkick to the throat that would bring him to the ground. And he certainly did not anticipate that she would have the force of will and the force of hate necessary to stomp his head to a pulp.

The moment Merciless finished stomping the life out of the Reichpriest, a figure emerged from the shadows. Blonde as Swastiken. More nude than Merciless. Duct tape swastika nipples. Smoothness between her legs, which seemed to be almost interminable. Freakishly small hips. The freak shouted at her, lips not even moving as she did.

"Merciless!"

She looked the woman over. She was one of the last people she would ever want to see again.

"Scornful!"

GODDESS' PROTECTION

Envious, Scornful, Frightening. Three sisters, formidable in the arts of combat and magick stood at the doorway to the reliquary, guided by Goddess and abbess alike to the spot where wicked Sister Merciless had been consorting with the Master-of-Arms… consorting with him. Killed him. Stole a powerful sacred relic, which would be rewarded to the sister that retrieved it from her cold, dead hands. These three were chosen by the abbess to undertake this task. Envious was a gifted mindreader and scryer, Scornful had amazing reflexes and was a vicious cunt who lived to hurt, Frightening was a snakehaired blotch-faced abomination whose hands had been replaced with piranhas by Milk of Creation. When Merciless caught sight of them, she knew that the abbess and The Goddess had set her up for a fall.

"Envious, Scornful, Frightening! This wicked thing has put me under its spell. Please, believe me…"

She could not finish her sentence before Scornful closed in and buried two sharp daggers in her thigh, backed off and threw a third that got her in the chest. Before Sister Merciless knew it, a hungry Gutrender was telling her to forget reason and shred the bitch. Scornful did not expect her to grit her teeth through the pain, dash across the room, tear through her chainmail bikini and mangle her vagina. Envious saw it coming but was too busy taking aim with her crossbow and thinking about how much she wanted Gutrender for herself.

As a bolt flew across the room, sinking into her right arm, Sister Frightful came up on her left side, piranha hand's mouth flapping hungrily. Gutrender sated its hunger before the piranha did, claiming the hand. Sister Frightful roared, punched and bit Merciless' right breast. Teeth that could skeletonize a cow were moving toward her heart. Merciless swung low, letting Gutrender take a big bite out of Frightening's hip. As the flesh on Merciless' breast regrew, Frightening's hand had to loosen her hold on it. Capable as it was at skeletonizing cows, the piranha hand could not eat nearly as fast as Gutrender could. Deprived of hands, Frightening backed off, hoping one of the snakes in her hair might be able to stretch out and get in a fatal bite. The quickness with which Gutrender separated the snakes from her head and the head from her shoulders. Crossbow sniping sourgrape prophetess remained. Not a shot in hell of making a shot.

Envious was frozen in horror in what she saw just ahead in time. She knew it would be only seconds before Merciless would chop her into bits. But when Gutrender touched her, she smiled. Although her body was being mangled, her heart was full of sick joy at something not far ahead in time. Sister Envious only smiled at the worst of occurrences.

In the doorway was the reason for Envious' bitchy smile. The abbess had arrived.

"Well, Sister, you've proven yourself quite the capable little heathen. You have killed the Master of Arms, you have stolen the foulest weapon ever forged and you have forfeit your life. The Goddess has willed it."

The abbess leapt forward, brandishing two swords and her cat o' ninetails, a three armed screaming harpy eager to punish Sister Merciless for taking what was hers, what The Goddess promised. With the will of Milk of Creation on her side and the extra arm she'd been endowed, the abbess thought the fight would end quickly, regardless of the weaponry at Sister Merciless' disposal. She was half right.

The fight ended quickly, lasting only seconds. The weaponry at Sister Merciless' disposal, however, was far from an insignificant factor. Gutrender bisected the reckless zealot, the moment she came close enough. The two halves of the abbess flopped anticlimactically to the floor in a puddle of blood and organs.

The blood spread out. The blood coagulated. The blood stank. Rotten breastmilk rained down from the ceiling onto the puddle, forming a much larger pool of pink, disgusting goo. The pink goo danced, bubbled, took shape, forming a shapely female figure with big milky batwings. Two tiny infant heads appeared on her bloody, milky face, opening their mouths to speak. The voice of Milk of Creation came from them.

"You have performed well, Sister Merciless and made the sacrifice I set you up for. And for this, I shall reward you. The Gutrender is a sublime weapon capable of killing the gods themselves. And you…"

Milk of Creation did not finish her sentence. Gutrender was hungry and Sister Merciless was mad. Drank milk, splashed blood, cut The Goddess. She had come quickly, shown no divine majesty, revealed herself to be nothing but a grotesque conglomeration of fluids. The Goddess pulled away, vanished quickly as she came, letting out a shriek of rage and pain that resounded through the abbey, sending every able bodied sister running armed to the rectory. She would get Merciless another day. Or the hundred someodd sisters, many of them bloodbathed and granted the strength and speed the virgin blood gave them would. A hundred someodd sisters that survived fifteen more minutes.

IT ONLY TAKES ONE NUT

"You left me there, Merciless, my home destroyed, the abbess killed. You ruined my cunt, Merciless! You ruined my fucking cunt!"

The air felt hot, toxic. Tiny pink sores began to bubble up on Merciless' skin. The pain from her open wounds was excruciating. She was wounded, she was melting.

"I was lucky, Sister. Though The Goddess abandoned me, I was granted a second chance. Thunder of Glory saw potential in me, gave me a smooth, glorious perfect pussy and the gift of the gas. I have Thunder of Glory to protect me and you… you have no gods to give you the strength to survive this. Unless, of course…"

Merciless backed up, toward Gutrender.

"I don't think so. I will not fail to finish you again, Sister Scornful."

Zyklon Barbie, once Scornful, practically flew at Merciless, jumpkicking her in the chest, sticking one of her toes into an open cut, twisting it, then withdrawing it before making her landing. Merciless hit the floor. She'd been spending a lot of time on the floor lately. She lamented somewhat that the one thing she had kept from her days at the convent was the vow to accept pain and not to scream. She wished to let out a shriek that sodomized Zyklon Barbie's eardrums til they bled. Thanks to the gas, Merciless' eardrums were bleeding. Merciless' everything was bleeding. Practically too injured to stand, she scuttled backwards, inches at a time toward Gutrender. Grabbed it. Cut the bitch on the leg. Found herself well enough to stand up and found Zyklon Barbie quite shocked.

"You would face Thunder of Glory? You would desanctify our temple as you did that of Milk of Creation, hmm? Very well, Sister. Your weapon would eat Thunder of Glory, so Thunder of Glory will eat you and I will take your fancy weapon and I will grind up his rivals."

Zyklon Barbie made a gesture and the double doors to the chamber of rituals opened. The bitch that was once Sister Scornful stepped out of the way so that Merciless could get a good look at the heavenly Fuhrer, the being Siegfriend Carcassfucker sacrificed his balls to become. It filled the entire chamber. A gigantic testicle twitching and pulsating with movement. Wirey black pubic hairs with wolfheads at the end of them undulated, snapping mindlessly at the air. The gas had bitten through most of the flesh over Merciless' calf muscles, which would melt away fast if something weren't done about the gas cloud. Skin melting, wolfheads snapping, she was near death, but Gutrender was just springing to life.

Zyklon Barbie wrapped her arms around Merciless' waist. She'd been slashed but the Reichpriestess still had a lot of fight left in her and Merciless was being torn apart by the second, the healing Gutrender had managed from what it had done to Zyklon Barbie would not keep her going for long.

"Take her, my Divine Fuhrer, take her!"

Three wolfheaded pubic hairs opened their mouths, full of quillish hairteeth, and though it was ropey pubebeast, those teeth looked sharp in earnest, crushing swallowing teeth, to deliver meat into the ball sac of reborn Fuhrer. She struggled with Zyklon Barbie, getting just enough momentum to slice into the pubebeast's head. Buzz buzz. The

Fuhrer's balls plucked of one wolf. Contented, Gutrender tasted a drop of godessence, just a hair, but a taste of what was to come. Stamped Zyklon Barbie's right foot. Elbowed her in the face.

Zyklon Barbie relaxed her grip, giving Merciless a chance to wriggle free. Hungry saw screaming for blood, lupine pubic hydra seeking to eat her, Sister Merciless advanced into the testicular sanctum. Outnumbered fiftyone to one, she cut through slavering godnut beasts, cutting conduit between testicle and mouth, absorbing tiny portions of soul. A berserk Zyklon Barbie behind her waited until Merciless was distracted by a multitude of pubic hair wolves coming at her to grab a sword from the wall and stab Merciless in the back.

Outnumbered fortyfive to one, Merciless had to decide whether it was more dangerous to turn her back on the Fuhrer or on Zyklon Barbie. The wolfheaded pubic hairs and the giant testicle could wait. Merciless turned, shoving the chainsaw into Zyklon Barbie's face. Scornful had not expected this, so had made the mistake of not trying to parry the attack or sidestep it. Gutrender tore her nose apart, ate through her cheeks, devoured her forehead, pulped her brain.

Spurts of blood and cum, threatening strawberry milk shake demise. Likely acidic. Likely corrode the soul. She sidestepped the spray, but did not for a moment let go of the saw. The pubewolves were getting lethargic, some not even able to reach her to snap at her. Let out a scream that sounded like jackboots stomping heads, racial epiphets shouted guttural at drooling cavebeast bloodthirsty beerhall zealots. Pandering promise of panzer divine position as goldentread valkyrie eternal. No! Fuck you! No! Wasn't about rewards. Wasn't about glory. Was about what she, right or wrong, called justice. It hissed that there would always be hate posing as valor. Tried to claim that they were one and the same. Might have been. Might not.

Fact was, Merciless didn't care what any of the gods thought about her. And Thunder of Glory was one of those gods whose opinion she cared about least. Kept slicing until the testicle opened up, spilling out the cumcovered skeleton of Siegfried Carcassfucker. Gutrender, having gorged itself on a god, fixed her body right up. She brought in the scorpion, let him eat his fill of werebear corpses, and they took off. Parter of Seas was next. She'd done a favor for the priest, but Sister Merciless didn't play favorites.

THINK TANK

DAN NICHOL

On Thursday we took a stroll down the Embankment to see if there were any cripples about. There were a couple of drunks, as per usual, but they scarpered when they saw us. We didn't follow. You get bored of drunks. We must have done hundreds, if not thousands, of those fuckers by now.

Anyway, apart from their drunkenness, there was nothing obviously crippled about them, and our research is specifically targeted towards cripples at the moment. A successful think tank needs to keep within the remit established by its financial backers. It's the only way you can maintain your integrity.

I looked out across the river to see if there was anyone likely-looking on the other side. I should have been watching where I was going.

"Jesus Christ!"

There was a dirty great nail sticking right through the leather of my shoe.

"Probably one of those piss-heads dropped it out of his pocket," said Farrier. "You know how much shit they carry around with them."

Some of the other lads laughed.

"It's not funny," said Farrier. "He's really hurt himself."

"No, no, I'm fine."

I pulled the nail out. As far as I could tell it had only scraped me. I was more pissed off about my shoes, a pair of nearly-new Churches. They don't come cheap. Fucking piss-heads.

Any other day we could have hung around and waited for some more of them, or maybe even some proper cripples, to show up. But we were due at Jobcentre Plus later to sit in on the Q&As. There are public Q&A sessions almost every day, of course, but we've been following the same bunch of benefit claimants for a good six months now, and they hold their sessions fortnightly on Thursday afternoons.

We stopped in at the pub for a spot of lunch on the way there.

"Can we claim for this?" asked Reggie.

"What the fuck do you think?"

"I don't know – is it ethical? I mean, we *are* within walking distance of the office."

We all laughed. Silly little twat. "Ethical"? When you consider the importance of the work we're doing? He needs to lighten up a bit.

They're good boys, though, this lot.

I left them to talk amongst themselves and retreated to the bathroom to take a look at my foot. I'd cut it worse than I'd initially thought. The nail had punctured the skin on the outer edge of my heel. There was blood. It was starting to congeal, gluing my sock to the floor of the shoe. Fuck it. It didn't matter now. I could still walk on it.

I joined the rest of the lads for a fry-up and a few swift halves. They started getting pretty boisterous after a while, and I was forced to play the adult and calm them down – perfectly understandable after the lack of action at the Embankment, but it doesn't do to waste all that energy before the Q&As.

Officially, I'm the boss. I've been on the team for longer than anybody else, too – joined straight out of university. So did the others, of course, but it was much more recent for them. That's not a bad thing. We try to foster a kind of collegiate atmosphere in the think tank. It's like being an academic, but with greater opportunities for self-expression – you know, within the remit.

The bar staff were grateful for my intervention.

Nice and calm again, we left the pub and made our way to the Jobcentre Plus.

*

Q&As are always exciting. It's the Big Society made flesh. You can't leave decisions like this up to the bureaucrats. There's always a decent turnout – people are very community-minded these days. Granted, most of them are over the hill. But that's no different from the kind of crowd you'd get at any public meeting. They've got the right attitude – I like to think our presence there, representing the younger element of society, gives them the confidence to really voice their opinions properly.

There were only a couple of seats left in the meeting room. I took one of them. Reggie took the other – cheeky sod. Farrier and the rest of them had to stand up at the back. There was a good quarter of an hour to go before proceedings were officially scheduled to get underway, but we like to push the time limit a bit. It keeps the cripples on their toes, so to speak.

Farrier started up a jeer, and the crowd got nice and noisy – even the old folks joined in. Actually, the old folks were louder than *anybody*. As I said before, I like to feel that it's our lot who give them that kind of confidence. In the end, the Jobcentre Plus Curator was forced to bring in the claimants ten minutes before they were due.

Just imagine: in the old days, this sort of thing used to be done on a one-to-one basis, where each benefit claimant would have an individual interview with a Jobcentre Plus employee. I haven't seen the figures, but it must have been an incredible burden on the DWP's resources. They certainly wouldn't have the manpower for it in *this* day and age.

I reckon we get better results this way, too. The wisdom of crowds, and all that. Most of the mentals, for example, don't even bother claiming anymore, because they know the crowds at the Q&A will see right through them straight away. Of course, a few always slip through. But you know what mentals can be like – sneaky cunts, most of them.

We had a couple of wheelchairs at the front of the line. A pair of droolers. Then there was a girl with half her head bandaged up. No good having a go at her, she was obviously going to elicit the sympathy of the ancients.

Next in the line was a tall, fat man with a newspaper under his arm. I hadn't seen him at previous Q&As. I scanned the line to see if there was anyone healthier-looking further on. There wasn't – just some visually-impaireds and a couple more wheelchairs. Potential crowd-pleasers, all of them.

You have to find the weak spot and dive straight in. Before anyone else had a chance to speak, I stood up and pointed at the fat man.

"What the fuck's supposed to be wrong with *you*?"

He muttered something about a "syndrome". That's always a good sign. Anyone who says he's got a "syndrome" is basically saying he hasn't been diagnosed with a proper medical condition. In other words, a bullshitter. Prime fucking target.

"What's that? Under your arm?" asked Farrier.

"The paper."

"If you've got time to read the paper, you've got time to work in a shop!" shouted Reggie.

The old folks in the crowd grumbled their agreement.

The time for voting came around. It's a pity the Q&As are so short – it would be nice to really get your teeth into some of these chancers. But there's just too many of them, and we need to move swiftly if we're going to get through them all.

The curator reminded us all of the rules – if we think that one of them's faking, the whole line loses their benefits. It sounds harsh, but it's the only way to safeguard the public purse.

Naturally, the results went our way.

"You can't even pretend to think that this is fair," said one of the visually-impaireds, as the curator hustled him towards the door.

"Look, I don't make the rules," I said, which wasn't strictly true. The think tank is pretty influential with the DWP – just as it should be.

The cripple wouldn't shut up.

"Why should my entitlement to benefit be determined by whether or not you happen to like the look of one of the people standing next to me?"

"How do you know it was one of the people standing next to you… oh, you can see, can you?"

"Just shapes and blurs."

"Cheeky fucking cripple. And you call yourself blind."

"No, I don't. I call myself visually impaired."

"Go on – fuck off," I told him.

I sent a couple of the boys to wait outside the doors for him, but there were too many cops about, so they didn't have the chance for any real hands-on research. Shame. Research is the life-blood of any decent think tank.

The afternoon wore on, and we managed to get pretty much every group disqualified. Towards the end of the day there was a line comprised entirely of quadriplegics. I swear that the curator put them all together like that just to give them a better chance. We should have that bastard investigated. If he'd been doing his job properly, he'd have slipped in a nice easy target – a bad back or something – amongst the rest of those lazy, supine fuckers.

Needless to say, the ancients all went soft on the quads. The boys were tired out by that point, so we didn't bother contesting it very hard. We'll make sure we're ready for them next time. Let's see what we can do about the curator… but I'm getting ahead of myself.

Farrier and I headed back to the office after the Q&A. I gave everyone else the rest of the afternoon off. It's emotionally exhausting, thinking all day. It's not like working with your hands. Your mind isn't free to wander.

Reggie wanted to come with us. I think he felt that I was letting everyone off too easy. He probably doesn't have anything in particular to do back at home. I don't really know. I've never asked.

"Oh no you don't – piss off home," I told him. There's nothing worse than having someone moping around the office when you're trying to get things done.

He gave me a funny look as he left.

That kid gives off a powerful impression of looking down on me. I understand, I suppose. Most of the lads felt the same, when they first joined the team. I used to be a day boy, on a scholarship, and once they know that (which they usually do after about three minutes of forensic small talk) it takes me a while to win them over. But I do win them over, in the end. I'll win Reggie over, too, eventually. It's not like I went to a fucking comprehensive or anything.

I let Farrier write up the report while I took another look at my foot in the bathroom. It wasn't too great. I should probably have seen my GP (in retrospect I should *certainly* have seen my GP), but spending all this time with cripples for the sake of work, it kind of puts you off wanting to be around them after hours - and I've been to the clinic before. Full of junkies and coughing babies. And that's even *with* my private subs.

They're reportedly building us our own waiting room, but they've been saying that for three years now. I would have gone with BUPA, but we're supposed to be supporting the new public-private initiatives and I thought I'd do my bit. To be honest, I wasn't anticipating any major problems.

I cleaned up my foot with some iodine, then saw Farrier out and locked up.

*

We all took a trip up High Street Ken on Friday. I treated everyone to new shoes, on the office account.

"What's the justification for this?" asked Reggie.

"Public relations," I said.

"And research," said Farrier. "And transport."

He had a point. You can't conduct peripatetic research without a decent pair of shoes.

I think some of the boys were a bit disappointed that we weren't out looking for cripples, but I promised them that we'd dedicate the best part of next week to properly-structured empirical exercises.

"We ought to be pushing the boundaries of our remit more strenuously," said Reggie. "What about people who exploit their toilet breaks and take sick days without a doctor's note? If they're state employees, it's taxpayers' money they're wasting."

"That's true," I said.

"In fact, if they're subcontracted by the state in any way, or receive subsidies…"

"You're right," I agreed. "I think we can safely say that the groups you've identified qualify as scroungers. I'm quite happy for you to expand the research in that direction if you feel like it."

That brightened everybody up.

I let them go (who works Friday afternoons, anyway?) then had a look around for a new watch, pressing the organisation's credit card to my thigh through the lining of my pocket.

*

True to my word, on Monday I sorted out a proper programme of research activity for the week. I stayed in the office Monday and Tuesday, taking care of the cerebral side of things with Farrier, looking for intellectual jumping-off points in the latest iteration of GTA. It doesn't actually come out for another fortnight, so we were pretty lucky to get our hands on it.

People who've never seen a think tank from the inside are often surprised at the unconventional approach we take at times, but honestly, it's amazing how often the best ideas come when you're immersed in an online fire-fight. And yes, I'm forty-seven, and no, I haven't grown out of it.

We let the boys roam around London – within the established research programme, of course – and as far as I could tell from their reports, there were no real problems.

The research is inevitably mainly qualitative rather than quantitative, so I'm naturally reliant on the boys to record their own feeling and instincts as to how things went down. The details of some of these reports is really not for the squeamish, but that's what I'm here for – to collate the information and make sure it's fit for purpose.

In that capacity, I do have an obligation to play some sort of supervisory role, at least occasionally, so I followed the boys out on Wednesday to see how things were going. We found a bench outside a day centre and waited there until they started leaving the building at around noon. I think they'd been having some sort of meeting. They all looked pretty grim.

The volunteers came out first. We heckled them a bit, but otherwise left them alone. Volunteers are strictly off-limits. They were followed by a stream of families. That was tricky – some of the adults were cripples, and some weren't. Some of the kids were cripples, and some weren't. I can pretty much guarantee you that all these people were in some way living off the welfare state, but it was hard to know exactly who, and whilst there is no restriction on researching children, if we accidentally got an able-bodied one, there'd be hell to pay.

Fortunately, the last guy out was in a wheelchair, and clearly didn't have anyone else with him, apart from a little terrier with its lead attached to the arm of his chair, so there was no chance of any able-bodies getting caught up in the fray.

As soon as he had finished locking up, the lads jumped him.

They researched him very thoroughly. I maintained a cool air of detachment throughout, allowing them to think that I was restraining myself for reasons of professional necessity, as a managerial observer. In fact, I had started experiencing a nasty tingling in my foot – the one I had scraped with the nail – which was gradually spreading to my ankle and calf. I didn't feel it would be wise to exercise it too strenuously.

We had to let the cripple keep his wheelchair in the end. It turned out he was a volunteer. I think he had been trying to tell us this all along, but couldn't get the words out (he was one of those, what-do-you-call-thems – spastics), so we only realised it when Farrier spotted the laminated card on a ribbon round the guy's neck. I told the boys it didn't matter – he was a volunteer *and* a cripple, and there's no question in my mind which category takes precedence there.

Still, we decided to quit while we were ahead, and, as I say, we didn't take his wheelchair (although I strongly suspect that it was purchased out of taxpayers' hard-earned money).

"We should probably let them say their piece before we research them," I said. "Just to be on the safe side."

Reggie nodded enthusiastically. There was an unpleasant glint in his eye.

It all felt like a bit of a let-down. I couldn't help thinking that the boys would have gone further if I hadn't been there, and that they blamed me for spoiling their fun. We walked around aimlessly for about half-an-hour, and were about to head back to the office, when Reggie spotted someone walking funny, off up the road we had just come down.

He's a pain in the arse, that kid, but he's got a great eye for deviants.

The others sped off after the cripple, and I followed behind at a slow lope, only catching up with them when the guy was already cowering on the floor.

"Can't you see that we're setting you free from these social democratic crutches?" explained Reggie, wielding said crutches in a single hand, raised above his head. "You don't really *need* them – you've just become dependent on them because we've *allowed* you to become dependent on them."

"I can't walk without them!"

"Of course you can, you wretched, weaselly scrounger!"

Farrier glanced at me as I approached. "Feeling a little worse for wear?"

I pretended not to hear him. He

looked down at my foot.

"Did you ever get that checked out by a doctor?"

"It's fine," I said.

"I'm sick of all this trudging round myself, too. Next time maybe we should hire a van for the day."

"Yes, maybe. Let's not talk about it now."

Farrier's a good chap. He just turned away, like it was none of his business – which it wasn't – but before he did I thought that perhaps Reggie had followed his gaze for a moment. Christ, I didn't want Reggie to start wondering about my injury.

"What's the name of this alley?" I asked. "I don't think it's part of the original research programme. Be sure to note it as extra-curricular when you write this up."

*

I didn't go out with them again that week. They finished up nice and early on Friday and we all went home after lunch. I was quite pleased to have escaped their scrutiny. My foot was still tingling, and now my jaw was starting to feel funny. I knew that I should have gone to the clinic, but… I was worried that my GP might tell me to take the day off work. Seriously. And *that* would not look good. It would not look good at all.

I stayed in over the weekend, but I did phone NHS Direct, and being as I'm a priority client, they sent someone round to give me a tetanus shot.

"When was it you hurt yourself?"

"Just over a week ago."

"It might be too late by now," she said. "You should have called earlier."

"Just do your fucking job."

*

We started writing up on Monday. I'd got used to having the office pretty much to myself – Farrier had joined the lads on Thursday and Friday, so I'd been completely alone for the latter part of the week – and I wasn't overjoyed at sharing again.

What's more, the tetanus shot didn't seem to be working. My foot still tingled – the nurse had told me that was nothing to do with tetanus, and could be psychosomatic, but fuck me if I'm going to let anyone tell *me* I'm a mental – and my jaw was getting worse. In fact, my whole face felt weird, as though I couldn't quite control it.

By lunchtime, I was convinced they were all whispering about me. They'd be deep in conversation, then as soon as I'd wander over to join them they'd all clam up. I didn't eat with them. For the rest of the afternoon, I kept to my end of the office and they kept to theirs. It was the only way to keep them from noticing the peculiar spasms that were starting to afflict me.

Towards the end of the day, Farrier came over to speak to me about hiring our own van for future research forays, but we were interrupted by the security desk calling through from downstairs.

It was the minister. He pops in from time to time to check up. I don't mind him – he's an odd looking chap, but he knows what he's doing. The lads had decided to play wiff-waff for most of the afternoon, in the creative space. I hadn't complained because it kept them away from me and – and, well, I didn't want to speak with them. I sent Farrier over to tell them to make themselves look busy, and asked reception to send the minister up.

He seemed angry. I thought at first that this was because I hadn't immediately invited him up, but had made him wait for a few seconds while the boys sorted themselves out at their desks. But that wasn't it.

Someone in the press had got hold of CCTV footage of the think tank researching a female Paralympian only a few streets away from Westminster. I hadn't heard anything about this. I hadn't seen all the reports yet, though. It would certainly explain how Reggie got that black eye.

"A woman?" the minister asked. "Really, a *woman*?"

He showed me the footage on his phone.

"She's still a cripple, though, isn't she?" I said, defensively. I wasn't about to let my boys take heat for something that was clearly implied as allowable – desirable, even – in the remit laid down by our backers, hashed out with the minister himself.

"Do you know what it looks like to the general public when they see a bunch of young guys picking on a woman? The opposition are accusing us of sexism now."

Political fucking correctness. The opposition front bench was fully committed to the principle of researching disability more thoroughly, so they had to find some other angle, like this, if they wanted to have a go at the government on the issue.

"Yeah, but the boys weren't researching her because she's a woman," I said, "– they were doing it because she's a cripple. It's exactly the same as we'd do for a man. There's nothing misogynist about it."

"The English public don't seem to mind when it's the cops doing it," said Farrier, who had slipped over to join us.

"The police have a free pass," said the minister, firmly. "*You* don't."

"There's a bunch of women already in the police force, anyway, isn't there?" said Reggie, the little suck up, who had also come along behind Farrier.

"That's right," said the minister. "That gives them legitimacy in matters like this. Anyway, the Home Office is beyond my purview. What I *can* say is that if you want to get away with this sort of stunt, you need to recruit some women to do it, or at least to get involved in some reasonably visible manner."

I tried to keep an expression of attentive deference as he spoke, but it was getting harder to control the mild facial spasms that had been afflicting me all day. I found myself constantly looking away for a few moments, or covering my nose and chin with my hands, desperately hoping that I would be able to avoid drawing attention to myself.

The minister regarded me oddly – as did Farrier and Reggie – but did not remark on my behaviour.

He proceeded to give us – in particular, me – a long dressing down. Our financial backers (including, as I have said, the DWP itself, though the department contributed very little in comparison with our principle individual donors) were very disappointed in us. As soon as something like this happened, some scumbag at the *Guardian* was bound to link it back to the money men. And the money men did not like their names in the papers. Names in the papers meant questions asked about tax status – which could lead to significant loss of income, and ultimately to the taps being turned off for the think tank, according to our guest.

I didn't believe that for a minute. Still, it is our duty as a competent and professional research organisation to conform to the wishes of our funders. I agreed with the minister that we should recruit some women to research the female cripples, and this seemed to satisfy him. I think he's just an old fashioned gent at heart. He went to Sandhurst. Maybe that's how they still do things there.

Before he left, he looked sadly into my face, and asked, "Are *you* all right?"

Unfortunately, I was prevented from answering immediately by a particularly violent spasm that co-opted my jaw, an eye and the right side of my mouth. The minister left without waiting for a reply.

*

Terror overtook me as I woke the following morning. My chest and throat were horribly tight. My legs felt stiff and were hard to move. I was feverish and sweating and my heart was racing. It had been like this on and off all night, though I had never been sufficiently awake properly to assimilate what was going on.

I looked over at the alarm clock. It was seven-thirty. I reached out and switched it off, then fell into intermittent sleep again for what felt like hours but was in fact only ten minutes. I pulled myself out of bed and tried to dress, but it was such a laborious task that I eventually abandoned my trousers and shirt, and went in search of food in my vest and underpants, in the thought that a little nourishment might get me going.

This was a mistake. My throat felt swollen and I could barely manage a few sips of coffee. I left my cornflakes to soak in the bowl for a good fifteen minutes, but still couldn't manage them. I realised that I was not going to be able to make it into the office.

"If you fail to report an accident within forty-eight hours then your insurance is invalidated insofar as it pertains to that accident," the receptionist at the clinic told me. "I'm afraid that your priority client status is suspended for the next four weeks."

How the hell did they know what the timescale of my accident was? The NHS direct nurse. That bitch must have informed on me.

"Well, I assume I'm still entitled to whatever's available within the public package."

The receptionist laughed.

"At least have someone come round and give me a sick note. There's no way I can make it into the office. And if there's no way I can make it to the office, then there's clearly no way I can make it to the clinic."

"And whose fault is that?" came the frosty reply.

The moment I put the receiver down, it started ringing. It didn't take any particular genius on my part to guess who it was. Reluctantly I picked it up.

"Farrier?"

"Hi." He paused for a moment. When I failed to respond he asked me, "Are you coming in today?"

"No. I don't think I can. Hold down the fort, will you?"

"Sure. Can you e-mail through your sick note – just for the records?"

"Well, about that…"

Farrier listened patiently as I tried to explain the situation.

"You know," he said sadly, once I had finished, "you really should have got checked out as soon as you trod on that nail. Maybe I'll see you later."

"I don't think so. I don't think there's any way I'll be in for the next couple of days, maybe longer."

"I know," he said. "I know… but anyway…"

I understood what was coming next. I settled down in front of the television. I couldn't face anything other than daytime chat. It was one of those days when the minister kept cropping up all over the place. Some policy initiative or other – in fact, I think it was something I'd been involved with, at the early drafting stage, but I was so sick I couldn't even bring myself to feel smug about it.

I finally succeeded in swallowing a few cornflakes, and another mug of coffee. I checked my Kindle for the papers, but the minister was all over those, too. He was right about that footage of the Paralympian. It didn't look good. If I'd been at the office, I imagined, I would have been fielding media enquiries all morning. I supposed that Farrier was dealing with it at that very moment. Or maybe not.

Outside, a horn squawked loudly,

echoing down the street.

I drew open the curtains. A white transit van was backing up so that the rear doors faced the gate of the front yard. I dragged myself to the front doorway, leaning heavily against the frame.

Farrier climbed out from the driver's seat.

"You see," he said. "We decided to get a van this time. No more tramping around."

I nodded.

Reggie stepped out from the other side of the cab and between them they swung open the rear doors. The back of the van appeared to me as a great, hungry maw, and the boys inside – my boys – as teeth.

"Go on," said Reggie, as they poured out of the transit and through the gate. "You might as well try and put your case. Everybody else does."

I mustered what strength I had, wheezed, "You can't do this to *me*! I'm in a THINK TANK!"

But were they listening? *Were they fuck*. They're good boys. They did the right thing.

CRESCENTS AND PENTAGRAMS

S. R. DANTZLER

Witchy shit! This map was driving him squirrely. Trapper couldn't let on he couldn't read the damned thing. Crumpling it back up into his sack, he headed over the ridge to get a bearing at the creek. He'd sent the pack to scout about. Time to make camp soon. Hotter than hell. No food in two days. Bugs eating his ass.

He knelt down by the stream to smell it and saw the track. It was her. Had to been a witch. Only ones crazy enough to go barefoot out here with the gators, moccasins, and traps.

Funny though, used to be he ran from witches, but lately since he been a little older and seen this one, bout his age, naked and wilder than a boar sow, he had been after her in some way that seemed to radiate from down where he peed. Kept in his dreams too. Sometimes he'd wake up stiff as a stump. That 'lil witchee magicked him good, and he was gonna track her down and make her stop it.

"Hoot! Hoot!" Hollerin' sounded like 'lil Pinecone tearin' in fast from the sunup side. Trapper hustled over the hill to see what the ruckus was. Some kinda serious. Pinecone couldn't talk for suckin' air. "Come fast! An old-timer… a real 'un… big as a bear… em boys got sticks on him, but he is ornery."

Trapper didn't hardly believe it, but Pinecone was sure riled up. Somethin' needed seein' for sure. Hurryin' through the thicket tryin' not to get the sacks stringed to his feet tore off in the briars, started him thinking about 'ol Biggun. Biggun used to lead the pack. Was the biggest and smartest too, 'for he run off after a witch and never came back. He was old enough to remember old-timers. Used to say that there was two of em that fed him pretty regular, washed him and made him clothes and such. Trap sometimes thinks he remembers dreams that go a little like that.

Pinecone caught his wind and was squirrely as all get out.

"Can you believe it, Trap? Hurry, he gonna bust loose. We betta tie em up, Trap."

Trap give him a look.

"I sorry. Shouldn't tell Trap what to do."

They were getting close. Trapper heard the pack squalling like they treed a racoon. He drew out his bat and ran to where them boys were hollerin'. Trap bout fell out when he seen the old-timer. Tall, scrawny, and one-armed. Had hair way down his face. Trap hadn't ever seen anything like it. Looked to be blind. He was swinging' back at the pack in wide circles. Them boys were

prowlin' him good. Bout had him passed out. Trap charged forward through the circle and stuck him on top of the head and dropped him straight to the ground.

"Reckon he's a Commie, Trap?" Gopher stood next to him. Had a way of pokin' his belly out that made him look like he was full a watermelon.

"Had him a can shell on his noggin, Trap. I knocked it right off him. Good thing, huh? Let you clobber him good." Rake was the next to chide in. It got real loud.

"Shut it! Y'all done enough racket to wake the woods. Y'all want to be fighting off Neegras all night? Want some witches makin' dolls out of your ugly heads and pokin' em with quills? Sickin' dem haints on us?"

Trap knelt down to the still old-timer. Hoped he hadn't killed him. Felt the knot on his head. No blood. He should make it. A leaf fluttered near where his nose mashed into the ground. He was breathing.

"Stick him up and bring him to camp. Be sure to string him good. This un knows how to stay livin'".

Pinecone dug some rope from his sack and made short work of stringing the old-timer's one arm and feet to a magnolia sapling that Rake hatcheted down real quick. That Rake had a way with tools. Trap made a little wish that he didn't get the idea of hatcheting him down anytime soon.

Trapper wasn't real sure what to make of this old feller. His tin hat had a curvy moon and a star on it like all them skeletons they had found in the Commie tanks. Skin and bone and dried up hide seemed like mostly, but it put a fear in him. Closer they got to the Big Place, the more strange stuff they had been findin'. Neegra packs were all around here. Ain't seen a pale pack in a handful 'o nights. Neegra witchees were a fright. He ain't never seen one, but he seen them dolls they made. He swore one of em was made just for him. The whole pack said so. Had a big spike stuck right in its head layin' sprawled on a rock along the creek they had been following for a few days. His head still hurt thinking about it, even though it had been almost a moon ago. They carved little haints too that looked like animals. Every time they found one, one of dem animal haints haunted em all night. One time 'ol Biggun tried burn one, and fell on the ground a screamin' said he felt on fire.

"No fire. No Meat." Trapper said as the pack made it to the camp he had picked between a fork in the river. High bluff on the sundown side. They'd back up into it and keep good guard tonight. Pack done howled up the whole woods. Sure be surprised if there were no Neegra packs attacking this night. "Pile up some rocks up on that ledge, Gopher, case them Neegras wanna bite. Prop that old-timer down fer in that bluff as you can. I want two of you stayin' on him all the time."

Besides that, the pack didn't need no orders. They liked to be ready for dark time. Lots to be scared of in these woods at night. All he'd seen trace of in the last three days though, had been his 'lil witch. He wasn't about to tell them boys about that. They was still riled up about Biggun goin' off huntin' one. If he couldn't hunt one nobody could. But Trap knew how bad he wanted to catch this one. Seemed pretty stupid because he didn't have a single thought about what he would do when he caught her, but ever since he saw her, all he could see was her. Her pale skin, hair long and dark as night. Her teets were bumped up a little, and she had hair down under her belly. Evil thing didn't even have anything to pee with.

Rake was over filing on his hatchet. Kept it real sharp. Trap had an eye on him. Rake, seemed to him, was getting the itch to take over the pack. Most of them boys thought him too brutal. Kept to himself mostly, scoutin' and killin'.

No fire meant cans and shoots. Gopher was over there opening cans and handin' em out. He kept track of what the pack ate. Right good at it, too. Beans is what Trap got. Just then he saw Rake take off into the woods like he heard somethin'. Dark was getting close. A sinking nervous feeling was all Trap tasted as he slurped cold beans from a can. Lil tater ran up quiet as he could and whispered, "He wakin' up, Trap."

Sun slipped away behind him as Trap made his way down into the shelter of the bluff to see the old-timer stirrin' and tryin' to uncross his eyes. That knot on his head was right big.

"Devil Spawn! Cursed little American Demons." Ol' Commie was just a talking' to himself.

"What's a demon? Old-timer, what's a Merican?" Trap demanded. "Better answer me too or I will put one on yer head you won't wake up from."

Old man's blind eyes homed in on Trap's voice and spit right in his face. "American Devils! You! Horrid Little Bastards!"

Trap kicked him hard in the chest, slammed his head back onto the rocks behind him. "Not sure what you are talking about, but you are bout to become like your other Commie pack. Dust and bones and nothin' else but your fancy tin hat."

"May I have some water?" Commie's forehead scrunched up. Must of had him a mean pain between them dead eyes.

"Watch him good, boys." Trapper scooped up his can and headed down to the creek. Moon was near full and shinin' pretty good. Good enough for him to see someone kneeled down by the creek before they heard him. Hid down by a palmetto, Trap tried to make out who it was. Rake is who he thought first. Wasn't drinkin' though, just a lookin' around. Bigger than Rake, even though he was squatted down like he was, Trap noticed that. Too Pale to be a Neegra. Then he saw her. Moon shined on her pale skin.

Long dark hair matched the darkness of the wood around her. The witch walked right up to the squatting figure, then he stood. They was talking' to each other but Trap couldn't make out what they said. It hit him then, it was Biggun. Trap could tell by the way he was shakin' his head and wavin' his arms around. Trap 'membered 'ol Biggun doin' that when he thought different than who he was a talkin' to.

From nowhere a hand squeezed against Trap's mouth and a strong arm drug him down real close to the ground. "It's me, Rake." Whispered the voice that caught him like a dumb rabbit. Beat, Trap nodded and the hand let him go.

"That's Biggun with that 'lil witchee of yours, you been a tracking," whispered Rake. They both looked at Biggun walk off, away from the camp way, just a shaken his head. The witch stood near the stream, then flinched and ducked down into the tall grass. Thinkin' they'd been heard, Trap tensed up and eased further behind the palmetto. Rake breathin' on his neck scared him pretty good. He knew all about the witch. Right he was to be worried about this one. Too much to make sense of. Too many things happening all at once.

They had sat a spell and the little witch seemed to have stalked off into the night. "Gotta get back to camp, Rake." Caught the meanest eyes he ever saw when he turned to Rake.

"I am tracking these two. I am gonna figure out what's goin on." It was right sure Rake wasn't asking' for permission, so Trap just nodded and headed back to camp.

At first he thought hard 'bout how he might never see Rake again, but down in his stomach, he felt scared and sure that he would. Got him thinkin' bout if it was a good idea of him leading his pack off away from where they came up. It had been that witch that had left him that map. Day after he seen her, it was right there, just sittin on his chest when he woke up. Nothin' but a haint could prowl up on him in the night... or a witch. Wonder if she had done something like that to 'ol Biggun too. She must have slaved him real good. Things were getting hard to think on out here the further away they got from their place. Might shoulda stayed. Food was easy 'nuff to find most times. Cans was gettin' hard to come by, but plenty of stuff growed out there. Trap wasn't sure if he was a good leader at all now.

Gopher looked like a haint had him. He was white as one himself when Trap arrived back at the camp. Had him a witchee doll in his hand. Held it up. Gave Trap a chill to his bone. Two dolls actually, a one arm oldtimer with a face full of spanish moss sewed together at the neck with one that looked a fright like Trapper.

Them witches sure know how to put a fear in you. "Found it right up on the ridge, there. Nobody heard nothin'," Gopher's teeth a chatterin' like bones on a strang.

"No sleepin' tonight. Keep them tools on ya. Gonna be a fight tonight."

"Yip!Yip!" Coyote call told the pack that same thing. Gopher sounded just like one.

Trap snatched the doll from Gopher and took it over to the old-timer. Tossed it in his lap. "What you make of this? Best to tell me what you know."

"Witchee winches, pudding pie. My, I love whats 'tween their thighs." Had him one crazy look about him when he sang that. Trap wasn't sure what to make of it. Startin' to wish they had never found this old coot. Had him more than enough to worry on.

"Best to start talking. I as soon stick you up on a fire to eat, as to hear you rant. Witches send you out here on us?"

"Witches. Boys always want to know about witches." They don't even know what they want to know. Burns them where they grow. Like to catch one, myself."

Trap had him a sharp knife he called the hawk toe. Pulled it out quick and stuck it to the old Commie's throat. Musta felt right serious to him. His mouth straightened out and he swallered, careful like, because the sharp blade was threatening to leave a mark when he did.

"Darwin was right. Nature has sure hardened you Godless little demons. What do you want to know, little murdering bastard?"

"I don't know no Darwin. I ain't never heard them names you callin' us. Is that what them witches call us? Is that who sent you?" Trap pulled back the knife but kept it fisted.

"U.S.S.R sent me here twelve years ago to exterminate what was left of you. My battalion was defeated by resistance. I am the last remaining."

"What's You,s,s,are? Whats sterminate?" Pacing back and forth, Trap's mind was spinnin'.

"Shit. I speak better English than... I came here to kill all you and your old-timers. My pack was killed. I am the only one left." The old Commie struggled against his binding.

"So Biggun and them older boys was right about you Commies. I should just kill you right now." Trap couldn't figure why he hadn't already. He wanted to know more about the witch and this seemed his best chance.

"You know where the Big Place is, Commie?"

"My name is Commander Dimetry Evanesavich." The Commie puffed out his chest like a struttin' grouse.

"I didn't ask yer name, Commie. Answer me. I am running out of reasons not to skin you." His trembling hand pressed the tip of the hawks toe into the Commie's leathery chest enough to draw blood. It was thick and dark like he ain't drank in days. Trap remembered the can and pressed it against his lips. The old Commie drank.

"Ah, so you do have a little heart in there." he licked his lips.

"I have a map. I am trying to get to the Big Place." Looked around to see that none of them boys was hearing him. "I can't read see."

"Oh, a map you say? I love maps. Where did you get it? Let me see." A wide grin showed Trap the old man didn't have many teeth left.

"You think me a fool? You can't read nothing. You can't see." Trap thought hard bout knockin' the rest o them teeth out.

"I can teach you to read, nonetheless." Trap smiled bigger than a bear in honey. Then was glad the old Commie couldn't see. Thought about fetching it from his sack 'for he 'membered he couldn't see it even in this moonlight. Mighty dark under that bluff.

"You better hope so. Mornin' comes and I can see it, you better show me or I leave you here strang up for the coyotes to pick on." Trap turned to check the camp. then stopped. "You hungry, I reckon."

Suckin' on his teeth made a call like a squirrel. Gopher ran over. "Feed the old un." Trap kept his voice real low. Getting bout the time them haints come out. Once they think a packs a sleeping'. They be in fer a surprise this time. Every tool in the pack would be on em quick as they snuck in.

But they never came. Trap went round and round to every one of them boys in the pack scattered here and there high and low. Just to make sure they was ready to fight and not sleepin'. Sun started to show it was gonna come up, and not a thing had stirred the wood.

Trap bird whistled to bring the boys in. They looked relieved to have made it through the night. "Go in pairs and scout 'round for any sign of witches or neegras."

Them boys paired up and took off. Trap took the chance to grab the map.

The old Commie was asleep. A nudge from Trap's foot woke him. "Alright old Commie. We ain't got much time."

"Right, Right." He rocked side to side. I will need my hand. You will use your hand to trace the letters and I will tell you what they mean."

Trap thought on it for a bit. Nothin' but his good sense told him not to trust this one. Keepin' his knife in the hand he used to hold the map might work. "Don't think you might try somethin'. I will bleed you out where you sit."

"You have my word. Give me your word that you will refrain from killing me if I help you."

"I won't kill you so long as you are useful." Trap untied his hand. Kept his hawk toe ready too.

"Which un do I start with?" It made Trap's head hurt. Only thing he could figure was the lines that was creeks and rivers. They was other lines up near the Big Place, but they was straight and Trap ain't crossed one yet. Straight things like that didn't seem natural. Truth is, Trap was scared to cross one. Thought he might fall off the land or somethin'.

"Is there any words along the top?" The old Commie grinned, excited like when you is about to get some cooked meat to eat.

"Yeah" Trap felt that excited too, but he tried to hide it.

"Start with that. It should tell me what the map is of." The old man made a pointer with his hand. Trap grabbed it and began tracing the letters.

"Q, U, I, N, C, Y, A, R, E, A, R, O, A, D, M, A, P. Quincy is a town, a small city. This is a map of the area. Is the Big Place where all the lines meet?"

"Yeah, What are them straight lines? The crooked ones is creeks and rivers. What is a city?"

"A city is a place where many people used to live together. Those straight lines are what used to be roads. You have never seen an old road?"

"Never seen one, stayed away from the ones on the map. Bein' straight and all didn't seem natural. Didn't trust em. What do they do?"

"They are wide stone paths people drove cars on." Trap had seen cars. Plenty of them and houses back in the place where they came up. Hated lookin' in em though. Always seemed to be a skeleton in one, or some witchee stuff. "So cars like big waggoons?"

The old Commie Chuckled. "Yes," he said.

"What is in the Big Place? In Quinceey? Have you been there?" Trap caught hisself getting' a might riled.

"Maybe some kids like you, more likely Negro kids. All the adults were eliminated by our Biological weapons. Lots of kids made it. Could never understand why. I have never been to Quincy, but I am sure it is no different than other small towns. They all got shelled hard, gassed good, and our tanks torched out as many of you little demons as we could. My battalion got pinned down by resistance up near Atlanta. I am trying to make it to the coast, then over to Jacksonville to get back home."

"I sure wish I knowed what stuff you talk about meant." All these words was makin' Trap's head hurt.

The old Commie was serious quiet for a moment. "No wonder. You kids raised yourselves." He started to cry. "What have we done?"

"Whats the matter?" He eased up then thought he might be playin' possum and gripped the knife tighter.

The old man said nothin'. Trap started worryin' on them boys comin' back and seein' the ol' Commie loose so Trap re-strung him. Kinda felt like cryin' himself, but couldn't figure why. He hadn't cried since he was a pup. Good way to get fisted on. He wanted to get to the Big Place... to Quincy more than ever. He wanted to know more about the world. Maybe there was more boys like him. Maybe there was more old-timers, not Commies. Mericans like him. Still wanted to get a hold of that witch too, 'cept now he was more scared of her than ever. She done magicked Biggun. She could do the same to him. She'd magic Rake as soon as she caught him prowlin' her.

Pack came back directly. Gopher brought him a string of hair he found. "Up near the cold side of the river,'" he said.

That witch was a leadin' him alright. Right to the Big Place, Quincy. The new word sounded over and over in his head. All them words that old Commie said. Some he still didn't know what they meant.

*

Trap pushed the pack hard all day. Pack was pantin' like dogs. Old man Looked 'bout to die when they found camp. Just shy of a road, Trap had seen on the map. He'd been right scared of em up til now, but they was no way to avoid them now if he wanted to get to Quincy. 'Sides he wasn't that scared of em now he knew more about what they were.

Wasn't much shelter. Cold weather comin' on knocked the leaves off most the trees. They had been as many cold times as there was fingers on one of his hands since he had been countin'. Not sure how many before that. Some though. Ol' Biggun used to say they was one hand and two fingers on the other before that. But Biggun was a bit older than Trap. He wished he knew them things, but wasn't sure why. Beauty berries and persimmons was about all they was to eat left wild. Green shoots and leaves was to be found, but they only ate them when they was grumbling hungry. Fire would bring every neegra in the area to em, but Trap didn't hardly care. Somethin' in him wanted a fight. Somethin' else bigger wanted to stay warm tonight. Pinecone clubbed a rabbit earlier. That sure sounded good.

"Stoke a fire, and be ready to fight."

Pack was eager to follow them orders, better to fight on a full belly and with warm blood. Trap let the boys get camp ready while he tied the old man to a Pine Tree. Half the sack he had strung to his feet had come off to so he sat there mending them while he thought on what to ask the old man. Finished up and put some water to the old dry lips.

"Tell me about witches. I mean everything."

Old man sighed as the water went down him. "Witches ain't no different than you. You Boys and they are girls. I never could make up why the girls seemed to split off on their own. Nature sure is funny, they are smarter than us you know. More civil by nature. They must have realized at some point that they could never get along with you boys so they made their own way and did well at keeping you at bay by scaring the mess out of you."

"Seems I 'member some." Older boys used to talk about witches livin' with them when they was pups. Trap seemed to think them right. "How they get their magic?"

"Your voice is crackling, you getting hair yet? That is when their magic really starts to work."

Trap felt his face get hot when he thought on the fuzz he had been sproutin'. "What does that have to do with it? They magic me and make me get hair all over? That what happened to your face?"

"Boys and girls are made to be together. It is the most basic part of nature. Where do you think you came from? Have you not seen animals give birth?"

"What's that got to do with us? We ain't no animals."

"We are all animals, son. We all chase witches for the same reason."

"Why won't you just tell me?" Trap kicked the ground. He felt a fight inside him.

"There is no way that I could tell you that you would understand." Old man got that look on him that told Trap he wasn't gonna say nothing else.

Trap stomped up to the fire. Dark was comin' on fast and the clouds was thick. He just sat there starin' into the flames. Felt them inside him too. He wished them Neegras would come tonight. Whipped out his hawk toe and snatched the rabbit off of Pinecones's pack and made short work of skinnin' it, and puttin' it on a stick to roast.

Smell of burning grease brought them boys to the fire quick. Trap got a funny feelin' when he looked at all of them. Wishin' he could be a better leader. He worried he might be leadin' them into somethin' they wouldn't come back from. "Eat up, boys. Feed em good, Gopher."

Gopher squatted next to his sack and started openin' up cans sat em in the coals next to the fire to warm em up. Trap shaved meat off the rabbit and stuck a piece in each can as Gopher sat em in the fire. Soon as they warmed up the line of boys picked them up and sticked at the warm food. Only sound was the boys smacking and fire crackin'. Air was still, cold and dark. Smoke didn't even have much of a way about it. Rose real slow in all directions.

Dog howl broke the silence and was followed by another one from another direction. A split pack meant they was on somethin'. Talkin' to each other they were. Comin' in on the smell of meat. Sounded trained. Trap was sure it was Neegras huntin' them. "Get them tools boys. Here they come. Spread some torches out to keep them dogs off us." He knew better than to think those trained dogs would be put off by a fire, but sayin' it made them boys a bit at ease. Them dogs was a brayin' knew right where they was. Knew right what they was after.

Neegras callin' each other came next. They was gettin' close. Hawk toe in the rope around his waist, bat in both hands, Trap charged out in the lead. "Spread out. Watch over there." Trap pointed in the direction of where he knew the road was. That was where they'd be comin' from. Started him thinkin' 'bout trustin' roads again.

Dogs came in first, bigguns. Strong and lean, and mean. A grey and black one charged right at Trap. His head was wider than it by twice. Trap put the bat hard and true right on that big head. Put an end to him. This made him think of the old man. He thought about untying him, but he seen one of them dogs get one of the small boys by the throat and shook him dead.

A spear stuck into the ground right next to Trap's foot. Felt like takin' it and stickin' it right through the neegra that chucked it at him, but he like his bat. Made his way swinging it. He'd a go out swinging it just the same.

Seemed like there was two or three on every one of them boys directly. Seemed like Neegras was poppin' out from behind every tree. Seemed most of them didn't have tools and was chuckin' big rocks. Trap chased a bunch of them down and made 'em wish they was a little better prepared.

Pinecone got one chasing him with a machete. Trap took off after him fast as he could. He ain't never seen no one run as fast as Pinecone. Right scared pinecone was about to be cut down when lil rooster cut off the neegra chasin' him with one of them spears they had throwed earlier. Stuck him right in the middle. Blood bubbled out of the Neegra's mouth. Before he fell still on his side.

Big ol' rock hit Trap square in the back. Hurt real bad. He turned, a lookin' for the one that had done it, just in time to

duck from a club getting swung at his head. In duckin', he dropped his bat. Big long Neegra had done it. Turned round and tackled him hard before Trap could get his bat. Wind came out of him as he got thumped into the ground. Neegra had his club in both hands sitting on Trap's chest. Raised it, and started to bring it down on his head when Trap pulled out the Hawk toe and stuck it right underneath the Neegra's jaw. Strangled scream and blood was the last thing that happened to him. Pushed him off and jumped back on his feet. Two Neegras stood looking at what had happened to the one Trap just killed. "Ezra dead!" one said. They made a strange call and took off the way they came. Lookin' round, they all was. That biggun they called, "Ezrey" must have been the leader.

"Squack's dead, fish is dead too, Trap." Gopher had blood from head to toe. "I put a hurting on a Bunch of them Neegras, Trap. They was so many of them. Them dogs musta been haints. They didn't die."

"I killed one, head big as a bear." Trap's mind stayed in the fight he had just seen.

The injured pack came back together near the fire. Many were bad hurt. Them that weren't carried those that were dead… four of them. Ain't never lost so many before. Trap's eyes got watery, then he stiffened up. Wasn't gonna cry for them dead boys. Wasn't gonna cry for nothin'. "Drag that biggun I killed last over here by the fire." Trap went to work on fixin' them boys that was hurt. Packed usnea in them big holes that was bleedin' hard, tyin' up smaller cuts with strips of cloth. Couldn't do nothin' bout them knots from them rocks. Gopher and Tater dragged the body of the leader next to the fire. Trap stopped what he was doin' and looked him over. Had curly hairs all under his arms on his chest, and down under his belly. He was big. Bout a leg taller than Trap. Almost as tall as the old timer. Had him a string round his neck that had bones and feathers on it. Looked a bit witchee.

"Let's go back, Trap." Little Rooster looked to be about to cry.

"Who YOU? Tellin' Trap what to do?" Gopher fisted him solid on back of the head. Now he did cry.

"It's okay, Gopher." Trap put his hand on Rooster's shoulder. His boys had them a beat look 'bout them. Their eyes was a shinin' too. "Anyone has somethin' to say, you say it now. Nobody gonna get fisted. We got whooped pretty good tonight."

"Back where we come up, ain't nobody hurt us like this." Tater sobbed. He and Squack was close. "Why we leave from there anyway?"

"We are going to a Big Place. There might even be old timers like us there. Not like that Commie. We are really close. One more hard day and we will be there. I promise." Trap bent over and took the witchy looking string off the neck of the dead Neegra. Put it on his own neck and stood up tall.

"How you know all that?" Tater got red in the face.

"Trap is our leader, and I trust him. You all better do the same." Gopher straightened out. Trap hadn't ever seen his belly so straight.

"Okay, Trap, but if we get to this Big Place and it is scary like this can we go back?"

Trap nodded. "You Boys get some rest, but rest on them tools and I will call loud if I hear anythin'."

Them boys huddled closer together than usual. Trap made sure they was finally asleep before he went to the old-timer. Nudged him with the end of his bat.

"It is a shame that you do not even know what that blood soaked weapon was actually made for. I would love to watch a baseball game… American pastime. I actually enjoyed it." Old man smiled.

"Are we going to make it in Quincy?" Trap wasn't smilin'.

"Those Negroes really did a number on you little muggers did they?" Old-timer's face straightened out.

"Why does that witch want me to come there? You think it is a trap?" His voice cracked. Tears actually came to the corners of his eyes.

"Doesn't make sense? They could get you wherever they wanted if they wanted."

"How did she get ol' Biggun all slaved? I saw him with her the other night." Trap couldn't shake her image.

"Made you jealous did it? He is where he wants to be."

"Just tell me if I am gonna get us all killed. I ought not to get them boys in trouble because of some witch magickin' me like a dumb rabbit." Trap felt his hand shakin'.

"I feel that you have made yourself respected tonight. By the sound of that attack, they sent the best they had. Just get into Quincy before dark, find friends if there are any as quickly as possible. If you don't. Go Back from where you came."

*

Trap pressed them boys hard. He even unstrung the old-timer with a threat to end him quick if he got any thoughts about running. They crossed many roads, many staring faces. Strange though. Neegras and pale boys like him ran together in twos, kept their distance. Even saw witches out and about and together with boys. Pack stuck close to their tools and to each other. Stray dogs even kept from them.

Trap kept that map out and studied them pictures on it real good. Got past where a few of them roads crossed close and got down to a place where they could follow a stream instead. By the time the sun was straight up, they got to a place where a road crossed over the stream. Smooth rock went right over their head. He looked up to see the top of it and saw a figure standin' up there, sun shinin' all 'round. Could barely make it out for squintin'.

"Hoot!Hoot!" It was Rake. Trap's stomach felt empty. "How you boys doing?"

The pack came to a dead stop like they had seen a haint. Rake disappeared into the sun then trotted down the side toward them. "Where you been, Rake? Thought them Witches got you, or them Neegras that got us last night." Trap did his best to swallow that scare in him.

"I have been tracking that Witch your leader has been trackin'. Biggun is with her to. She done magicked him just like she has magicked Trapper. She is leadin' him, y'all right into a Neegra den. A trap it is. I seen it with my own eyes."

Them boys started a lookin' at each other and whisperin'. Trap went toward Rake, Hoping to get to talk to him in quiet. No need to get them boys all scared. Rake gave him a mean look though and put his hand on the hatchet at his waist. Trap stopped.

"Ain't no trap. If they wanted us, they'd have got us last night. They sent the best they had at us and we stopped em. Look here." Trap held out the witchee string round his neck. "This one came off the leader. Bigger as any I ever seen, bigger than Biggun."

"Yeah, we fought off more of them Neegras than we ever have. Trap ain't leadin' us to no trap. We are gonna find old timers. Like us." Gopher puffed his chest out like a little rooster crowin'.

"Ain't seen no old-timers" But Rake looked sideways when he said that like he wasn't telling the truth. Made Trap excited to think Rake had seen actual old-timers.

"You lookin' sideways when you say that. You seen old timers in the Big Place?" Trap turned to look at his pack. Seemed split. Most didn't like Rake too much, but those that had seemed to be the most scared seemed to be listenin' real good.

"No, but I did see that witch, lots of witches. Cats everyplace. Biggun was with her too. She got magic on em good. Slaves him all around like he is on a string. They even sleep next to each other. She got the same Magic on Trap. He don't even know it." Talk of cats and witches did good to scare them boys. Cats was bad magic.

"I am takin' y'all back to where we came up. Who is comin' with me?" Rake held his hatchet in the air.

"Ain't nobody goin' nowhere, Rake. We goin' to the Big Place to find the old-timers. There is more to this livin' than we know and we goin' find out more about it." Trap slapped his thigh like he did when he meant business.

But most them boys had done headed over to side with Rake. All except Gopher, Pinecone, and a few of the older boys. "Y'all do what you like. I am goin' to the Big Place. Quincy is its name. Lots of people used to live there together. Still do maybe." Trap grabbed the old timer by the arm and started walking with his lil pack. Just as he got under the road, hollering scream raised up. The lil witch was runnin' toward him. He turned to see Rake running after him with his hatchet ready. She jumped right in front of him screamin', "No!"

Time slowed down. Trap tried running to save her, but Rake put that hatchet right in her chest. Nothin' he could do for her. She was gone. Rake turned his glare back to Trap.

"Run!" Trap yelled. He and his few took off down the river. Wasn't far before Trap felt the pain in the back of his shoulder. Rake's hatchet split him good. Felt the blood running down his back. Good hand grabbed the hawk toe from his belt and turned to fight, but there was Biggun just a clubbing on old Rake.

"Run!" Biggun screamed. "Go to the

big fence. Find Noah."

Trap got dizzy. Gopher grabbed his arm. Them other boys got the old-timer and they made tracks. Things got real fuzzy for Trap, felt he was bout to pass out when they got into the Big Place. Lots a boys and witches looked at em. Neegras, pale boys all together. One little witch ran up to them. She looked scared.

"Where do we find Noah?" Gopher asked her.

"Come with me," she said. Trap didn't remember much else til they got to the big fence.

Two big tough lookin' boys guarding the gate opened it. Trap seen a big tall old Neegra and a little Neegra witch. Youngest he'd ever seen. She looked as she'd seen a haint. Smoke come off metal machines all around. Loud sounds, unnatural sounds like metal rubbin' together fast was everywhere. Hurt Trap's head real good between the noise and the smell.

"It is Ezra's necklace, Papa!" said the little witch. "Where did you get it?"

Trap could barely talk. "Off a Neegra that attacked us night ago."

"Who you callin' nigger, Cracker?"

The old Neegra grabbed her arm hard. "Watch your tongue, Jessie. He doesn't know any better. You do." He turned to Trap. "So it is true. You killed my son?"

Dark was comin' on and there was little glass balls strung everywhere that lit everything. So bright it hurt Trap's head. Powerful magic here. Trap was just too beat to be right scared. "Just fendin' em off us, mister. He woulda killed me had I let him."

The old man looked sad. "Ezra chose his path when he left the compound. You are welcome to join us here. Let me take care of that wound."

*

Trapper awoke in a warm bed covered in clean cloths. The old Commie was sittin' next to his bed in a wood chair. Right startled, he tried to push himself up but the pain in his shoulder made him wince.

"Easy, lad. You are safe. Been sleepin' for two days. Cried out for that little girl that saved you many times. Easy now, lad. You are safe here. Gopher and the other boys are learning how to plant seeds and talk to girls. Learning to talk better. Learning to be boys. Rake is dead. The one you call Biggun brought the pack here. They are all safe."

Girls... Trap remembered his dream and how it wasn't a dream. That little witch. That little girl he had never met. Saved him, led him here.

"What was her name, Deemeetree?"

"I think it is best you rest now, lad. I think it is best that you ask her what her name is when she awakens." Dimetry pointed to a bed on the other side of his where the young dark-haired girl lay healing and sleeping.

FOOD FOR THOUGHT
MEDUSA GRAVES

What kids deface, I must repair and restore. A few years ago I was exhaustedly sandpapering some ink penises from a library desk when I suddenly had an attack of the vapours. Some weeks previous to this, several antiquarian volumes in the Special Collection had been found vandalised with outrageous marginalia – a sight that shook me to the core. Ink projectors are routinely used by little rascals to imprint photos of genitals into important and rare books. The cumulative effect of this ever-materialising filth took its toll on my health, until I could literally stand it no more. After the memorable collapse and subsequent hospitalisation, I opted for neuronal reconfiguration and paid a substantial amount for a controversial clinic to burn out my libido with their special machine.

Following the 'burnout' procedure, I was asked by the chief neurologist to keep a personal log, accessible to both myself and the clinic staff. The libido burnout procedure is a lot safer than it used to be, but certain aspects still remain clouded in uncertainty. Lapsing is a genuine concern, therefore it is vital that post-burnout convalescents are monitored for many years. For unknown reasons, in rare cases libido can return with a vengeance after a latency period, and a couple of post-burnout super-paedophile rampages have cast the procedure in a bad light. I found that the benefits outweighed the risks, proven by the fact that now I can do my job efficiently and behold crude sexual imagery without becoming severely flustered, upset, aroused and intimidated as I used to.

As I come into contact with schoolchildren regularly in the library, my progress is monitored especially carefully, but I feel generally 'on the ball'. My motor skills have improved considerably, and at weekends a new-found creativity prompts me to sketch a series of studies: fragile likenesses of our local supermarket branches rendered in charcoal and sulphur.

Years ago, when the Martian paintings inside the vaulted chamber of Arcadia were beamed to Earth from the Dawkins rover, many businessmen committed suicide. Among them was a property developer, later identified as Dave Burke, who plunged his light aircraft into a giant cowshed near our council estate. Social commentators said that the discovery of Martian art caused many people to rethink their lives, sometimes drastically, recklessly and fatally. Most people either took to religious mania or hedonistic abandon – but it didn't really affect me at the time, as I was too young to truly appreciate the implications of the Martian vault. Pretty paintings, though. As a child, the sight of Dave Burke's naked corpse shredded by corrugated iron surrounded by cows crushed in agony had a profound effect on my development (I recoil when presented with sexual matters). At this time, 'incident management' teams were understaffed and overworked, so the corpse and cow carcasses were left to rot for many weeks. Poring over the mess were a local gang of boys and girl-tomboys who stole my doll, Greta. They said I could have my Greta back if I ventured into the shed and cut off the dead property developer's penis with a shard of glass. I hacked at the corpse for the floppy member until darkness fell, but sadly, flies were feasting and the shape of his body was becoming syrupy, cow-gnawed and ill-defined. I didn't get my doll back.

It was weird how people quickly forgot the significance of the Martian paintings. Perhaps this was due to their demoralising effect? Reconciling transcendental ideals with baser instincts is impossible for some. Humankind's most incredible discovery couldn't stifle the habit of millennia: that self-cannibalising tendency to diet on death and horror. Life continued as before, as crass as ever. Comedians of the day made jokes about the Martian artworks; burying an incredible discovery in vaudeville dirt. Nobody can be sure what the Martian images signify, but to suggest crude ideas for comedy's sake is just foul. Everybody except the deeply religious swiftly forgot about the strange and beautiful Arcadian murals. Even the space scientists, I understand, decided to stop examining the artworks in the chamber due to the religious hysteria they were causing, and reassigned the Dawkins rover elsewhere to contemplate moisture. I once saw pastiches of Martian symbols drawn on the walls of a public lavatory (for a joke presumably) which was such a discomfiting sight I had to return later with paint stripper to remove the graffiti. I'm not a religious person, but I just hate that destructive crassness associated primarily with teenagedom – the urge to soil the mysterious. Whether my prudishness was a reaction against alienation, or whether it was a pre-existing prudishness that alienated people I don't really know. Throughout school, college and uni, nobody invited me to parties or functions. Whilst my peers were revelling in their own smut, getting drunk and doing all kinds of high jinks, I felt disgusted at humanity in general, as well as myself. Graduating with a degree in Data Inputting wasn't as happy an experience as I'd imagined – the realisation came: my entire pre-adult life had been wasted in solitude, seemingly through no fault of my own.

I do hold old works of art in high regard. Even the mass-produced stuff. When they dredged the nearby flooded lowland estates, some well-preserved old Sega Megadrive videogames were found, and I persuaded them to donate these to the library's Special Collection. More recently, landfill burrowing pirates dumped a pile of 20th century crisp packets on a lay-by. I carefully put as many of these historically important items as possible into my bag and carried them home to restore, later accessioning them into the antiquarian section of the library. Quavers, Frazzles, Skips, Monster Munch, Hula Hoops and Nik-Naks are well-represented in this cache.

My post at the library is a voluntary one, as are the vast majority of public-service posts. Librarians (the old-fashioned paper-touching ones) are a dying breed of awkward individuals, and I've certainly felt myself physically dying here! The adjoining decayed school with semi-official ownership of the library building treats the space as a 'cooling down zone' for its unruly pupils. A hail of disrespect comes from all quarters. The stress of the job, the thankless unpaid grind and the sense of desolation all conduce to depress the soul. This depression occasionally gives birth to monstrous bitterness, most notable when I once found youngsters having apparently great sex in a storage cupboard. Even the meditative hum of the dehumidifiers could never dispel the nagging 'highly-strung' mood. Thankfully, all this tension has completely dissipated since the libido burnout procedure. I am a new person! Now I open the storage cupboards quite regularly, hoping to see those lovebirds at it again, simply so that I can blithely say "carry on!" or "carpe diem!".

As long as I patrol the library, maintain upkeep and clear the donation boxes regularly, the environment seems peaceful enough. Before libido burnout I was always on edge; worrying over the constant threat of oversexualised vandals ruining the library for all posterity.

Horror stories circulated some years ago about the fate of some big city libraries. Various unstaffed self-service libraries, in conditions of near-obsolescence, became increasingly decorated with layers of photograffiti, tags and ink. The graffiti continued unchecked. An unsuspecting reader would enter the grotto, pick up a book on, say, dressmaking, and the contents would consist of the most shocking ink-projections and sayings overlaid on the original text. Many libraries became populated by gangs. All items of value stripped. All surfaces covered in graffiti of all kinds. I saw a picture of one library resembling a cross between a zoo and a super-toilet. Many news outlets celebrated this "reclaiming" of libraries by "the people", salivating over these "new guerrilla art galleries", but such sentiments were swiftly cut short with the brutal murder of beauty queen Puritee Tumisang Mamelodi in Birmingham Central Library (she herself put photograffiti into books for self-promotion, but she never lowered herself to printing mucky stuff). Journalists descended upon the defunct libraries in the hope of interviewing the new representatives of desecration – anxious to portray the murder as a tragic one-off accident. At least seven journalists from major news establishments were violently dismembered for their naivety; the photos of their deaths being circulated and injected into demented scrapbooks and noticeboards.

The defaced books, packed with unintelligible jargon, sickmaking gore and genuine obscenity, were viewed as collectors' pieces by wealthy creeps – actively sought by millionaires living in gated communities. The so-called 'Vivaldi book' was a "classic" (utterly overlaid, depicting most of the journalists' mutilated bodies annotated with obligatory crotch photos, blab and gumph), selling for an incomprehensible sum at auction. Somewhere I read an art critic describe the 'Vivaldi book' as being noteworthy for its strong irony (surely he wrote this with a smirk?). Terrifyingly disgusting as all this seemed to me at the time, the burnout treatment has almost given me a blasé outlook. Hateful as I once was of masculine symbols of oppression, I now feel evolved beyond all that carnal tumult, nevertheless I dutifully continue erasing juvenile rubbish here in this library.

Libido burnout is not a cheap procedure by any means. As well as being a popular choice for people for whom sex is either an addiction or an irritant (for me it was certainly an irritant!), the procedure is also a rite of passage for highly paid nanoelectricians whose profession demands tempering of emotion during extremely delicate work over periods of days. Sadly I'm not in such a well-paid line of work. Over the years I had tried to retain as much Poverty Allowance as I could, knowing full well that one day I must surgically or electromagnetically rid myself of this grotesque sex-millstone. Maybe I'm a prude, but it really isn't right, all this sex foisted onto innocent objects. In this forsaken library, the dirty children, with their graffiti-lasers and air-printers, constantly provide poisonous food for silent and secretive mental hunger. Jobs are non-existent in the poverty stricken sectors where I perambulate, and I knew that my interning at the library would be a long-term tenure, if not eternal. The Royal Family's horrific dissolution in the acid baths of inhuman anarchy was a fortuitous event for Poverty Allowance claimants, raised as it was by eighteen percent following their extermination, thus enabling me to save more money for libido burnout treatment.

Since the treatment, my library work has become rather blissful. Whenever I find that kids have been air-printing photos of their genitals onto objects, I diligently scrub at the ink-projection without a second thought. Like mould growth around windows, I now view it to be a natural by-product of the passing of time; similarly, the dirt can be discouraged with vigilant tidiness. Very occasionally there is a stirring of resentment when a uniquely valuable item has been found impaired with muck, but the whole buzz of sexual frustration – the blush of the loins – has wholly vanished now. Without libido, the horizon becomes clear and beautiful universal truths stand out in their superb significance.

I even venture to assert that the erasure of sex drive uncovers previously hidden human faculties. Dreamlike premonitions have aided me during meetings with government officials to secure funds for library resources. Premonitions become indistinguishable from telepathy. For instance, during one begging-for-money meeting, I was facing the back of our councillor Atticus Wa Njiriri when I mentally heard the words "my tea's gone a bit cold". Instantly, I offered to heat up his tea, and he exclaimed that I had read his mind! Near the end of the meeting, I telepathically heard the trustee Chris Thompson murmuring worriedly about a metamorphic substance he'd discovered on his property that very morning. I told him not to worry, as I had had a psychic vision of the substance on his driveway, which I could clearly see was merely an abandoned electronic pet writhing inside a wet silvery handkerchief with a malfunctioning electrochromic element. The interest of the funders was aroused by my intuitive powers, and the sum of 500 EU credits was successfully secured for the library.

"Spend it on whatever you like," grinned Chris Thompson!

One of the most intriguing ideas I received telepathically occurred during one of my weekend sketchings of supermarket landscapes. As I sat on the hillock overlooking a store, I suddenly received the impression that the Dawkins rover (to my knowledge still communicable on the Martian surface), along with subsequent rovers, had found more Martian vaulted chambers than the authorities had let on, each containing new artworks, and that this knowledge had been deliberately kept secret. I imagined scientists had discovered hundreds of other Martian murals but were withholding the information from the whole population for fear of economically destabilising an already compromised world order. A strange plausibility struck me. New symbols came before my eyes. I couldn't detect from whom this thought had come. True, it might've been the emanation of some Mars-worshipping conspiracy nut, but equally it could have come from someone who actually *knew* something. I spotted, outside the supermarket, a group of violent looking male and female youths – one of them had shaken up a fizzy drink and was holding it to his groin creating the comic impression of a spurting orgasm – all this being filmed by other group members using various devices. No – their minds weren't on Martian art – the thought emanated from somewhere *inside* the supermarket. Entering the supermarket would mean passing this uncouth gang with my expensive paper and drawing implements. Despite a certain fearlessness instilled in me post-burnout, I resisted the urge to trace the source of the thought. I regret this now. I had missed a golden opportunity to uncover a possible conspiracy of silence around what must surely be one of most important discoveries of humankind. As the moronic theatre of delinquents played on with its phallic prop, I did wonder if the wider human race was considered by elite space scientists too infantile to deal with knowledge of new Martian art. Yet who are they to decide? Furthermore, could the withholding of such amazing knowledge actually be responsible for stifling enlightenment?

I didn't mention the premonitions and psychic experiences in my log for the clinic. It seemed unnecessary, and might alarm the neurologists. Besides, the new power, although inconsistent, was wonderfully uncanny. Often when people entered the library I knew precisely what they were looking for, and so I could direct them to the appropriate terminals or shelves before they'd even uttered a word, much to their surprise. I also knew what people thought of me – but even the most stand-offish thoughts didn't faze me. With the libido erased, appearance angst vanishes.

Furthermore, I could sense immediately when troublemakers were in the vicinity. A dull throbbing heralded the arrival of teenagers hell-bent on mischief. One afternoon I calmly focussed my attention on such a group, dressed in the sickest electrofluorescence. Their presence made me rush my mid-afternoon aerosol snack. The youths draped themselves over the sprawling pipework in the dark corner nearby the iReaders. My psychic vision unravelled their hidden motives with complete lucidity. Once the bane of my life, they were now as readable as books. It all made perfect sense, whereas in the past their ominous actions irked and offended me deeply, I now discerned their moods as the inevitable outcomes of obvious formulae. Hooray for psychic vision! Their inner thoughts ran as follows: they were dimly aware of the overarching presence of oldfashioned paper-lovers, and a primal urge to attract attention coupled with a contrarian disregard for paper items compelled them to deface items they deemed overly venerated. Through this, they sought to experimentally verify their existence as living, conscious, social beings. All this was intermixed with various sexual fixations and simplified ultramodernist postures.

A bald member of their gang had moved elsewhere in the library. Suddenly, I could actually telepathically sense him scanning the old book shelves for an item worthy of defacing. Up came an expectant, rising sensation. Simultaneously, from another direction, a different youth was preparing to photograph his genitalia for the purpose of imprinting it into the chosen book: rubbing the groin into a photogenic semi-erect state. Damn these silly, ignorant boys! I coughed a cough only a librarian could cough, but they were impervious to sound. With the hastening palpitations and sensations of imminent book-desecration, I had to decide whether to tip-toe toward the group – a hub of tacky pseudo-depravity – or to move towards the stacks where the malcontent was stalking items of value. A sudden click, translated as a mental detonation in my psychic vision heralded the camera's blink. A second click – one for luck. Looking over to the group, I could see one of their number facing the wall with a cameraphone to his privates. Then, from the stacks, the bald bozo came into view with an expensive-looking green folio under his arm. It was the collection of 20th century crisp packets!!! A volume I felt personally attached to!! Outrage coupled with channelled nervous energy charged me into action. Without hesitation, I ran towards the boy with the cameraphone – so vital for their photograffiti – and snatched it from his grip. In this moment, all tensions blew up into a dangerous uncharted vacuum. Barks of "give it back" and garbled invective encouraged me to increase the incursion into their personal space. His penis was still half-exposed, and for some reason I grabbed at it with my other hand. Shouting caused panic. He was half-immobile thanks to the stupendous neon boots he sported, but he clawed my pullover with a vigour reciprocated by my grip. Childhood memories came flooding: hacking at the cowshed plane-crash corpse with the shard of glass…. My doll Greta… Searching for the lifeless urethra. Tables were upturned. My nails were drawing blood as I struggled to uproot the stressed penis from the gristle, but it wouldn't come out. The idea persisted that I must rip it out from his body. As I looked back to locate the other boy with the valuable crisp packet folio, I unexpectedly saw its green buckram binding hurtling towards my face. That's all I remember.

At a recuperation facility, two junior neurologists from the clinic, standing beside my bed, informed me the news had arrived of my undignified behaviour, which had deeply concerned clinic officials. The previous day's incident at the library was considered so singular that an eminent doctor was planning to write a paper about it for a journal. Asked why I had tried to "molest" the teenagers, I replied that there was absolutely no sexual motive whatsoever – I was trying to stop them damaging rare materials with their obscene photograffiti. Anger would seem a natural response. I quipped that those tawdry imps would each benefit from a libido burnout of their own. The two neurologists appeared sceptical at my protestations, suspecting a possible 'lapse' into libidinous frenzy. Firmly, I rubbished this theory. After much questioning, I told them of my psychic episodes. This interested them a great deal. In my groggy state, I couldn't ascertain whether I still possessed this faculty. I wanted to know where the 20th century crisp packet folio was. This had been temporarily confiscated by the local marshal as evidence (after it was thrown at my face).

The neurologists insisted on me undergoing a second 'deep pass' libido burnout. For some reason, I signed a document to give my consent for them to perform this. Frankly, I had entirely lost what little motivation I once had to interact with people. All personal upkeep and hygiene was now firmly on the backburner. A letter shown to me in bed later that day detailed my suspension from library duties. The library would activate a self-service device. These devices are the death knell for libraries, and within weeks the library would inevitably become desecrated: a tomb of apathy. But I didn't seem to care anyway. All life is roadblocked in these dismantled times. Rather than U-turn into degeneracy, my thoughts were hovering over the roadblock toward loftier things: alien symbols, exalted states of the nervous system, our perception of time, the lost antiquities of landfill, the quality of light on chrome supermarket roofs in the morning…

A dim glow of motivation came. I asked the trustworthy-looking neurologist with the shock of ginger hair if he would kindly retrieve, when possible, my 20th century crisp packet folio.

THE SECRET STEALER
SAM WOOD

The Captain dealt in secrets at the end of eternity. He hunted them in the marketplace from the junk traders and memory merchants. He teased them out of whores for a coin and a kind word. He stole them from the mouths of sleeping babes. It was not his natural trade but he was good at it.

When he learned that there was only one free vampire left in the city of Wreckage, he sold the secret to Parliament for over two-hundred ducats. Most went to pay off old debts and some went on dreamsmoke and breathing in fear from a handful of dust. Anything to escape for a few captured moments chasing the door in his dreams. It had been lean these last few months. The Parliament had been cracking down and he'd had to pay plenty in bribes, and fines, and licenses.

He clinked together some of the money in his pocket as he walked down Grey Lane, past the mewling forms of three vampires nailed out on crucifixes. The buildings here were tumbledown and ruined, wattle slums next to featureless concrete boxes. The air was blue from the large ultra-violet strips shining and bubbling the creatures' flesh. He could smell the puss, but kept his face resolutely turned away from the twitching figures. He was heading towards Undercross and the Wraithyards, and this was the quickest path.

'Red.' One of the vampires spat. 'Please. Just a bit of red. Delicious red.' Its voice was cracked with a thick accent. To the Captain, it sounded Russian but there was no Russia where this thing came from.

The Captain looked at it then. It was female shaped, its body burned to a single open wound. Its jaw lolled.

'Please sir,' it said. 'Just a bit of red. Crimson. Even burgundy or maroon.'

'Sorry,' the Captain said. He walked on. These things wouldn't last much longer. They and their kind would be another thing rendered extinct.

'Secrets!' the thing said. 'I have knowledge! For just a bit of red. I will tell you.'

That made the Captain pause. He looked around carefully, but he was alone. Very few people had the guts to walk past the prisoners on Grey Lane.

What could it hurt? He reached into one pocket for his grubby handkerchief and the other for his gutting knife. With a wince, he cut the flesh of his thumb and bled onto the rag. Quickly it turned crimson.

He leaned up and pressed it to the vampire's mouth. It gasped in broken pleasure, sucking desperately. When every bit was gone it dropped it to the ground. Its broodmates hung unmoving.

'Thanks,' it said.

'Your knowledge?' The Captain picked up his handkerchief and wrapped it tight around his thumb. He concentrated on a healing sigil in his head and as he did so the bleeding stopped. The Captain was from England, and an England without witchcraft. But he had taught himself quickly after the world had ended.

'Closer. Come close. Saying it will kill me.'

'Why? What is it?'

'It is the Seventh.' It gave a hacking, rotting sound that might have been a cough or a laugh.

'The Seventh?'

'Yes. The Seventh Great Secret of the End. This one was given to the erythrophage. I tell it to you. For the red. And so it will not be forgotten.'

The Captain's heart thumped. This was undoubtedly a trick. Yet still he stood on his toes and pressed close to the hissing vampire.

It had taken the Captain years to even hear of the Nine Great Secrets. It had taken him two more decades to learn them. Even then he had only managed to find five. He could feel them now, brooding quietly in the back of his mind.

His search grew more frantic with every new one he unearthed. He was always hunting rumours of the last four. The city of Wreckage sat in the eye of an apocalypse, the last lashed together flotsam of a hundred-thousand universes. Beyond that was nothing. Every second the Maelstrom, the storm of the unmaking, sucked away his leads and made it so the secret-keepers had never been at all.

The Captain leaned close. The vampire told him. As she spoke the words, her body cracked. Thick black ichor gushed from the rents. The Captain jumped back as she collapsed and dissolved. He mopped a spot of vampire off his face and scowled. She hadn't finished her revelation.

He looked at the other two vampires, but they could do little more than drool and moan. He needed to know how it finished. He had to know the rest.

There was only one thing left that could tell him.

The Captain couldn't sleep. That was rare; normally he slept like a guiltless man. But the unfinished secret had infested his dreams, leaving him lying in his bunk wide-eyed and wide awake. There was no sun to mark the days or the nights any longer but he worked for hours in the tumbledown streets of Wreckage, seeking the erythrophage.

He listened by the pillars in the Circle to the agitative cries of the Revolutionary Ghost Brigade, the spirits of those who had hung on after Parliament had them executed for their beliefs. He cloaked himself in magic and sneaked into the shadowy vaults of the Museum to read the ancient records. When his raid proved fruitless, he stole documents and bartered them in the Steel and Candle Inn for scraps of hearsay.

An old grindylow in a copper bath had given him a lead. In return it had demanded the scrawled hieroglyphs on the back of a takeaway menu.

He followed the grindylow's rumour, which led him to cross the rickety bridge to Fourth Cambridge. He patted his chest, checking on the pistol in his right breast pocket and the small tin box in the left.

The cobbled streets were lined by strange mausoleums, all domes and spires of slick piscine-shining stone. The Parliament had set up a stark black and white sign at the edge of the district.

WARNING: UNSPEAKABLE HORRORS WITHIN

The Captain walked past it with barely a glance. There was a drone in his head, the voice of the dead vampire, getting ever louder. The secret was muttering to him in words he did not know.

Lamps lined the street, looking like

great spinal columns. All were dark except for one at the far end which burned with a red glow. The Captain was pleased. The Parliament refused to send their agents into Fourth Cambridge even to deal with chroma crime. It was probably one of the few places the erythrophage had left to hide.

His footsteps echoed as he walked toward the lamp. He kept his eyes dead ahead. He could see the residents of the district clustering at the edge of his vision. They wafted, rippling and hungry. Their forms changed when he blinked.

As he reached the lamp, he realised a great gash ran across the street beyond it. It was twenty feet across and seemed to grow wider as it stretched to the void.

There were stairs set into the cliff face, which led down to a simple wood shack and balcony clinging to the rock. It looked like it had been built hastily out of scrap and could fall down at any second into the rippling expanse of the Maelstrom and the winds of the unmaking.

The locals moved closer. They were right on top of him, ethereal and blurred in the periphery of his vision. He refused to look at their ulcerous faces and too-long fingers. You weren't supposed to look at them; they took it as proof of your belief. What they did then had never entirely been documented but you didn't survive in any meaningful way.

The Captain sucked in air through his teeth. Fourth Cambridge tasted like dust and iron. Carefully, he began to climb down the staircase. Rust flakes fell as it creaked under his weight. As he descended it got cold. Very cold.

A step cracked and fell as he put his weight on it. The Captain leapt backwards, grasping the staircase. The new gap between steps was too far to jump.

There was a stub of Babylon candle and an old lighter in his coat. He pulled them out, sparked fire on the wick for just a moment, and stepped in one movement across the five hundred yards to the deck outside the shack. His breath frosted in the icy air as he landed without a sound.

Mouldy curtains were pulled over the windows. The Captain drew his pistol and raised his hand to knock at the door.

Something stopped him. A prickly shadow swooped and looped in the corner of his eye. He froze as he heard it land behind him.

'You can turn, secret stealer,' a quiet voice said. 'I am real even if you don't look at me.'

The Captain masked his anger with a grim smile. 'Hello, Raoul,' he said.

The figure was tall and monochrome with a beaky nose. The man wore a long cloak of black feathers. 'You're brave coming here,' he said.

'Not as brave as yourself. I thought your kind refused to risk your necks. In fact, I thought it was against protocol.'

'The Parliament of Rooks has granted me extensive authority in order to locate the final erythrophage.'

'So you tracked me.'

'It became apparent in the course of my investigation that I was not the only soul engaged as such. Rather than waste my resources, I concluded it would be more prudent to merely utilise yours.'

The Captain frowned. 'Normally I charge.'

'Take it up with the Parliament. They might take pity on your poverty. Or they might throw you in the Deepgate.' Raoul shifted from foot to tridactyl foot.

'Lovely. So what do you want?'

'I would have thought that obvious. I am here to bring in the erythrophage for trial. Crimes against Parliament. Agitation of the masses. Violation of chroma laws. Such perverted violations. How could we suffer them to exist? Despicable things. Colour-eaters.

Foul.' Raoul shook his head, choking a little. 'But what I am not sure is why you are here.'

'Oh, you know. Information.' The Captain shrugged. The secret was wriggling like a parasite in his brain.

'I see. We keep a file on you, secret stealer. We know what you do. We know about your contact with vanguards and terrorists. It benefits us to let you operate with impunity. Don't let us rethink that benefit.'

'You know, where I came from,' the Captain said, 'Rooks were dumb birds. No authority at all.'

'That as may be, Captain,' Raoul said. 'Whatever place you came from is gone. Here in Wreckage, the Parliament has every authority. Now stand aside.'

Raoul strutted to the shack. The Captain moved behind him.

'If you provide me with some backup, there might be a shiny ducat for you,' Raoul said, pushing open the door. His head exploded like a bursting egg. For a second, his body stayed standing. Then it collapsed down into a gloomy pool of ink.

The Captain lowered his pistol. 'I steal the secrets. Nobody steals them from me.' The words in his head muttered something that might have been agreement.

'Blood?' The voice was weak and shrill. The Captain ducked over the threshold through the sticky slop that had been Raoul. He held his gun out ahead of him.

The vampire was crouched in a corner under a grimy sheet. It did not breath but it shivered. Its skin and hair were almost colourless, hanging in folds, and its eyes were raw. The Captain recognised the signs. It had not fed for a while.

'Blood,' it said, muttering, 'but no red. No red. Blackblooded bird. Blackblooded Parliament bastard. Witchfinder. Kinslayer.'

'You're the last,' the Captain said. 'But why are you here? There's a red lantern just up the steps. You could feed on that for days.'

'Don't you hear them? In the walls? Outside the door? The things from the next world being reborn from the one that came before? They are in the street. They are in the air. Waiting in the gap right behind your head, the bit where you can't see. Waiting for you to turn and look at them. But you mustn't look.'

Excellent, the Captain thought. It had been driven mad. That would make this easier.

He lowered his pistol and took out the tin box. He popped it open with a thumbnail. A single bright and fresh red rosehead sat nestled within.

'You see this?' he asked. The vampire was gagging, twitching at the sight. It nodded. A string of drool trickled down its chin.

'I will give you this. For the secret.'

'Secret?' The creature clutched at its face. 'I don't know any. They have stolen them all from me. Along with my wits.' It gave a shrill laugh. 'Please. Give me the flower. So bright and beautiful.'

'Your broodmate told me. Your kind was given one of the Nine Great Secrets. It told me half of it. Now I need you to tell me the rest. Then you get the rose.'

Shaking, the vampire rose. 'That silly little thing? Barely a secret. And given to us? No. Sputtered by the Blinded Queen. We learned it by chance, listening to the swansong of Prometheus as he burned on the pyre of his own making. We nicked it from a little girl who might have been an oracle. I wonder why we have not traded it for a lick of crimson before?'

'I wonder. Well. The secret, then the rose?'

'First the rose. I need my strength to speak.'

'Fine.' The Captain tipped the flower to the dirty floor. The vampire leapt on it, stuffing it to its mouth to suck.

The colour dribbled out of the petals into the vampire's lapping tongue. It moaned like a lover as it drank. Eventually it lowered the rose, a translucent ghost of a flower.

'That is better,' it said running its tongue wide around its chops, lapping up the last taste.

'Now. My payment. Tell me the secret.'

'I said I shall and so I shall. But indulge me. Why do you wish to know?'

'I'm a collector. That and…' The Captain knew better than to give information out for free. It was one of his few principles.

'And?'

'And nothing. Now fucking tell me.' There was buzzing and scratching in his mind. Gates and chants, weights and measures, whispers and words. A single candle burning down to wax in a darkened room. A night which had never seen stars. The ends of empire. A door.

'I am the last, aren't I?' the vampire said.

'Yes. I told you that before.' The Captain grew impatient.

'So I am the only person left in all of the Wreckage that knows this?'

'Unless your broodmates told someone else. We had a deal.' The Captain raised his gun again. The vampire shrunk back.

'Yes. Yes we did. Come then. Let me share my knowledge.' It sat back on its heels.

'There is just one path through nightmare. It leads back on itself like a children's tale…'

Hours later, the Captain stumbled out. The first vampire, nailed up on a cross, had barely begun the telling. At one point, the windows of the shack had flashed an unearthly orange. The Captain's hair was tangled and his eyes were wild. Behind him the vampire laughed long and shrill.

He used the Babylon candle stub to step right to the top of the cliff. The residents of Fourth Cambridge clustered close. He kept his eyes half closed, looking dead ahead. They seemed more solid than before. He realised that he could hear them muttering.

He used up the rest of the Babylon candle to run all the way to the docks in thirteen rapid steps.

The ships rose and dipped in the buffeting winds of the unmaking. There was a sudden crack and a crimson flash. One of the boats at the edge of the dock had broken up and vanished from existence, sucked away by the storm.

He looked to check on his own rusting vessel. The *Oblivion* floated between a void barque and a half-rotted pleasure barge. He doubted that it was still seaworthy. Luckily there was no sea left, only the lapping waves of the void stretched out like a black ocean.

His candle was used up and he was forced to dodge from deck to deck and clamber across rigging. When he finally put his boots down on his ship he went immediately to the map room. The door was half stuck and a layer of dust covered everything. He hadn't been in here for years, having traded the charts for dreamsmoke long ago.

He rifled through draws and files until he found a large sheet of spare paper. He spread it out on the table and began to sketch the signs and symbols that appeared in his brain. The voices were gone now. Instead was a sense of purpose and an idea.

When he was done he had a chart.

Two days later, having traded every secret but seven for food and supplies, he took a hatchet to the rope holding his ship to the barque next to it. After half a dozen blows it burst apart. The *Oblivion* slowly moved, bumping its way through ships and boats. Apocalyptic tides drew it out into the swirling Maelstrom.

The Captain put his hands on his wheel. The windows were open and there was, somehow, a cool breeze. As his ship muscled the last few ugly vessels aside and set off into open space, he checked his chart and corrected his course.

He sailed towards a patch of blackness that might, just might, have been a door.

FIREFLIES
RICHARD THOMAS

When the winds come, the hut shakes and I grab the tabletop, the heavy wood carved centuries ago, scarred and pitted by time. I wait for the roof to rip off, exposing me to some giant hand, pulling me into the sky to be punished for my sins. The beams creak and moan, and in the gaps I hear her voice. I beg her to shut up, to leave me alone, but the dull ache that wraps around my plodding heart, it trembles and hesitates, apologizes for snapping at her, my love, and asks her for forgiveness. And she gives it, freely.

The scrap of paper dances in the wooden bowl, the printed type from another time, so long ago, when machines still ruled the world. It nestles into the handful of buckeyes, their dull red orbs rolling around–a fluttering eagle feather next to the pink fleshy lining of an aging conch shell. I've memorized the serial number that runs along the bottom, the bent edges of the stained slip, once a shiny white stock, now a dull, faded yellow. The solitary word used to make me laugh. Isabella and I would dance in their glow, mocking the insects, asking them to take us home–to smother us in their amber. I don't laugh about them anymore.

After the winds start up it isn't long until the black rain beats down upon the tin roof, sheets of metal scraps stolen from ruptured airplanes that dot the island, bent and fastened by my tired, mangled hands. When the door swings open, I'm not surprised–the latch has been busted for days now, and my hope was that it would fix itself, the wood warped and swollen, praying for the doorframe to shift back to its former self. Shadows drift in from the field, lightning fracturing the night. The long grass bends, rippling in the flash of light, photos taken as her arms raise and lower, long legs extended, leaping, and I shake my head, squint my eyes shut, and beg for more time. Not tonight. I'm too fragile to handle the haunting.

And then it is quiet. She is gone, my memory of her body, her giving curves and gentle fingers fading into the night. Beyond the field lies the edge of the cliff, and beyond that is the water of a never ending ocean, black as tar, a universe expanding, calling me to take the long swim home.

At the edges there is a history, a blur of wagons and horses, bodies piled high, the stench taking on a physical weight, splintered doors slamming shut like gunshots as the dead were taken away. She was taken away, and for nothing more than a ripe peach hanging from an abandoned tree, the orchard ripe with flies and decaying nectar. But the disease had taken hold already, whatever we called the mutation then, the plague had come home to roost, to rest–to unfold.

"Isabella," I sigh, a wave of moonlight crossing the field, crawling over the lush grass, wandering inside the hut. I light the candles that sit in a melted pile, now that the winds have died down. The box of matches is running low, a trip to the town square near at hand.

The howling will start soon, the rabid pack of mongrels coming to sniff at the cracks of my homestead, licking at the sap that plugs the gaps, snuffling at the door, rattling the frame with their dark, wet snouts, pissing on it and moving on in a sickening mass of dark, hairy flesh. There is little time to fix the latch, but I must.

On the wall hang a few handmade instruments–bent metal and wood stained with the slick oil of my flesh. I am not a blacksmith nor am I a carpenter. These tools are about all I have. Heavy rocks work just as well and sometimes I get lucky in the wreckage, a steel beam or bar changing the way that my life staggers on. So many times I've frayed the flesh of my fingers just to steal a bolt or two, a handful of nuts and nails taken from the bent and empty metal birds. And to what end? In a few days when I'm drained by the sunlight that beats down on this solitary rock, the heat will push me down until I collapse in the sand on the east side of the island, seashells spilling from my hands. Or the exhaustion will leave me in the meadow, covered in tiny cuts from the sharp blades of grass that surround me, lost to time and place. The black winged beasts will descend on my homestead, pecking at the shiny objects, these diseased children of the raven and magpie. The dogs will take what is left, I don't know why, scattering the bits of metal far and wide, the dull pieces of steel picked up by the deformed rodents that live in the caves down by the water. They mock me. But I continue. She tells me to carry on.

I take down the bastard screwdriver and malformed hammer and push at the lock that protrudes from the door, trying to straighten it out, to solidify this pitiful lock, so that the demon beasts will not get in tonight.

The wind picks up again as I crouch in the doorway, the coolness washing over my slick skin, and the grass waves back and forth, telling me to come lay down in the damp finery of their offerings, and for a moment, I stop and consider doing just that.

No. The latch.

I lick my lips and bend the piece of metal, the rusted tongue eluding my clumsy fingers, the metal in my hand slipping, running a gash through my left hand. I shove my palm into my mouth, cursing as I sup the liquid, knowing that it will surely draw them out. And at the edge of the field there is a flickering of lights, dots of yellow fading in and out–they've smelled the humanity that drips onto the stone porch, the slab of grey rock dotted with discs of red and I hurry to bend the metal straight.

To my left the glowing circles meander across the night sky, taking their time. They have all night to play with me and I have nowhere to go. My eyes stay on them, watching as they pulse in and out, slowly moving across the field, the cool metal in my hands finally bending. I check my work, lifting the latch up and down, my eyes drawn back to the field and to my handiwork. I step inside and close the door, their night music fading behind the dense wood. Sliding the lock in place, I tug on the brass knob and it holds, it is solid, and the shadows pour over the edge of the cliff, stretching and shrinking, eager to test my work. I rattle the knob one more time.

I sit down at the table, the old wooden chair creaking under my weight, as the panic drains out of my skin, my face falling into my open hands, muffling a sob that has been building all day.

"Oh, Isabelle," I moan. "Help me, my love."

I can hear them circling the house, their hot rancid breath coming out in gasps, the wet lapping of their tongues in the air, teeth clicking, snapping at each other as their hackles raise and a heavy wind pushes against the house. I don't want to blow out the candles—they give me comfort and warmth. I've only just lit them with my dwindling supply of matches—but I do it anyway.

"Go away," I yell, and they yip and bark, excited by my anger, hoping to lure me outside, wanting the confrontation—willing me to take them on tonight. I hear a clang of metal on the slab outside and creep over to look between the cracks. A body slams against the door and I fall backwards, my heart stuttering, a long bit of rusted rebar lying on the rock like a sacrifice. I smile against all logic. I grin in the darkness despite my need to piss, my stomach rolling and unfurling—they want me to take this weapon, they're trying to even up the odds. Manipulative bastards.

Another heavy weight is flung against the door and I worry the latch will not hold. There is a sharp cry and the furry beasts move away from the front of the hut, and I hear the animals disappear behind the house. A gathering of yellow lights hovers in front of the door, and this may be my only chance tonight. I flick the metal latch up and step forward, flipping my head to the left and then the right, the wind gusting, grasses sighing, and I bend over to pick up the bar. The glowing dots gather before me and I stand upright as they fill the frame of my Isabella, just for a moment, her curves and slender legs, her long hair blowing in the darkness, and then they break apart. I take a step outside.

The fireflies head back across the grassy field, a line of yellow dots, expanding into slashes, and I follow this lost highway out into the night, a wave of peaceful inevitability washing over me, the hounds coming back around to the front, yapping at me, nipping at my feet, my knees, as they bound in and out of the grasses. I swing the bar lazily towards them, and they retreat. Moments later they are back at my side, escorting me through the lapping blades. I fling the bar out into the grass and it lands with a dull thud, the animals descending on it, confused. They sniff at the metal, something off, standing still now, and they let me continue, rotting flesh that I am—they let me go.

When the blinking lights drift out over the water and up into the sky, I follow them. She whispers in my ear, her mouth on my neck, and the tears come, the dancing lights pulling me over. Her laughter is with me and I take it, I hold it, and let it cushion me as I fall to embrace the rocks below.

THE GUILTY PARTIES
OR
CONTRIBUTOR BIOS

GARRETT COOK is a writer of Bizarro and Neopulp fiction that's not that bad. He is the Winner of the First Annual Ultimate Bizarro showdown. His books in print include the Wonderland Award nominated *Archelon Ranch* and *Jimmy Plush, Teddy Bear Detective*. His persecution complex knows where you live.

DAN NICHOL lives in Herefordshire. This is his first published story.

MARSHALL PAYNE has written over 100 short stories and sold 43 of them to markets such as *Aeon Speculative Fiction*, *Talebones*, *Brutarian*, and *Polluto Magazine*. A former pro musician, he lives in San Antonio, Texas with novelist Jaime Lee Moyer, their two cats and three guitars. None of the guitars he has had to pawn lately - life is good!

NICOLE CUSHING's short fiction has appeared alongside stories by Neil Gaiman and Chuck Palahniuk in the anthology *Werewolves & Shape Shifters: Encounters with the Beast Within*. In 2010 Eraserhead Press published her first collection of dark satire *How to Eat Fried Furries*. Later this year, the podcasts *Cast Macabre* and *Pseudopod* will be presenting audio versions of two original tales. Nicole would like her readers to know that no actual anthropomorphic clods of mud (or sweaty, over-tanned wrists) were harmed during the writing of "The Meaning".

GARETH DURASOW lives in Huddersfield. His poetry has recently appeared in *The Rialto*, *Cadaverine*, *Shearsman*, *French Literary Review*, *PANK* (U.S.) and *Critical Documents*' 'That Merciless and Mercenary Gang of Cold-Blooded Slaves and Assassins, Called, in the Ordinary Prostitution of Language, Friends'. He was born in the year of the pig.

GIO CLAIRVAL is an Italian-born writer and translator who lives in Paris, France, and writes in English. Her stories have appeared in *Weird Tales* and *Postscripts*, among other places. Visit her at www.gioclairval.blogspot.com — **ERIN E. STOCKS** is a writer living in Oklahoma City, OK. She can be found on www.erinstocks.com.

STEVE CONOBOY has been writing for years and waiting for an opportunity to unleash his work. A five minute horror entitled *Billy Rae Smith* is floating about somewhere. He's currently building a collection of short stories and scripts on jottify.com under the username steveconoboy. Feel free to check it out and leave a comment. Nice comments only.

ROBERT LAMB spent his childhood reading books and staring into the woods -- first in Newfoundland, Canada and then in rural Tennessee. There was also a long stretch in which he was terrified of alien abduction, but such are the trials of puberty. He earned a degree in creative writing. He taught high school. He wrote for the smallest of small-town newspapers before finally becoming a full-time science writer and podcaster. He was named a Doghorn Fiction Prize winner in 2010 and is currently working on a book-length project. You can learn more about his work online at http://rjlamb.com and follow him on Twitter @Vomikronnoxis.

ERIK T. JOHNSON's work has appeared in or is forthcoming in periodicals such as *Electric Velocipede, Space & Time Magazine, Shimmer, Tales of the Unanticipated*, and *Morpheus Tales*, as well as several anthologies including *Box of Delights, Dead but Dreaming 2, The Shadow of the Unknown, WTF?!, Pellucid Lunacy*, and *Best New Zombie Tales 3*. The highlight of his writing life to-date (and likely forever) is when D.F. Lewis called one of his stories in the Winter 2010 *British Fantasy Society Journal* "perfect, in my eyes." Oh those eyes! Those eyes! You can learn more about Erik's work and get in touch with the author at www.eriktjohnson.net.

DAVID MORGAN has been an arts worker and literature officer, organizer of book festivals and writer-in-residence for education authorities, Littlehay Prison and Fairfield Psychiatric Hospital (which was the subject of a Channel 4 film, Out of Our Minds). He has had two plays screened on ITV and over 200 hundred poems published in National and International Poetry Magazines.
His books for children include: *The Strange Case of William Whipper-Snapper*, three *Info Rider* books for Collins and *Blooming Cats* which won the Acorn Award and was recently animated for BBC2's Words and Pictures Plus as well as a Horrible Histories biography: *Spilling The Beans On Boudicca*. David has also written poetry books, including: *The Broken Picture Book, The Windmill and the Grains* (Hawthorn Prize) and *Buzz Off*.
His poetry collection *Walrus on a Rocking Chair*, illustrated by John Welding, is published by Claire Publications and his last adult poetry *Ticket for the Peepshow* was published by *art'icle international*. His latest collections : *Beneath The Dreaming Tree* was published by Poetry Space Ltd in October 2011 and *Lightbulbs In The Sea* by *Knives, Forks & Spoons Press* was published in November 2011.

CLAIRE T. FEILD is an English composition instructor. She has had 235 poems accepted for print publication in 101 literary journals, such as *Runes, The Carolina Quarterly, Birmingham Arts Journal, Hurricane Blues: Poems about Katrina and Rita, The Mochila Review, Folio*; *South Dakota Review*; and most recently, in these print journals: *Perceptions: Magazine of the Arts, Turbulence Magazine, Black Magnolias Literary Journal, The Toucan Literary Magazine, Windmills* (Deakin University, Geelong, Victoria, Australia); *The Chaffey Review* (Chaffey College,

CA); *The Eclectic Eel* (Hull, England); *Eye Contact* (Seton Hill University, Greensburg, PA); *Polluto* (U.K.); and *Spillway*. Her first poetry book, *Mississippi Delta Women in Prism*, is set in Mississippi. Excerpts of her memoir, *A Delta Vigil*, have been published in Boston's *Full Circle: A Journal of Poetry and Prose*.

ALIYA WHITELEY was born in Devon in 1974. Her first two novels were published under the Macmillan New Writing imprint, and her short stories have appeared in places such as *The Guardian*, *Strange Horizons*, *McSweeney's*, and various anthologies. Her first short story collection will be published at the end of 2012.

Canadian poet, fiction writer, and playwright **J. J. STEINFELD** lives on Prince Edward Island, where he is patiently waiting for Godot's arrival and a phone call from Kafka. While waiting, he has published fourteen books — ten short story collections, two novels, two poetry collections — along with five chapbooks, the most recent ones being *Misshapenness* (Poetry, Ekstasis Editions, 2009), *A Fanciful Geography* (Poetry Chapbook, erbacce-press, 2010), and *A Glass Shard and Memory* (Stories, Recliner Books, 2010). His short stories and poems have appeared in numerous anthologies and periodicals internationally, including in two previous issues of *Polluto*, and over forty of his one-act plays and a handful of full-length plays have been performed in North America.

JACOB EDWARDS studied at the University of Queensland, graduating with a BA (English) and an MA (Ancient History). He stacks deckchairs at *Andromeda Spaceways* and currently is editing #55 of their *Inflight Magazine*. Jacob lives in Brisbane, Australia, with his wife and son, and may be found online at www.jacobedwards.id.au

MICHAEL ARONOVITZ published his first collection titled *Seven Deadly Pleasures* through Hippocampus Press in 2009, and Bad Moon Books will publish his first novel *Alice Walks* in 2013. His short story How Bria Died recently appeared in "The Year's Best Dark Fantasy and Horror 2011," published by Prime Books. Aronovitz's latest collection titled *The Voices in Our Heads* has recently been completed, and various "Voices" stories have initially appeared in *The Weird Fiction Review 2011*, *The Turks Head Review*, *Death Head Grin*, *Kaleidotrope*, and *Black Petals*. Aronovitz has also published short fiction in *Midnight Zoo*, *The Leopard's Realm*, *Slippery When Wet*, *The Nighthawk*, *Crimson and Gray*, *Fiction on the Web*, *Philly Fiction*, *Studies in the Fantastic*, *Metal Scratches*, *Demon-minds*, *Weird Tales*, and *The Weird Fiction Review 2010*. Michael Aronovitz is a professor of English and lives with his son Max and his wife Kimberly in Wynnewood, Pennsylvania.

CHRIS KELSO is a 23 year old writer/illustrator who has been printed frequently in small literary and university newspapers across the UK and Canada - such as *Evergreen Review*, *AlterNation*, *Is This Music?*, *Trisickle magazine*, *Trouser Press*, *Heart and Lungs*, *Profane Existence*, *Re-Gen*

Magazine, *Lost Boy Zine*, *Sabotage Times*, *Beard Rock*, *Total Football Magazine*, *Dead Man's Tome* (August issue), *Duality* (Issue4), *Salzberg Review*, *Firstwriter Magazine*, *In Bed With Maradona*, *The Edinburgh Journal* and the *Strathclyde Telegraph*. He works as a voluntary copy/editor for Eraserhead Press, Deadite Books and Dog Horn Books.

DOUGLAS THOMPSON's short stories have appeared in a wide range of magazines, most recently Albedo One, Ambit, and PS Publishing's "Catastrophia" anthology. He won the Grolsch/Herald Question of Style Award in 1989 and second prize in the Neil Gunn Writing Competition in 2007. His first book, *Ultrameta*, was published by Eibonvale Press in August 2009, nominated for the Edge Hill Prize, and shortlisted for the BFS Best Newcomer Award. A second novel *Sylvow* was published in autumn 2010, also from Eibonvale. His third novel *Mechagnosis* was published by Dog Horn in 2011. His new novel *Entanglement* will be out later this year from Elsewhen Press. In it, Douglas explores some of the other stories that arise from the 'dupliporation' technology introduced in "Dissemblance."

J. MICHAEL SHELL, a frequent contributor to Spectrum Fantastic Arts Award winning *Polluto* magazine, is a serious and dedicated artist. At the University of South Carolina (B.A. in English) he studied under the great American poet and novelist James Dickey. Internationally published, Shell's fiction has appeared in *Tropic: The Sunday Magazine of the Miami Herald*, Space and Time Magazine, Hadley/Rille Books' *Footprints*, the *Panverse Two All Novella Anthology*, and the Shirley Jackson Award nominated *Bound for Evil* anthology (Dead Letter Press), to name just a few. His fiction has also been audio produced for MP3 download by *Sniplits: Audio Shorts to Go*, and his novella "An Occidental Book of the Dead" was podcast by *Nil Desperandum*. Shell's fantasy novel *The Apprentice Journals* is scheduled for release in 2012 by Dog Horn Publishing. Though he has been characterized by the anachronistic title "Old Hippie," Shell insists the correct appellation is "Last Hippie."

RICHARD THOMAS was the winner of the 2009 "Enter the World of *Filaria*" contest at ChiZine. He has published over fifty stories online and in print, including the *Shivers VI* anthology (Cemetery Dance) with Stephen King and Peter Straub, the *Warmed and Bound* anthology, *Speedloader* (Snubnose Press), *Murky Depths*, *Gargoyle*, *PANK*, *Weird Fiction Review*, *Pear Noir!*, *Word Riot*, *3:AM Magazine*, and *Opium*. His debut novel *Transubstantiate* was released in July of 2010. In his spare time he writes for The Nervous Breakdown and Lit Reactor. Visit whatdoesnotkillme.com for more information.

MAX T. HAWKER was born in 1987 and lives in Croydon, South London, with his wife Johanna and his daughter Freya. He has had poetry appear in several publications and his current interest is in trying to find a bloody agent for his first novel, *Breaking the Foals*. He is a graduate of Kingston University and his influences include Gene Roddenberry, Louis de Berniéres and Thomas Hardy. He likes to use his writing to tackle uncomfortable issues in a tragi-comic way, and believes the whole world would be a much better place if everyone watched *Star Trek*.

CRIS O'CONNOR is just another writer.

SAM WOOD lives and writes by the sea in Aberystywth, Wales, where he studied for his Creative Writing Masters. He writes weird fantasy and science fiction, as well as poetry about werewolves. His work can also be found in *The Strange: An Anthology of Speculative Literature*. His favourite Pokémon is Cyndaquil.

KHK A.K. was educated at the University of California, Berkeley and Santa Clara University. He earned his MA at UC Davis where his poetics thesis was titled "THE JOY OF HUMAN SACRIFICE." He is a current MFA student at UC San Diego. The poems included here are dedicated to Lucy Corin.

S.R. DANTZLER is a fledgling writer of speculative fiction. When he is not spinning twisted tales he can be found foraging, or cultivating his own food.

MEDUSA GRAVES is a volunteer librarian, cat lover, polymorphic activist and writer of skew-whiff psycho-hauntological non-romances. She graduated from Middlesex in 2007 with a first class honours degree in Sociology, in which she studied the influence of household pets on human relationships. Her key interest is in the concept of futility.

Thank you to our
Supporters:

NO SELL OUT PRODUCTIONS

JASON DUKE

ELLIS FRANCE

DHPLM

PUNK ASS KIDS PRODUCTIONS

BEYONCEHOLES.COM

HALF LIGHT STUDIOS

BLASPHEMYLEEDS.CO.UK

(To see how you can support Polluto, check out pollute.com/subscribe.html)

Polluto is in no way responsible for its own output and is compiled entirely by dust-dealing Dream Pirates. Don't tell the Sandman where we are!

POLLUTO

Out Now:
Women Writing the Weird
Edited by Deb Hoag

WEIRD

1. *Eldritch*: suggesting the operation of supernatural influences; "an eldritch screech"; "the three weird sisters"; "stumps … had uncanny shapes as of monstrous creatures" –John Galsworthy; "an unearthly light"; "he could hear the unearthly scream of some curlew piercing the din" –Henry Kingsley
2. *Wyrd*: fate personified; any one of the three Weird Sisters
3. Strikingly odd or unusual; "some trick of the moonlight; some weird effect of shadow" –Bram Stoker

WEIRD FICTION

1. Stories that delight, surprise, that hang about the dusky edges of 'mainstream' fiction with characters, settings, plots that abandon the normal and mundane and explore new ideas, themes and ways of being. –Deb Hoag

Featuring

Nancy A. Collins, Eugie Foster, Janice Lee, Rachel Kendall, Candy Caradoc, Mysty Unger, Roberta Lawson, Sara Genge, Gina Ranalli, Deb Hoag, C. M. Vernon, Aliette de Bodard, Caroline M. Yoachim, Flavia Testa, Aimee C. Amodio, Ann Hagman Cardinal, Rachel Turner, Wendy Jane Muzlanova, Katie Coyle, Helen Burke, Janis Butler Holm, J.S. Breukelaar, Carol Novack, Tantra Bensko, Nancy DiMauro, and Moira McPartlin.

RRP: £14.99 ($28.95).

POLLUTO

Out Now:
Bite Me, Robot Boy
Edited by Adam Lowe

Bite Me, Robot Boy is a seminal new anthology of poetry and fiction that showcases what Dog Horn Publishing does best: writing that takes risks, crosses boundaries and challenges expectations. From Oz Hardwick's hard-hitting experimental poetry, to Robert Lamb's colourful pulpy science fiction, this is an anthology of incandescent writing from some of the world's best emerging talent.

Featuring
S.R. Dantzler, Oz Hardwick, Maximilian T. Hawker, Emma Hopkins, A. J. Kirby, Stephanie Elizabeth Knipe, Robert Lamb, Poppy Farr, Wendy Jane Muzlanova, Cris O'Connor, Mark Wagstaff, Fiona Ritchie Walker and KC Wilder.

Out Now:
Cabala
Edited by Adam Lowe

From gothic fairytale to humorous pop-culture satire, five of the North's top writers showcase the diversity of British talent that exists outside the country's capital and put their strange, funny, mythical landscapes firmly on the literary map.

Over the course of ten weeks, Adam Lowe worked with five budding writers as part of the Dog Horn Masterclass series. This anthology collects together the best work produced both as a result of the masterclasses and beyond.

Featuring
Jodie Daber, Richard Evans, Jacqueline Houghton,
Rachel Kendall and A.J. Kirby